CW00645867

The Hope She Found

LK Wilde

PART ONE

1941-1942

Chapter 1

July, 1941

Her body lurched forward as the train juddered along the track. Marnie gripped on to the armrest, not wanting to attract attention to herself. The carriage was packed with soldiers, and Marnie felt vulnerable among so many young men. There had been stares, nudges, and lewd comments from battle-hardened boys who'd been out of civilised society for too long.

Marnie wrinkled her nose against the smell of sweat and cigarette smoke. The countryside beyond the window lay flat and burned beneath a strong summer sun. It was as though she could hear the parched ground cracking beneath its brown and yellow crops. Gone were the rolling hills and lush green fields she'd become used to. Each mile of separation from her children tightened Marnie's chest a little more.

Slut. That's what these young men would call her if they knew what she'd done. Marnie swallowed down the lump in her raw, scratchy throat and coughed into her hand. She allowed her blonde curls to fall around her face, using them as a shield to wipe away the lone tear that tumbled from her eye.

If someone had told her a few years ago how her life would turn out, Marnie wouldn't have believed them. First she'd been widowed, then one foolish encounter with a man she should have steered well clear of had resulted in her giving birth to a daughter, Grace. A daughter

Marnie knew she could never keep. Marnie prayed her older daughter, Annie, would never find out the truth about what she had done.

Marnie missed Annie more than she thought possible. She remembered the last time she was on a train, Annie by her side as they embarked on the long journey west. It had only been a few short years before, but felt like a lifetime. Compared to today, that journey had been luxurious. The absence of Annie brought some relief as Marnie imagined trying to squeeze her daughter into a seat amongst the soldiers and sailors. No, she'd done the right thing, leaving her in the relative safety of Padstow. At least, unlike other evacuees, Annie knew and loved the family Marnie had left her with.

Grace, though, was a different matter. As the miles slipped past, Marnie's resolve faltered. Had she done the right thing in abandoning her illegitimate daughter? She pictured the baby lying in her friend Helen's arms. Helen loved Grace with the fierceness of a natural mother and Marnie harboured no doubts she would prove an excellent guardian. But would Grace ever question where she came from? Would she feel that part of her was missing?

"Travelling far, love?"

Marnie snapped her head up. A broad-shouldered soldier took a puff on his cigarette as he waited for her answer.

"Lowestoft."

"Lowestoft? What are you going there for? I thought they'd forbidden visitors to the town? Taken a right battering, has Lowestoft."

"I have to look after my in-laws," said Marnie.

"Ah, right, well, good for you, but couldn't you get them evacuated? It's not a safe place to be these days."

"They wanted to stay in their home."

"*Pfft*," said the soldier. "You want to give them a talking-to. They won't have a home to stay in if the enemy keeps up their rampage."

"I'll bear that in mind," said Marnie, turning her eyes back to the dusty window.

A thread of worry thrummed deep inside. Her friend Kitty had warned her of what she was going back to. Nevertheless, when she thought of Lowestoft, Marnie could only picture the town as she had left it a few short years before. In her mind's eye she saw fishermen arriving and departing the dock, barefoot bairns running through the streets of The Grit, herring girls singing in the pickling plot.

A familiar tingle beneath her blouse caused heat to rush to Marnie's cheeks. "Excuse me," she said, jumping to her feet and pushing past soldiers to reach the facilities in time.

Marnie locked the cubicle door and grabbed a handful of tissue. The milk should have stopped by now, but still it came from time to time, taking her by surprise, reminding her of what she'd given up. Marnie unbuttoned her blouse and shoved pieces of tissue inside her bra. She dabbed at the silk, trying to dry the small damp circle darkening the fabric.

Her dabbing turned to scrubbing, but it only made the stain worse. It was stuffy in the train carriage, but there was only one thing for it. Marnie buttoned up her cardigan, then smoothed a hand across her chest, making sure the tissue wasn't sticking out. She forced down tears. If only there was someone she could talk to, but she had to keep recent events in Padstow a secret.

"Everything alright, miss?" asked a moustached middle-aged man in a uniform smarter than his companions.

"Aye, thank you."

"Private Lewis tells me you're travelling to Lowestoft."

"Aye."

"You have all the correct paperwork to enter the town?"

"Aye," said Marnie, clutching the bag that contained her ticket into the town and all the paperwork her brother Jimmy had advised her to bring.

"Good."

Marnie lowered her eyes to prevent further conversation. No one troubled her again, and she tuned out the metallic screech of the train, and the raucous chatter of soldiers grateful for a moment's reprieve from the battlefield. She closed her eyes and kept them shut until the train slowed, its squeal mingling with a shrill whistle.

"Best gather your belongings, miss," said the moustached soldier. "We're pulling into Lowestoft station."

"Thank you."

Marnie stood, steadying herself against the train's lurches and grabbing her suitcase from the luggage rack. The train creaked to a halt, and Marnie joined the queue of soldiers desperate to get off the stuffy train.

A young man reached for her hand and helped her step down onto the bustling platform. This was it, she was back on Suffolk soil. Marnie sent up a silent prayer, took a deep breath, pulled out her official papers, and headed to the exit.

Chapter 2

July, 1941

"I t will be alright. Everything will be alright."

Kitty held her son's head to her chest as he dampened her cotton blouse with sorrow and frustration. She kept her eyes on the bed, trying to ignore the shouts of pain and smell of disinfectant which filled the surrounding air.

"It will never be alright." Stevie's voice came out gruff and low, his words tinged with bitterness.

"There's no need to be thinking so far ahead, Stevie. You need to concentrate on the here and now. You have to get yourself well."

"And how am I supposed to do that? It's not like I can grow another leg."

Kitty looked down at the flat area of bedclothes, where a limb should have bulged the fabric. She held Stevie at arm's length, clasping his cheeks in her palms and staring into his eyes. "You've lost a leg, but you've kept your life. I'm not saying what's happened to you is easy, but you've fared better than some. Think of your brother..."

"Oh yes, Al the war hero. I'd have rather died in battle given the choice. Now I'm consigned to live the life of a cripple depending on my mother like a child."

"Now listen here," said Kitty, her accent thickening to its original Scots as she struggled to contain her frustration. "There is no need for you to rely on your mam, and even if there was, I wouldn't let you. The doctors are going to help you build your strength and you'll soon be able to walk with crutches. And yes, your brother is a hero, but I'd far rather have him here with me missing a few limbs than have his name scratched into some monument for the fallen. You need to pull yourself together, Stevie. Visiting hours are almost over, so I'll leave you with that thought, and I'll see you tomorrow."

Stevie sank back against his pillow, scowling. His bright red hair stuck up in clumps against his pillow and his bottom lip jutted out like that of a petulant child. Kitty's heart swelled as she saw not the battle-hardened soldier but the small boy he had once been, now scared and in pain. She leaned forward, kissed the top of his head, and gathered up her coat and bag.

Kitty kept her eyes fixed on the ground as she walked through the ward, only lifting them to say goodbye to the nurses at their station. She emerged onto a wide landing, a sweeping staircase lined with old family portraits leading down to an expansive hallway. Kitty wondered whether the rich family that once lived here minded their home being packed to the rafters with wounded soldiers. Perhaps, the moment Stevie realised the opulence of his surroundings would be the moment she knew he was on the road to recovery.

Her hand ran down the wooden banister, and for a moment Kitty allowed her mind to forget reality and pretend she was the heroine of a book. She was snapped out of her reverie by a blank-eyed one-armed soldier climbing the stairs in nothing but a hospital gown. A nurse spotted him, taking the stairs two at a time to guide him back to his ward.

Outside the hospital the sun beat down, spilling golden light onto the gravel driveway and extensive gardens which someone still kept well manicured, despite the dearth of men to care for the rose bushes.

Kitty's feet crunched along the driveway. She kept to the edge, grateful for the shade provided by ancient conifers lining her path. Her legs already ached and there were still two miles to cover before she reached her lodgings in the nearest village. Tomorrow would be her last visit. Her finances were already stretched to breaking point and one more night's accommodation was all she could afford.

After leaving the grounds of the stately-home-turned-hospital, Kitty set off along a narrow country lane, the overgrown hedgerows tickling her bare arms. The delicate wildflowers filled her with a sense of hope. Stevie would be alright. Once he came to accept his injuries, he could move on with his life.

Kitty could never voice her true thoughts aloud, for although she wouldn't wish Stevie's injuries on anyone, it meant he'd come home. Not only that, he wouldn't be able to return and fight. Her heart had shattered at the loss of her firstborn. If it took losing a limb or two to keep her other bairns from the same fate, so be it.

The hedgerows parted to reveal a rickety wooden gate. Kitty leaned against it, pulling out a handkerchief and wiping it across her brow. She squinted against the sun and spotted a group of women sitting on the back of a trailer drinking what she assumed were cups of tea. They must be the land girls she'd read about in the paper. One of them spotted Kitty and waved. She waved back, wondering if she could help with the war effort once Stevie was better.

The land girls jumped down from the trailer, returning to their work. Kitty continued along the road, only meeting one car before she reached the outskirts of the village. She sent up a silent prayer that Mrs

Finnegan would be out. The owner of the boarding house liked to quiz Kitty on her hospital visits, although Kitty suspected Mrs Finnegan was more interested in the goings-on at the once stately home than in Stevie's progress. It seemed to bring the spinster untold joy that the army had requisitioned the house for the war effort, much to its owner's displeasure.

Kitty clicked open the front door and waited. The house was quiet. No wireless, no sound of a kettle, no gossip filtering through the sitting-room door. Kitty dashed to the stairs, racing up to her attic bedroom and closing the door firmly behind her. Although little over five foot, she still had to duck to cross the room, flopping down on the single bed and removing her shoes.

Aside from what had happened to Stevie, Kitty found the loneliness of her southern excursion the hardest. All her life she had been surrounded by people; growing up in a large Highland family, life was never quiet, then as a herring girl, eating, sleeping and working alongside her friends. And then her own family, her beautiful bairns and Bobby. Kind, gentle Bobby. How she wished she were in his arms right now.

Kitty pulled a letter from her handbag and frowned as she read her friend's news. She understood why Marnie needed to return to Lowestoft, but wondered if her best friend knew the risk she was taking. Lowestoft was not the place it once was, and most locals were fleeing rather than returning. With a sigh, Kitty folded the letter and placed it back in her bag. If there was one thing she'd learned about Marnie over the years, it was that she was stubborn, and no warnings from Kitty or anyone else would change her mind once it was set.

Chapter 3

July, 1941

The destruction she witnessed on stepping out of the station tempered any relief at Marnie's papers passing scrutiny. The swing bridge remained, but the harbour master's residence had been reduced to a pile of rubble. As Marnie moved closer, she could see more destruction around the area and it seemed a miracle the bridge itself remained intact.

A thunderous roar filled the sky. Marnie screamed as several aircraft appeared overhead. She ducked against a wall, cowering as the sound of the engines increased around her. Someone tapped her on the shoulder, and Marnie looked up to see an elderly man in a raincoat standing beside her.

"It's alright, miss. They're ours, though it's not always easy to tell, I grant you. Thought you'd be used to the sound of planes by now?"

"I've only just arrived in the town," said Marnie.

The man's eyes widened. "Just arrived? Well, I never. Most are fleeing this place, not coming here through choice."

"So I've heard," said Marnie. She smiled at the man, then stumbled her way along London Road North. She longed to glimpse the department store which once felt like home. Marnie hoped the sight of something familiar might help her pull herself together before arriving at Sally and Roy's house.

Eyes to the ground, Marnie pressed on further until, without needing to look, she knew instinctively she had arrived. Marnie lifted her eyes and felt a rush of love for the place that had once spelled freedom and independence. Anyone else would see a department store, no different from others scattered around the country. But Marnie saw memories. Happy memories from a simpler time. She held her palm against the window. The shop remained unchanged, from the outside at least. Inside was a different story. Brenda had moved north, and Marnie had heard that Mrs Sinclair had finally retired, and suspected she had left town.

Beyond the dresses and bags displayed in the window, Marnie watched young girls attending to customers' needs, cheerful in both appearance and attitude. How could the people inside the shop behave so normally? Did the destruction all around not affect them, or had they grown used to it, oblivious to the chaos wreaked on the town?

Marnie tore herself away from the department store, moving further up the street. She stopped in her tracks as she took in the space where Woolworths had once stood. Twisted metal hung like ribbons on a carpet of rubble, broken glass catching the bright summer sun and twinkling amid a sea of grey. Timpsons' was gone too, another victim of the unscrupulous enemy.

Further along the street, a large poster had been nailed onto the window of a boarded-up shop. Marnie stopped to read the words, her breath catching at the grim proclamation.

DANGER OF INVASION

LAST YEAR ALL WHO COULD BE SPARED FROM THIS TOWN WERE ASKED TO LEAVE, NOT ONLY FOR THEIR OWN SAFETY, BUT SO AS TO EASE THE WORK OF THE ARMED FORCES IN REPELLING AN INVASION. THE DAN-

GER OF INVASION HAS INCREASED AND THE GOVERN-
MENT EXPECTS ALL WHO CAN BE SPARED, AND HAVE
SOMEWHERE TO GO, TO LEAVE WITHOUT DELAY...

Marnie shuddered, whipping her head around, half expecting someone to come and cart her off back to the railway station. Two young
girls, walking along arm in arm, gave her a strange look, giggled, then
crossed the street. Did she really look so out of place in the town she
thought of as home?

With a sigh, Marnie made her way down Rant Score towards The
Grit. Kitty was still away, so Marnie wouldn't stop at her friend's house,
but she wanted to check on her own house before turning up on Sally's
doorstep.

The streets were quiet, and after walking for ten minutes Marnie was
almost used to the craters in the ground, rubble-strewn pavements, and
burnt-out buildings with sky showing through their roofs. As Marnie
turned a corner, a hand reached out and grabbed her, pulling her into
a shop doorway.

"Hey, what are you doing?" shouted Marnie, struggling against the
arm that held her captive.

"Protecting you," said a male voice.

The man released his grip, and Marnie spun around to face him.
"Protecting me from what?"

"There are soldiers training down that road."

"Training for what?"

"House-to-house combat."

"They're using the homes of ordinary folk?"

The man sighed. "Those homes have been abandoned."

Marnie placed her hands on her hips. "And do you know for a fact
that the owners intend not to return?"

"Look, miss, in case you hadn't noticed, there's a war on. I'm sure Mrs Smith or Mrs Jones or whoever owns those houses won't mind if their tea-set gets chipped, if it means our lads know how to fend off the Germans."

Marnie had a feeling Mrs Smith or Jones would return to find more than a chipped tea-set, but held her tongue. She felt a foreigner in her own town, as though in her absence the place had changed beyond recognition. It was only after witnessing the changes that she realised how sanitised Kitty and Jimmy had kept their letters to her. Had they been trying to protect her, or could they not bear to put down all that was happening on the page?

The man doffed his cap and wandered off down the street. Marnie returned to the corner of the road, poking her head around a building. Young men in uniform rushed in and out of houses, guns hoisted on their shoulders.

All was quiet until a sudden burst of shouting followed by the popping of guns exploded into the still summer's day. Marnie pulled her head back and leaned against the wall. She heard the thud of boots, the slam of a door, a small explosion, then the sound of ordinary conversation as the soldiers spilled out of houses.

Marnie risked another look. The soldiers were at ease, guns no longer poised, shoulders no longer hunched and tense. Men clapped each other on the back, some shook hands. One man ducked beside a house to relieve himself.

Soldiers stood smoking beside burnt-out cottages. As she continued walking, Marnie passed a terrace where one house was missing a roof, and another's door hung drunkenly from its frame, exposing a hallway whose walls were pockmarked with bullet holes. Every few steps she climbed over a pile of rubble. Bombs had devastated some homes, but others looked like they'd suffered at the hands of British soldiers, as they honed their skills to prepare for face-to-face combat on Suffolk soil.

The newspapers were full of news from London, but walking through the once thriving streets of Lowestoft, Marnie felt she was walking through an unseen casualty, whose suffering went unreported, hidden from the minds of most of the country. No wonder everyone's faces were etched with worry, their shoulders slumped, feet moving in scampers rather than strolls. An air of terror lingered over The Grit.

Chapter 4

July, 1941

Kitty sat blinking back tears as she tried to take in the doctor's words. *Making excellent progress. Home within the next month.* Could it really be that the home which had become so deathly quiet would once again welcome one of her children? An anxious tide of questions swiftly followed any relief Kitty felt. Would Stevie manage the stairs? Would he be able to move to the nearest shelter quick enough to avoid the torrent of bombs being dropped on the town? Would he allow her to provide the help he so clearly still needed?

"We've been very pleased with your son's progress," the doctor was saying.

Kitty nodded. "And his mind, doctor, will that heal too?"

The doctor frowned.

"I mean, he seems to struggle to come to terms with his injuries. I just wondered..."

"Mrs Thorne, these young men have witnessed things we can't begin to imagine. The attack young Stevie was caught up in will have left scars far beyond those physically present. The best thing to do is give him time. And please believe me when I say Stevie is among our more positive patients."

Positive? Kitty thought of the screams and howls she heard each time she visited Stevie, of the dull-eyed men roaming endlessly around the corridors. She decided to trust the doctor's assessment and count her blessings. Things could be far, far worse.

"Will he need any specialist care once he returns home?"

"His stump will need regular checks, but the local nurses will take care of that. It's important Stevie keeps up the exercises we have introduced during his time here. It's too soon to be considering a prosthesis, but this will be something to think about once his leg is fully healed."

"Thank you."

"I will write to you with a formal discharge date, but you can expect to be taking your son home within a matter of weeks rather than months."

"Thank you, doctor, that really is wonderful news." Kitty stood up and reached forward to shake the doctor's hand. She left the office and headed to Stevie's ward, wondering if Bobby would be allowed leave to help her bring Stevie home. The thought of helping Stevie on and off trains alone was daunting, and there was no way she could afford a taxi, even if they could find one with enough petrol to make the long journey.

Kitty found Stevie sitting up in bed, staring into space. She pulled two magazines from her bag and laid them beside him on the bed. He glanced down and then fixed his gaze once more on the far wall.

"The doctor says you'll be home within the month," said Kitty, perching on the edge of her son's bed. "Isn't that good news?"

"Hmm."

"Stevie." Kitty lifted her son's fingers to her lips and kissed them. "It will be a new start. We'll get through this together."

Stevie continued his unfocussed staring. Kitty picked up a magazine and started to read aloud.

"If you don't mind, I've got a headache," Stevie said.

"Oh, sorry. I'm afraid this will be my last visit before we come to take you home. I'm hoping Dad will come with me next time."

Mention of Bobby caused Stevie to look up. "Will he get leave?"

"I hope so. He's hated not being able to visit you."

"I worry about him."

"So do I." Kitty reached across and squeezed Stevie's hand. The thought of Bobby out minesweeping on his trawler was too much to bear. The only way she could cope with the worry was to pretend he was out fishing, chasing silver darlings like he used to before the world turned on its head. "Right, I'd best be off. I'll see you soon." Kitty leaned down and kissed Stevie's cheek. To her surprise, he pulled her closer, wrapping his arms around her neck.

"Thank you for being here for me. I know I've not always made it easy."

Kitty swallowed back tears. "I'm your mam. It's my job to look after you, whether easy or not. Goodbye, love."

Kitty pulled away and turned to leave before Stevie could witness the tears breaking free.

Chapter 5

July, 1941

O n shaking legs, Marnie walked the short distance to the street which for so many years she'd called home. As she approached the house, she wondered if this was her punishment. The windowsills her husband Tom had lovingly painted were tinged grey. The windows themselves had fared no better. Some were missing all their panes, and one had a small circular hole in its centre, a spider's web of glass cracked around it.

Marnie stepped back to get a better look at her home. Paint peeled from the door, the wood splintering, a boot mark imprinted in its centre. With trembling hands, Marnie pushed against the door. It creaked open, and she stepped inside.

Someone had emptied the house of most of the furniture. Marnie wondered where it had gone, but decided it was best not to know. She hoped they had given it to a deserving family, but feared it had been burnt. The floor was covered in dust and grime, scuffed boot-prints telling of many feet having passed through.

In the sitting room, Marnie ran her hand along one wall. Peppered among the flowers of the wallpaper were small round holes, plaster and dust spilling from them as her fingers disturbed them. The mirror which had hung above the fireplace had fallen to the floor, and as

Marnie walked across the carpet, fragments of glass crunched beneath her feet.

Marnie entered the kitchen and closed her eyes, trying to relive her first morning as Mrs Hearn, when she had proudly shown Clara around her new home. The crockery and glasses were safely stored in Roy's shed, but there could be no cooking in the kitchen even if she had utensils. The cooker-top had rusted, sharp pieces of metal crumbling as her finger ran across it.

A line of lime scale ran from the top to bottom of the sink, a reminder of all the potatoes scrubbed and dishes once washed. Marnie turned the tap, but no water emerged from it. She supposed either the previous tenants or the army had disconnected the water.

Marnie opened the pantry door and crouched down. It seemed unreal, the faint pencil lines she and Tom had drawn to mark each of Annie's growth spurts. Marnie sank to the floor, her finger running up and down the measurements. How tall would Annie be by the time she next saw her?

Pull yourself together, Marnie told herself. *You're not the only mother separated from her child.*

Questions of the future clustered in Marnie's mind. She had assumed she would return to this house one day with her daughter, but now, in its crumbling, battle-scarred state, she couldn't imagine a time the house would ever be habitable again. Marnie climbed to her feet and brushed her skirt free of dust and grime.

The kitchen held too many memories; her and Tom laughing over breakfast, welcoming Tom back home from sea with a home-cooked meal, and most poignant of all, the evening Annie had been conceived. The weight of what might have been stole Marnie's breath, and she stumbled through to the hallway. She held a hand against the banister and pulled herself up, one stair at a time. The carpet was only a few years old, a present from Tom after he took over his father's boat and their fortunes had improved. Despite its youth, the treads had worn thin, and mud and dirt clung to the patterned fibres.

Dirty palms had coloured the magnolia wall with a line of grey. At the top of the stairs, Marnie paused. What was the point of walking from room to room when she knew what she would find? She slid down against the wall and looked at the two bedroom doors in front of her. Was it really less than two years since they'd been living here as a family of three? Now Tom was gone, and Annie was as far away as it was possible to get while remaining in the country.

Marnie clambered to her feet. Brooding would solve nothing. She ran down the stairs and out of the front door, almost knocking an old man to the ground.

"Watch it," he said, steadying himself against a wall and pulling a pipe from between his teeth. A small terrier tugged on the piece of rope that served as a lead and the man cursed under his breath.

"Fred Hargreaves?"

The old man squinted at Marnie. "Mrs Hearn? Is that really you?"

"Aye, Fred, it is." Marnie bent down and gave the dog a scratch under its chin.

"Last I heard, you'd moved down west."

"I had, but now I'm back."

"I was very sorry to hear about your Tom. The sea can be a cruel mistress. I couldn't believe it when I heard the news from Roy. It seemed like only yesterday I was watching the pair of you wed in Christ Church."

"A lot's happened since then. How's Maggie?"

"Up north with her sister. She tried to persuade me to go with her, but I'll not leave The Grit. I've signed up as a Local Defence Volunteer."

"Good for you," said Marnie, wondering how much help the elderly man would be should the Germans invade.

"You'll be staying with Sally and Roy, I expect."

"Aye, that's right."

Fred shook his head. "They've had more than their fair share of grief have those two. It will do them the world of good having a youngster around the place again."

"Oh, Annie has stayed in Cornwall."

Fred let out something between a laugh and a cough. "I wasn't talking about your daughter, Mrs Hearn. I meant you. You're still a spring chicken in my eyes. Alright, alright," said Fred, struggling as his dog pulled hard against the string lead. "I'd best get this one home for his dinner. Take care of yourself, Mrs Hearn."

"And you, Fred."

Marnie set off down the street, feeling nothing like the youngster Fred viewed her as. She kept her eyes to the ground, unwilling to see more of the destruction wrought on her hometown. As she walked on, Marnie squared her shoulders. This was her new reality, and there was no choice but to face it head on. All she could do was pray that the next time she saw her daughter, the world would be set right and humanity would have prevailed.

Chapter 6

July, 1941

Marnie knocked on the door and waited. Through the mottled glass, a dark shape appeared, blocking the light. The door opened and Sally's hands planted on her cheeks, her mouth gaping open as she stared at Marnie.

"Hello, Sally. Aren't you going to invite me in?"

Instead of stepping aside, Sally rushed at Marnie, throwing her arms around her and clinging tight as though establishing she was real and not a hallucination. "I can't believe you're actually here," said Sally. "Me and Roy thought we'd never see you again."

"Didn't you get my letter?"

"Yes, but we couldn't believe you'd really come back here, or that the authorities would let you."

"Aye," said Marnie, "I saw the poster in town."

"At least you didn't bring Annie with you."

"No, but she's very upset not to be seeing you. Shall I put the kettle on?" asked Marnie, glancing at Sally's hands that were gnarled and misshapen at the joints.

"It should be me making tea, seeing as you've just arrived, but since you offered, I won't say no. Everything's in the same place as when you were last here."

"I'm sure I'll find my way around. It's good to be back," said Marnie, rubbing Sally's arm and forcing a smile.

Sally tried to return the smile, but her face dropped into a frown, her swollen fingers twisting together. "Marnie, as happy as I am to see you, I wish you hadn't come. I couldn't live with myself if anything were to happen to you after coming back here on our account."

"Sally, you're family. War is affecting the entire country. I didn't tell you as I didn't want to worry you, but we had a near miss with a bomb in Padstow last year."

"What?"

"See, nowhere is safe from that evil Hitler. Besides, it was my decision to return. You hold no blame or responsibility for what happens to me. Now, come on, let's get that kettle on."

Marnie walked into the kitchen and turned to the sink to hide her shock. Cloth marks in the dust showed that Sally had tried her best to keep on top of the housework, but grime clung to the windowsill, and a layer of lime scale had accumulated around the sink. Cobwebs hung from the ceiling light and month-old food stained the floor.

"Is Roy home?"

"Yes, he's up in the bedroom. He finds it so hard to get out and about these days."

Marnie placed the kettle on the stove and opened a cupboard to find a near empty jar of tea leaves. "Do you have any milk?"

Sally's cheeks turned pink. "I haven't been able to get out to the shop yet this week."

Marnie opened further cupboards, finding them bare. "Sally, what have you been eating? There's no food in the house."

"We've been managing," said Sally, some of her old pride coming out in her voice. "With rationing and all the soldiers around, shopping isn't as easy as it once was."

"No, I understand. Well, let's have a nice hot cup of black tea, then I'll head out to the shops for you."

"Why don't we take it through to the sitting room, as this is a special occasion?" asked Sally.

Marnie placed two cups and saucers on a tray and followed Sally through to the sitting room. As she laid the tray on the coffee table, a plume of dust filled the air, causing Marnie to cough.

"Sorry," said Sally. "We don't use this room much these days, so there seemed little point dusting. Besides, the soldiers running in and out of houses with guns cause so much dust and dirt, it's dirty again the second I've finished cleaning."

"They don't come in here?" asked Marnie, horrified at the thought.

"Goodness no, but there are plenty of empty houses a couple of streets behind us, so we often hear them scurrying around, practising for battle."

"It must be dreadful having them running all over the place."

Sally sank into a faded armchair. "I fear it's a sign of what's coming. The fact they think they can use The Grit as a training ground suggests its days must be numbered. Have you seen your cottage yet?"

Marnie nodded and swallowed the lump in her throat. All the work Tom had put into the house, at least he wasn't here to see what had become of it. "I'm sure it can be patched up somehow. What will happen to all the other families when they return to the town? From what I saw, other houses are in even worse condition than ours."

"They'll be put into those new council houses most like. If any of them are still standing by the time this dreadful war ends."

Marnie stood up and opened the curtains, looking out onto a deserted street. It felt like a ghost town, with so many women and children of fishing families evacuated to safer areas.

"Some families have stayed," said Sally, "but plenty have gone and who can blame them?"

With more natural light spilling into the room, Marnie took a good look at her mother-in-law. Sally had visibly shrunk, her clothes hanging off a gaunt frame. Her hair looked as if it could do with a wash, and her clothes had stains down their front. It was a far cry from the neat woman of only a few short years before.

A heaviness settled on Marnie as she sat on the sofa drinking her tea. Over Sally's shoulder, on the mantel, was a row of photographs. Sally and Roy's three precious sons, black and white images, all that remained of them. Marnie turned her eyes away from the photograph of Tom, feeling a mixture of longing and shame at the way she had conducted herself since his death.

"Is it alright if I pop upstairs and say hello to Roy before I head out to the shop?"

"Of course it is," said Sally. "He would've come down, only he's probably slept through your arrival. He finds it hard to stir himself for much other than his volunteering at the Seamen's Mission. Take your bags up with you when you go. You're in the herring girls' old room."

"It's such a shame they've not been able to return since war broke out."

"I know. *HMS Europa* are desperate for locals to take in some of their sailors, but I've not been feeling up to it."

"Perhaps now I'm here to help, it's something to consider?"

"Perhaps. Oh, and, Marnie?"

"Aye?"

"Just... well... Roy may be a little different from how you remember him."

"Oh?"

"Ignore me," said Sally. "He's just frail after the stroke."

"Alright, well, I'm sure he'll be the same old Roy to me."

Marnie smiled and Sally returned it, but her hands wrung in her lap and her cheerfulness felt forced. Closing the door behind her, Marnie leaned against it, eyeing the staircase. Had Roy really deteriorated that much? There was only one way to find out.

Chapter 7

July, 1941

M arnie collected her bags from the hallway and climbed the worn treads of the staircase. She pushed open the door to her new bedroom, surprised to find the herring girls' bunk-beds removed in favour of a single bed, wardrobe, and dresser. The room was a reasonable size, and despite its musty unused smell mingling with a lingering scent of fish, it was more than enough for Marnie's needs.

After unpacking her clothes into the drawers and wardrobe, Marnie stepped onto the landing and knocked on Roy's bedroom door.

"Hmm?"

Marnie opened the door and poked her head around. "It's me, Roy, Marnie."

"Marnie?" Roy shuffled in his bed until he was half sitting against its headboard. "It's really you?"

"Aye. Sally seemed surprised to see me too, but I wrote."

"Yes... yes. B... but...what with... with them refusing... visitors entry to the town..."

"I know, but I'm not visiting, am I? I'm back for good."

Marnie tried not to show alarm at Roy's laboured speech, or the way one side of his face seemed to hang down.

"Annie?"

"Annie's safe living with Helen and Richard in Padstow. She'll join me here as soon as it's safe." *But not Grace*, thought Marnie, a dull ache reaching her heart.

Marnie crossed the room and sat beside Roy on the bed. The light in the room was dim, but even so, Marnie could tell he was in terrible shape. Even ignoring its new uneven form, his face had thinned, the skin around his jaw sagging almost to his chest. His eyes looked at her with a creamy dullness, and each time he drew breath, Marnie heard a scratching sound in his chest.

"How are you, Roy?"

Roy let out a laugh, which turned into a cough. He banged his chest with a balled fist until the coughing subsided. "Wonderful, as you can see." He chuckled again, the loose skin around his eyes creasing as he smiled. "It's tricky to get around these days. Ever since I gave up fishing, it's like all those years straining my muscles have caught up with me."

Marnie worried it was more than old age ailing Roy. The stroke seemed to have done lasting damage, not to mention the rattling in his chest and stiffness of his limbs. Goodness knows how many ailments he'd been nursing in silence and for how long.

"Well, I'm off out to get some shopping in, and I'll cook you something to strengthen you up this evening."

Roy reached out and squeezed Marnie's hand in his own. "It's good to have you home."

Marnie smiled, unable to return the sentiment due to the conflicting mass of thoughts and emotions swirling through her mind. Given what she'd experienced since arriving in Lowestoft, she wasn't even sure she was home anymore.

Sally was waiting for her at the bottom of the stairs. "How was he?"

"He seemed in good spirits."

"You're a kind girl, Marnie, but I can see the shock in your eyes. I've been trying my best to look after him, but my wretched joints don't make it easy."

Marnie placed a hand on Sally's arm. "Like I said, Roy seemed in good spirits, and I could see no evidence you've been neglecting him. You've been doing all you can, and now I'm here to share the load. Does Roy get out much?"

"He's actually not too bad walking once he gets going. Getting him up and out of bed's the hard part. Once he's upright, he uses his walking stick to get around without too much difficulty. Every Monday, Wednesday and Friday, come rain or shine, he toddles off down the Seamen's Mission. I'm not sure how much help he is, but it certainly helps him to go. There's always a bit of a twinkle in his eye by Wednesday evening. I think it's being around old sea dogs that does it. He misses the fishing life so much, even after all this time."

"I'm not surprised. Once a fisherman, always a fisherman, or so they say. Does he get out much other than the mission?"

"Days he's not at the mission he rests and collects his strength for the next time he goes. Yes, I leave him be on his rest days. On Sundays, I try to coax him out for a walk. It isn't good for him to be sitting in one position for too long. In fact, it makes things worse. We used to go to church on a Sunday, as you know, but since Tom died, neither of us feels much like being in the presence of God."

"I can understand that."

"Of course you can, love," said Sally. She pulled Marnie into a hug and gave her back a brisk rub. "It really is good of you to come back here."

"You're family," said Marnie. "Of course I'd come back."

Sally's hands stopped rubbing and her arms tightened around Marnie. "Family." Her voice came out in a rushed, hoarse whisper. She gave Marnie one last squeeze, then shooed her out of the door.

Chapter 8

July, 1941

Kitty waited for the soldiers to exit the carriage before stepping off the train. Her mind was frazzled by the noise and cramped conditions she'd experienced during the journey. Tiredness threatened to overwhelm her, but a cloud inside had lifted. The next time she had to make the journey, it would be to bring her precious son home.

It was slow going getting her papers checked, but the officials recognised her by now and greeted her news that Stevie would soon be home with congratulations and warm smiles. Everyone welcomed good news during these dark days, and Kitty was grateful to have some to share.

"Kitty."

Kitty spun around. "Bobby?" She dropped her suitcase and ran towards her husband, wrapping her arms around his neck and burrowing her face in his neck.

"Hey, it's alright," he said, tilting her chin and wiping tears from her cheeks. "Was it bad news at the hospital? Has something happened to Stevie?"

"These are happy tears," said Kitty, planting a kiss on Bobby's lips. "Our boy's coming home, Bobby."

He held her at arm's length and studied her face. "Home? Are you sure?"

"Aye, I am. In the next month, the doc said."

Bobby grabbed Kitty's waist and lifted her off the ground, spinning her around until both were dizzy. When he laid her down, she had to swallow back more happy tears, for she'd glimpsed the man she had married, before grief and war stole his optimism for life.

"How about a fish supper to celebrate?"

"You mean you've not prepared a welcome home meal for me?" Kitty teased, linking arms with her husband.

"No, I... um..."

"Bobby, I'm teasing. I wasn't expecting dinner, or a welcome party. I thought you'd be out on the boat?"

A familiar shadow passed over Bobby's face and it was as though Kitty could see the happiness from moments ago seeping out of his skin. "Night off," Bobby said, picking up Kitty's suitcase.

"Has there been any news from the bairns while I've been away?"

"Yes, a letter came from Derbyshire, but I haven't opened it yet. I thought I'd save it until you got home."

"Thank you," said Kitty.

"Tell you what. Why don't I see you home, then go out and get our fish supper? It will give you a chance to read the boys' news, then you can tell me all about it, and what's going on with Stevie over fish and chips."

"That sounds like a wonderful plan," said Kitty, desperate to read any news of her boys. "I don't suppose there's been any news from Simon?"

Bobby shook his head. "No, but no news is good news, don't you think?"

Kitty plastered a smile on her face. "Aye, you're probably right." She tried to ignore the knot tightening in her stomach. The last they'd heard, Simon's regiment was in France, but there'd been no word for over two months and after receiving the horrific news about Al, Kitty wouldn't relax until she knew he was safe.

They walked the rest of the way to the house in silence, each lost in their own thoughts. Kitty enjoyed the warmth of Bobby's hand on her arm, and the stillness of a sky that was more often than not humming with danger.

Bobby unlocked the front door and carried the suitcase inside. "I won't be long," he said. "The letter's on the mantelpiece."

Bobby closed the door behind him and Kitty picked up the letter, sinking into an armchair and pulling several sheets of paper from the envelope.

Dear Mum,

How are you, and how is Stevie? Tell him he's a hero to us then maybe give him a punch on the arm so he doesn't think we've gone too soft just 'cause he's injured! Things are going well here. Life on the farm is as busy as ever. I tell you, some chaps from my class have got a raw deal with their host families. One poor lad comes to school black and blue and others are growing so thin I don't think they're getting fed. There's no chance of getting thin here. Mrs Burrage gives us three square meals a day. She keeps us busy with jobs too, and I've never slept so well as I do on the farm. I've grown several inches since we left and I expect I'll have overtaken you, and perhaps even Dad by the time we come home!

Anyway, I must dash as Mrs Burrage is calling me. I've told the others to write too, and we'll put all our letters in together. Love, Chrissy.

Kitty smiled and folded the letter on her lap. She sent up a prayer of thanks that four of her seven children were safe, five now, if you counted Stevie. After their initial separation, it had come as an immense relief when Mrs Burrage had agreed to host all the boys together on her farm.

The writing on the next letter was not as neat, as if the writer was in a hurry to get to more fun pursuits. Kitty checked the name of the writer and smiled. Mark had been in a rush ever since he left her womb.

Dear Mum, Chrissy probably asked after Stevie so I'll get the latest from him when you reply. I've joined the school cricket team and Mr Burrage says I've got the makings of an England player. Can you believe it, a Lowestoft lad playing for England? Let's hope Mr Burrage is right! Don't worry about me playing too much sport, I'm still doing well with my schoolwork, although it has been marvellous to have a break for the summer holidays. There's a river at the edge of the farm where we swim most warm days. Mr Burrage found an old tractor tyre and has tied it to the strongest tree. You should see us. We can all fit on there and it's a fight to see who can stay on the longest without falling in the water. You'd think Sam would be the first to go, but he's tough for his age, not that I'd tell him that. I'd better sign off here, as I've got cricket practice in half an hour. Love to you and Dad, Mark.

Kitty closed her eyes and tried to picture her son in cricket whites. She'd not seen where they were staying, but imagined a cricket pitch with rolling hills in the background. Kitty sent another prayer of thanks that her boys had been housed together. After speaking to the mothers of other evacuees, she knew this was unusual and extremely fortunate.

The next two letters in the envelope were much shorter. Peter asked after Stevie, told her about the weather, then signed off. When she reached Sam's letter, Kitty felt a pang of loss as she studied his handwriting. He'd been a small boy of five when he left her. Now the loops and curls from his pen spoke of a child growing up fast, and she was missing it all.

Dear Mum, I hope you are well. We all miss you and Dad. Have you heard how Annie is getting on down in Padstow? I miss her too. Sam.

Kitty smiled. Time and distance hadn't dampened the affection her baby felt for Marnie's daughter. Was Marnie serious about coming back to Lowestoft? Kitty supposed she would soon find out.

Chapter 9

August, 1941

Marnie's back clicked as she straightened up. She'd been cleaning for two weeks straight and now the end was in sight. Both Sally and Roy were now in clean clothes, and sleeping in fresh bedding. Her cleaning felt like a penance, a way to salve some of the guilt she'd hoped to leave behind in Padstow.

The letterbox clicked and Marnie threw her damp cloth back into the bucket of water and went to collect the post. There were only two letters, and by their postmarks she knew one had come from Cornwall and one from Derbyshire. Marnie opted for the Derbyshire letter first, deciding she'd need to steel herself before reading Helen's news.

Dear Marnie,

I've sent this letter to Lowestoft as, by my calculations, you should have arrived there by now. How are Roy and Sally? Please pass on my love and best wishes to them. You may have seen by now that some of the local schools have reopened to children not evacuated. For the time being, I have been asked to stay here and continue my work, but if more children return home, that could all change. I'll keep you posted.

Are you alright for money? I don't imagine Roy's seaman's pension stretches very far these days. Please let me know if you need any financial help. You've given up so much to return to Lowestoft, it's the least I can do.

I met with Clara last week. She is well, although losing several young island men has brought much sadness to the community there. It also saddened me to hear that Mam has been in poor health. I know it's to be expected at her age, but I suppose part of me had always hoped we could make our peace one day. Between them, Clara and Rachel are caring for her and I'm hoping she will rally. If you would like to write to Mam, send your letter to Clara and she will see that she gets it.

Anyway, on that note, I will leave you. I hope you are well, Marnie, and the separation from Annie is bearable. You are all in my thoughts. Jimmy.

Marnie thought back to the last time she had seen her mam, over ten years ago, on her honeymoon. She sent up a prayer of thanks for Rachel and Clara and decided she would write, but not before facing the latest news from Padstow.

Dear Marnie,

I hope your journey east wasn't too arduous. How are Sally and Roy? How are you?

You asked me to be honest about Annie's wellbeing, so I shall. She has struggled with your absence more than perhaps you would expect. She has been withdrawn, quiet, and finding it difficult to settle at any activity for long. I think she will feel much brighter once she returns to school next month. Yesterday she went out to play with friends and some of her usual vigour had returned when she arrived home. It's a big change for her, but she will cope. She's a strong young thing, just like her mother.

Grace is thriving and smiles more than she cries these days. Annie has got used to her presence in the house and enjoys making her laugh by tickling her under her chin. Grace has brought such light into our home during these dark days of war. Your gift to us will never be taken for granted.

Richard is in good health, and the shop continues to be busy. There have been no more attacks on the town, thank goodness, and folk are continuing as normal, in as far as that's possible. We see a lot of Jack, who finds it hard to stay away from Grace. I've seen a softer side to him, one I'd not witnessed since childhood. That little girl is the apple of his eye. Not that Grace gets all his attention. He's a firm favourite with Annie for bedtime stories, and has promised to take her out on his boat when it's safe enough to do so.

I'm much the same as when you left. Still knitting socks for soldiers, still attending whist drives, and the many fundraisers Mrs Keswell ropes me into.

You are much missed, Marnie, but I hope you have settled well up there. I will write again soon, and please don't worry about Annie. She will be right as rain in no time. Your loving friend, Helen.

"Is everything alright, love?" asked Sally, shuffling into the kitchen and making Marnie jump.

"Aye, just a couple of letters from Jimmy and Helen." Marnie turned her head and brushed tears from her eyes.

"Can I see? I'd love to know how my granddaughter is getting on."

Marnie clasped the letter from Helen between her fingers. Was there anything in there to arouse Sally's suspicions? Before Marnie could decide, Sally mistook Marnie's hesitation for acceptance and took the letter from her hand.

As she read, Sally's forehead creased. "Oh, love, I feel terrible for poor little Annie."

"She'll be fine," said Marnie, hoping it was true.

"And you? Will you be fine too?"

Marnie sniffed and swallowed the lump in her throat, before plastering what she hoped was a convincing smile on her face. "I'll miss Annie, of course, but you know me, I'm always fine."

Sally crossed her arms and looked at Marnie. "You're right, I know you and I see how events of the last few years sit heavy in your heart. First Tom's death, now having to be separated from Annie."

"I'm no worse off than plenty of other women. Besides, you've lost far more than me."

"That's true," said Sally, "but I'm an old lady now. I'll carry my loss with me to the grave. You're still young, Marnie. Tom wouldn't want you grieving him at the expense of happiness."

"I'm not sure I understand what you're saying, Sally?"

Sally sighed. "All I'm saying is, don't close your heart off when you've still got plenty of years ahead of you. I know you've got a lot on your plate, what with this damned war, caring for us, and worrying about Annie. But, in times like these, it's important to seek happiness wherever you can find it."

"I'll bear that in mind," said Marnie, not entirely sure what Sally was trying to tell her.

Sally glanced at the letter again. "Who's this Grace Helen keeps talking about?"

"An evacuee. Helen took her in. She's still a baby." Marnie hoped she sounded convincing, but couldn't stop colour rushing to her cheeks as she told a blatant lie. Sally could never find out about the illegitimate child Marnie had conceived in a moment of madness.

"I see, and what's the gift Helen wrote about?"

"Gift?" Marnie took the letter back and scanned through. "Oh, Helen must be talking about a blanket I made for her as a leaving present."

Sally seemed satisfied by Marnie's explanation. "What a kind gesture." Sally leaned over Marnie's shoulder, her forehead creasing as she looked again at the letter. "What a dreadful thing for a baby to be parted from their mother so soon. Poor little mite. This war is evil. The sooner it ends, the better."

"I couldn't agree more."

Chapter 10

August, 1941

Marnie stared up at the ceiling, waiting for dawn to arrive. With blackout curtains at the window, the bedroom felt like a cave, and a hot one at that. The thick black curtain framing the window did its job blocking any light and also just as good a job blocking any fresh air. Wearing a thin nightdress and with the sheets kicked off, Marnie had resorted to keeping a small bowl of water and a cloth beside her bed to relieve some of the insufferable heat.

Her hand felt along her bedside table, her fingers brushing against paper. Marnie gathered the paper up and scrunched it into a ball, flinging it across the room in frustration. She'd made five attempts at writing to Helen and Annie but could still not muster any thoughts to send to either her friend or daughter. What could she tell them? That she hated herself for leaving? That she missed Annie so much it hurt? That her body still leaked and ached from giving up her baby? That she couldn't look in a mirror because of the shame she felt at her recent actions?

Of course, she could describe the events surrounding her return, but neither the ill-health of her in-laws nor the destruction already wreaked on the town made for cheerful reading.

Marnie crossed the room and peeked around the curtain. Dawn was breaking, the sky hazy with a pearly glow. Gulls swooped like white arrows against the silver sky, enjoying a rare moment of calm before more planes came to invade their airspace.

Marnie let the curtain fall and began dressing with renewed purpose. Now she'd seen to the immediate needs of Sally and Roy, she needed to make a plan of action for how she could sustain the household.

The thought of joining the WRENs was appealing. Marnie had seen pictures of young women in smart navy uniforms doing their bit for the war effort. But the practicalities of joining the fight would defeat the purpose of coming back to Lowestoft. There would be training, somewhere beyond Lowestoft, and the work would take her away from the household she had come to care for. No, a different course of action was needed, something that would bring in a much needed income but also help the war effort in some small way.

Downstairs in the kitchen, Marnie laid out cups and saucers and poured the tea. Roy had made it out of bed by himself that morning, the prospect of a day of volunteering stronger than his need for rest. Looking at his pale face and shaking hands, Marnie wasn't convinced he was up to it, but knowing it was the only thing to give him a sense of purpose, she kept her thoughts to herself. Roy leaned heavily on his walking stick as he moved around the kitchen, each step resulting in a wheezy breath. Sally appeared in her dressing gown, rollers still in her hair, and Marnie asked her in-laws to sit at the table.

"Is this going to take long?" asked Roy. "Only, I'm supposed to be at the mission by ten."

"No, it won't take long. But we need to have a conversation about our finances."

Both Sally and Roy squirmed in their seats. Money and politics were considered vulgar topics of conversation, but given their current circumstances, neither could be avoided.

"As you know, I have some savings from my work in Richard's shop," continued Marnie. "But those savings won't last much longer, and it's clear you've been struggling on Roy's pension."

"We manage," said Sally.

Marnie sighed. "I know this conversation makes you uncomfortable, but we have to make a plan. I've been speaking to some of the local women and they said they've swapped their net mending for making camouflage nets. It seems there's a growing call for them, so I thought I might offer my services."

"I wish I could help," said Sally, "but my arthritis…"

"Sally, you have to put your health first. I'm happy to take on the work alone. Besides, you've made and mended more than enough nets over the years. I thought I'd also pop into Chadds and see if they have any shifts that need covering. And there's another thing. You said *HMS Europa* needs accommodation for their sailors?"

"Yes." Sally's cheeks reddened. "I've not been shirking my duty, it's just with my joints as they are…"

"Sally, you have nothing to feel guilty about. But now I'm here, there's no reason not to take someone in. It would replace some of the income you've lost since the herring girls stopped coming."

"That sounds like a lot to place on your shoulders," said Roy.

"Perhaps, but I've not got Annie with me, and to be honest, it's best I keep busy. Besides, I'd like to help with the war effort any way I can. Would you be happy to let out the third bedroom?"

"Of course," said Sally. "Anything we can do to aid those brave young chaps. It will need a bit of freshening up, though, and it's full of junk that needs clearing. It shouldn't be too big a job if we all muck in."

"Wonderful. Well, I'm going to head off and speak to Caro Shaw this morning. She seems to have her finger on the pulse with anything to do with nets. Then I'll head to Chadds, and then I'll go up to *HMS Europa*, although I still can't get used to calling it that."

"It will be back to *Sparrow's Nest* soon enough," said Roy, expressing more optimism than any of them truly felt.

Marnie cleared away the teacups and left the house. The streets were quiet, but Marnie soon spotted a woman walking along the other side of the road carrying two string shopping bags.

"Excuse me," said Marnie, crossing the road and running to catch the other woman up. "I don't suppose you know where Caro Shaw works these days? Is she over at Beetons'?"

"No, you'll find her over at The Shoals, bottom of Lighthouse Score."

"Thank you," said Marnie, pleased her assumption that everyone knew Caro Shaw had paid off.

Marnie walked the length of Wapload Road, praying the air raid siren wouldn't sound when she was so far from home. She passed the net drying racks on the Denes and was almost at *HMS Europa* when she finally glimpsed The Shoals.

As Marnie approached, the sound of women's chatter reached her from the net store. Marnie stepped inside a long, low-ceilinged room. A row of women stood in front of nets hung from hooks on the walls. Their fingers blurred with speed and none took any notice of Marnie as she walked the length of the room. At the very end, she spotted the familiar rotund figure of Mrs Shaw.

Marnie stepped forward. "Hello, Caro."

Caro Shaw looked up and grinned a toothless grin, her fingers continuing their work with no sight. "If it isn't Mrs Hearn. How are you, Marnie love? I heard you were heading back to these parts. But without your man, you poor love. And what about that lovely daughter of yours? I hope you've not brought her with you?"

"No, I've left her behind in Padstow. She's much safer there, and it seems Hitler hasn't got you yet."

Caro cackled. "He's had a fair old crack. Had a bomb fly in one side of my bedroom and out the other. Caused a right old mess, but I'm still here. Are you after some work?"

"Aye. I'm heading up to Chadds too, but thought I could take in some mending at home. I hear you're making nets for the army these days?"

"You heard right. I'm sure we could set you up with plenty of work. You're staying with Sal?"

Marnie nodded.

"So you'll have everything you need. Shame her hands aren't what they once were. She was a fine beatster in her day."

"Aye, she was. I'm not sure I'll match her speed, but I'm willing to try."

"Well, we can do with all the help we can get. The nets have to be dyed green these days, but other than that, it's much the same as it's always been. I'll drop everything you need round this evening if that suits?"

"Aye, that would be grand. Thank you."

Caro turned her attention back to the net in front of her and Marnie left the beatsters to their work. Given her proximity to *HMS Europa*, or *Sparrow's Nest* as she still thought of it, Marnie decided she would enquire about hosting a serviceman before making her way to the department store. With a deep breath, she turned left on the street and headed for the naval base.

Chapter 11

August, 1941

Of all the changes she'd witnessed in the town, the transformation of *Sparrow's Nest* from place of leisure to the headquarters of the Royal Naval Patrol Service was so great, Marnie struggled to believe it was the same place she'd visited with Tom just a few short years before. The place teemed with bodies, men and women in smart uniforms, all purposeful as they moved around the site. Marnie walked to a small hut at the entrance of the complex.

"Excuse me," she said.

"What can I do for you, madam?"

"I'm here to enquire about hosting one of your sailors."

"You've been a landlady before, have you?"

"My mother-in-law used to host herring girls before the war. I'm now living with her and we have a spare room."

"Well, we're always on the lookout for digs for our boys. Write your name and address down here and I'll make sure it's passed on to the relevant department. Someone will be in touch sooner rather than later to check the accommodation and discuss details."

Marnie wrote her name and address down on the paper provided and handed it back to the man. "Thank you."

"Thank you for offering your services."

Marnie left with an added spring in her step. She smiled at people she passed, pleased to have accomplished two important tasks on her list. It wasn't far to the department store, but halfway there the piercing screech of a siren filled the air. People out on the street began running, and before Marnie knew what was happening, a man rushed up to her, grabbed her arm and pulled her down the side of a building.

"Get off me," shouted Marnie, trying to tug herself free.

The man let go of her arm, turning his head but continuing to run. "You'd best come with me, miss, unless you want to be slap bang in the path of the bomber. I'm trying to help you, not hurt you."

It only took Marnie a second before she decided that following the man was the lesser of two evils. She ran to catch him up, finding herself in a small grass-covered back garden. The man was struggling with a corrugated-iron sheet.

"In here, quick."

Marnie ran towards the shelter, finding it already occupied by a woman and two small children.

"Who the hell are you?" asked the woman.

"I found her out on the street," said the man, shutting them in and making sure the entrance was fully covered.

"Bloody hell, Mick. It's enough of a squish in here already."

The children stared at Marnie, and the woman scowled.

"Thank you for sharing your shelter with me," said Marnie. "Hopefully, we won't be down here for too long."

"Hah, fat chance," said the woman. "Last time we was in here twelve hours."

The woman lit a paraffin lamp and pulled a pack of cards from a box. Marnie perched on the edge of a narrow camp-bed, its blankets damp to the touch. One child reached into a box and pulled out a packet of biscuits.

"Oh, no you don't," said the woman, slapping the child's hand. "We need to save the food until we're starving."

"I'm Marnie, by the way." Marnie smiled at the child nursing their stung hand. "What's your name?"

"Ruth. That's James," she said, pointing to the small grubby boy beside her.

"Oh, I have a brother called James too, but no one's ever called him that. We all call him Jimmy."

"I call my brother Jim sometimes," said Ruth.

"And I'm Mick," said their father, holding out his hand. "Sorry for grabbing you like that, I was only trying to help."

"I'm sorry I assumed otherwise," said Marnie. "I've not been back in town long, and this is the first raid I've experienced since I arrived."

The woman let out a cackle. "You'll get used to them soon enough. I don't know why they bother ever turning the siren off, it sounds that often."

"It must be hard living under constant threat."

The woman shrugged. "We're used to it. Closest town to the enemy and all that. It's to be expected." The woman's laissez-faire attitude was at odds with the way her leg jiggled up and down and her fingers tapped against the camp bed's blankets. Her eyes had the sunken look of someone who'd lacked a good night's sleep for quite some time, and darted around the shelter as though expecting the enemy to tunnel through the floor and grab them from their safe haven.

"Were your children not evacuated in the early days?"

"They were, but it made them miserable, so we brought them back. Do you have children?"

Marnie nodded. "They're, I mean *she's* in Cornwall."

The woman tutted. "I couldn't bear to part with my kiddies, whatever the government says. It's not right, kiddies being separated from their parents."

Marnie felt the implied criticism like a slap in the face.

"Each to their own," said Mick. "None of these choices are easy. You said you'd not long arrived back in town?"

"That's right. I was in Padstow with my daughter, but my in-laws are in poor health, so I came back for them."

"You were down there for the fishing?"

"Aye."

"Did your husband join up?"

"No, he died before the war."

An awkward hush descended on the shelter. Marnie's ears strained for the sound of enemy bombers overhead, but all seemed quiet.

"I'm sorry," said the woman. "I wasn't friendly when you arrived in here. We're all a little on edge these days. And please don't think I judge you for being parted from your daughter. To tell the truth, I was terrified bringing my two back here, but they were so unhappy…"

"Being a mother has always been about making hard choices," said Marnie, "and never more so than now." A familiar throb lent its deadened ache to her chest as she thought back over the events which had led her here. Marnie wondered if she'd ever be free of the guilt, and if she'd ever be free from the need to atone for her mistakes.

A second siren sounded.

"That's the all-clear," explained Ruth, helping her brother gather up the cards they'd been playing with.

"Thank God for that," said the woman.

"I'd best get home to my in-laws," said Marnie. "Thank you for your hospitality."

The woman looked around the shelter and laughed. "If we meet again, let's hope it's between four solid walls with a nice hot cup of tea. I'm Mary, by the way."

"Well, thank you, Mary. Thank you, Mick, and Ruth and James. I'll leave you in peace now."

Mick helped Marnie climb out of the shelter and she brushed herself off. This time might have been a false alarm, but with no saying when the next air raid siren would sound, Marnie decided to make her way to Chadds while she had the chance.

Chapter 12

August, 1941

I t was ridiculous to feel so nervous, and yet, as Marnie stared at the double-fronted department store in front of her, her heart hammered and she had to rub her sweaty palms against her skirt. The window display was pretty, but not up to the standards Marnie once upheld. But that was another lifetime. Marnie tried to imagine a time when her greatest worry was whether the outfits in the window display were coordinated. Had she ever really been a carefree shop girl, or had it all been a dream?

The ring of a bell startled Marnie from her reverie as a customer walked out of the shop. It was no good standing on the street staring, that wouldn't get Marnie any work. She allowed herself one last glance at the impressive three-storey façade, then marched across the street and opened the door.

The smell was just as she remembered it, a delicate floral perfume mixed with furniture polish. Her heeled shoes tapped against the varnished floor, and she held her head high as she walked to the large wooden counter with its sparkling built-in glass cabinets.

"Good afternoon, madam. Can I help you?"

The woman behind the counter was younger than Marnie. Her brown hair hung in waves that tickled her shoulders and her perfectly made-up face was free of lines and blemishes. Marnie felt suddenly old and frumpy as she forced a smile onto her face.

"Hello, I've recently moved back to the town after a couple of years away and..."

"Moved back to the town? My, that's rather bucking the trend around here."

"Aye, well, I had to come back for family reasons. Anyway, the reason I'm here is that I was wondering if you had any work going?"

The woman frowned at Marnie and chewed on the corner of her lip. Marnie wished she'd worn a smarter outfit and added some rouge to her cheeks and lips before leaving the house.

"Do you have any experience with shop work?"

"Actually, I was assistant manager of the women's department here until a few years ago."

"Really?" The woman raised a perfectly plucked eyebrow and folded her arms across her chest. "It must have been quite some time ago as I've been here for the past five years and don't know you from Adam."

"Aye, I left when I had my daughter."

"You're an unmarried mother?"

Marnie flushed at the woman's assumption. What about Marnie's demeanour had possessed the woman to ask such a question? "No, well, aye, I suppose I am, but only because my husband died recently. Not in the war," Marnie added, "he died while out on a fishing expedition." Marnie could have kicked herself. Why did she feel the need to tell this stranger her entire life story? "Mrs Sinclair was the manager when I worked here. I'm sure she'd give me a reference if one is required."

"Have you worked at all since you left Chadds?"

"Oh, aye, I used to help my husband with nets and such like, but most recently I've been helping at a shop down in Padstow."

"And the shopkeeper in Padstow would give you a reference?"

"Oh, certainly. Do you have a piece of paper and a pencil? I can write the address for you?"

The woman pushed a piece of paper and a pen across the glossy countertop. Marnie wrote Richard's name and address in her best handwriting, once again sending up a prayer of thanks that her brother Jimmy had taught her to read and write all those years ago.

"We have a few spare shifts going, but nothing close to full-time hours. Also, the shifts wouldn't be regular. You'd need to be prepared to work as and when you were required."

"That wouldn't be a problem."

"It wouldn't interfere with your family responsibilities?"

"No, my daughter is living down in Padstow. I came here to care for my in-laws, but they're still fairly independent, so as long as I'm home to cook them their supper, I will be free to work."

"Very well. I suggest you come in next week for a trial day and to get yourself acquainted with the latest lines we're stocking. A lot will have changed since you were last here. Would Monday morning suit you?"

"Perfectly."

"Wonderful. My name is Mrs Marjorie Ruthers, and I am the manager of this department. If I am not on the shop floor, tell one of my assistants I'm expecting you and they will come and find me."

"Thank you. Oh, I almost forgot, my name is Mrs Hearn, Marnie Hearn."

"Right, well, Mrs Hearn, I shall see you at nine o'clock sharp on Monday morning."

"I'll look forward to it."

"Please be aware that this is not a firm offer of employment. We'll have to wait and see how you do on Monday, and hear from the shop in Padstow before making such a commitment."

"I understand," said Marnie. As she walked out of the shop, she thought back to her old boss, Mrs Sinclair, and how she'd often come across as a bit of a dragon. Well, it seemed Mrs Marjorie Ruthers could give Mrs Sinclair a run for her money. But a job was a job, and Marnie wasn't about to let her frosty reception get her down. She had just crossed another item off her list, and in times like these, all small victories were to be celebrated.

Chapter 13

August, 1941

Marnie was about to turn back and head home when the door finally opened. Kitty stood there blinking, shielding her eyes from the sun's glare. Marnie noticed that the sitting room was dark, the curtains still drawn despite being almost midday.

"Marnie?"

"Aye, it's me."

Kitty burst into noisy tears, falling to her knees and burying her head in her hands.

"Oh, Kitty, come here." Marnie scooped her friend up in her arms and half led, half carried her towards an armchair.

"I'm s... s... sorry," said Kitty. "It's j... just...so... wonderful to... see you."

"You daft old thing," said Marnie, pulling a handkerchief from her pocket and dabbing it against Kitty's cheeks. "I'll make us a cup of tea."

Marnie left Kitty and walked through to the kitchen as familiar as any she'd been in. The weight of others' grief lay heavy on her shoulders and she leaned against the kitchen counter to take some deep breaths. Pretending to be strong was taking its toll. Marnie wanted to find a quiet corner somewhere and scream and cry her own pain out without witnesses. But that couldn't happen. Instead, she shook herself down and set about boiling the kettle and filling the tcapot with leaves.

"Here you go," said Marnie, walking into the sitting room carrying a tray. Kitty had her knees pulled up to her chest and her sobs had reduced to snuffles.

"Sorry," she said with a sniff. "That wasn't much of a welcome home, was it? I'm not usually a blubbering mess. I pride myself on holding it all in."

"Has something happened?"

"Only Bobby, heading back to sea this morning. You'd think I'd be used to it by now, but just last week there was an entire crew lost to a mine just off the coast of Yarmouth. I've not been sleeping too well and having to wave off Bobby again... well, I think the constant worrying toppled me off my perch. Added to which, there's talk at the base he may be sent down to somewhere called Queenborough, and could be gone for months. Oh dear, I am sorry. It's lovely to see you."

Marnie smiled. "You have nothing to apologise for. I'm just sorry I've not called around sooner, but I wasn't sure you'd be here at all. I thought you might still be down south with Stevie."

"I've been back a little over a week, so I should have called on you, but with Bobby on leave, I wanted as much time with him as possible."

"I completely understand. I've been up to my eyes in cleaning since I got back, so wouldn't have been much company. How is Stevie?"

Kitty blew her nose and managed a weak smile. "He's getting there. And at least he's alive."

"Will he return to active service once he's better?"

"I don't think there's much call for one-legged soldiers," said Kitty.

"Oh, Kitty, I'm so sorry. That was a silly thing for me to say."

"Like I said, at least he survived. He lost his two best friends in the same attack."

"How is he coping?"

"I don't know. Some days he's bright, talking about making the most of the life he's lucky to have, but the next day he'll be brooding and will barely speak a word. The doctor says that's normal."

"I'm sure it is. How long will he be in hospital for?"

"The doc reckons he'll be home in a couple of weeks. I couldn't afford to stay down there any longer, and I wanted to see Bobby. We're praying he's granted leave so we can fetch Stevie together."

"And how's Bobby been managing without you?"

"Well, the house could do with a dust," said Kitty with a smile, "but his mother's been making sure he gets fed, and he's worked out how to wash his own drawers."

Marnie laughed. "Good for him."

"So far, he's not been gone longer than a few days, a week at most. I thought the news about Queenborough was bad, but some sweepers are getting sent much further afield. Bobby knows of a crew sent to the Arctic, if you can believe it. One of our old neighbours is somewhere near India. I'm just praying the south coast is as bad as it gets for us. Even that would see Bobby gone for months on end. To think only a few years ago we were both part of complete families. Look how the war's torn us all apart." Kitty sniffed and dabbed at her eyes. "How've you found the return to Lowestoft? It's different from when you left..."

"That's an understatement," said Marnie. "I couldn't believe it when I saw how badly the town has been hit, not to mention all the soldiers running around The Grit treating it like their personal playground."

"That's unfair."

"I know," said Marnie, "it's not their fault, they're just following orders. But it's heart-breaking to see homes being destroyed as though they're worthless. What a shock those poor families will have when they return."

"If they return. From what I've seen, your own house hasn't fared too well."

"No," said Marnie. "It breaks my heart when I think of all the love Tom put into that house. At least he isn't here to see its downfall. But hopefully it will still be standing once the war's over and we can begin repairs. And we're more fortunate than plenty of folk. Roy and Sally's home is still untouched and all being well, me and Annie can stay there while our own house is being fixed up."

"You must miss her terribly."

"No more than you miss your bairns, or half the women in town miss their own evacuees."

Marnie considered that this would be the perfect opportunity to admit the truth about Grace, the illegitimate child she had abandoned, but Kitty had enough of her own strife to be dealing with, without Marnie piling on her own. And if she were honest, Marnie feared Kitty's reaction. How could someone so comfortable and content with motherhood understand the reasons for abandoning a child? No, Kitty and Marnie needed each other, now more than ever, and there was no way Marnie would risk breaking the bonds of friendship.

"I'd best be getting back to Sally and Roy. I've got myself work on the nets and Chadds will throw a few shifts my way."

"Crikey, you have been busy. Have you heard anything from Jimmy?"

"Aye, I had a letter from him this week. He's staying in Derbyshire for the time being. I miss him, but things are so fraught here, he's probably best off out of the way. I'll call round again tomorrow. I want to make the most of you being here before you have to go south again."

Kitty pulled Marnie into a hug. "I'm pleased to have you back," she said, "despite the circumstances."

Marnie kissed Kitty's cheek and let herself out of the house.

Chapter 14

August, 1941

Marnie rubbed her fingers, trying to tease out the stiffness and cold. It was still summer, but the weather had taken an autumnal turn, the mornings and evenings becoming cooler, a crispness in the air which hinted at the changing of the seasons. She'd been working on the nets for four hours straight and still had several more hours of work to go.

The work was repetitive, tedious, and left Marnie with far too much time for thinking. More often than not, she pictured Helen and Richard's home, full of warmth and love, Annie and Grace comfortable and well loved. In Marnie's darker moments, she wondered if falling victim to the war would be such a bad thing. Wouldn't Annie be better off staying with Helen and Richard forever? After all, Marnie had made that choice for Grace. Why not for both her daughters?

"You look like you could do with a cup of tea," said Sally.

Marnie jumped, pushing away the awful scenarios that filled her head with increasing frequency. "That would be lovely."

"Is everything alright?"

"I was just thinking about Annie."

"You must miss her."

"Aye, but Helen and Richard are good people. By the time this war ends, I'm not sure Annie will want to come back to me." Marnie laughed, trying to hide the truth in her words.

"What nonsense. You're a wonderful mother and Annie adores you. She'll be desperate to be reunited as soon as she's able. I'm so sorry I can't help you with your work." Sally rubbed her swollen fingers.

"Making tea is as good a help as any," said Marnie with a smile. "What time will Roy be back?"

Sally glanced at the clock. "Any time now, although I wouldn't put it past him to stop off at the Rising Sun on his way home, especially as he's been feeling so much better since your return."

The kettle whistled, but before Sally could take it off the stove, the familiar whining of an air raid siren filled the surrounding air.

"Not again," said Marnie, dropping the net she was working on and grabbing her coat.

Sally looked around her in a panic. "Roy should have been back by now. What if he doesn't make it to a shelter in time?"

"You go straight to the shelter and I'll have a quick look for him, then follow behind."

"No. That would be beyond foolish. Come on," said Sally, moving with more determination than Marnie had seen her muster since she arrived.

Sally rushed along a street, which had suddenly become a hive of activity. Folk spilled out of their houses, used to the now regular call of the air raid siren, compelling them to reach safety.

"Where are we going?" asked Marnie.

"The Eagle Brewery."

"Why?"

"Their cellar."

"Oh."

Marnie could tell from the look on Sally's face she was struggling to move with any speed. With each step a grimace flashed across her face, her uneven gait a sign of the arthritis which had now reached her knees. To Sally's credit, she pushed past the pain, fighting her way along the street until they reached the long, low brewery buildings.

At the entrance to the brewery, they joined a group of locals, pushing and shoving to get below ground. A handful of children jostled with women and elderly couples. One of the brewery workers stood at the entrance to the cellar, shepherding people down the steep flight of stairs.

"Down these steps," said Sally, clutching tight to Marnie's hand. "Let's pray to God Roy's already down here."

Lamps hung from the ceiling of the cellar, a series of makeshift beds lying against its walls. Some people had already made themselves comfortable, perched on beds, leaning against barrels. Marnie waited for her eyes to adjust to the gloom as Sally led her towards the far wall.

"We'll have to share a bed," she said. "There'll be more bodies than beds by the time everyone arrives."

"Hopefully we won't be needing a bed at all," said Marnie. "This is probably just another false alarm. The previous raid lasted a little over half an hour."

"I heard the planes," said an old man on the bed beside them, stuffing tobacco into the bowl of his pipe. "There'll be no getting out of here tonight."

Sally strained her neck, looking at the stream of bodies filling the cellar.

"Roy's probably gone to another shelter," said Marnie.

Sally remained quiet, scanning faces in the gloom to no avail. In the opposite corner of the room, a man pulled a fiddle from its case, scraped resin across a bow, and struck up a jolly tune hoping to lift spirits. The old man beside them began clapping along. A few women joined hands, turning the middle of the cellar into a makeshift dance floor.

"How can they be so calm?" asked Marnie.

"They're not, not really. But what else are we supposed to do? Cower in a corner? Cry? We may not be out there fighting the enemy, but the least we can do is not let these scare tactics break us. You know what Gritsters are like. We've suffered our fair share of hard times and always come out the stronger for it. Hitler's no match for fishing folk, you'll see."

Marnie tried to share in some of the calm and good spirit, but couldn't muster anything but feelings of fear and hopelessness. Her earlier daydream taunted her, an image of Helen and Richard assuming parental responsibility for Annie and Grace stuck firmly in her mind.

Two beds along, a woman was boiling water for tea on a small stove. Steam rose in the air, meeting the cold cellar wall and turning to drops of water that trickled to the floor. Beside her, an elderly couple played cards, humming softly to the fiddler's tune. Everyone seemed so at ease.

By ten o'clock the fiddler was still playing his tunes, but his lively numbers had been replaced by gentle, lilting folk songs, acting as a lullaby to the many bodies crammed into their makeshift beds.

Marnie and Sally lay top to tail on the narrow bed. A rumble reached them through the thick cellar walls, sending a confetti of plaster-dust onto their heads. The fiddler paused his tune, casting his eyes up to the ceiling. Seconds stretched out. Another rumble. Quiet.

The fiddler resumed his playing, and Marnie pulled her blanket tighter around her, trying to stop shivering, which was just as likely to be caused by fear as by the cold. She squeezed her eyes tight shut, praying she could get some sleep. When morning came, they would need all the strength they could get for whatever destruction would face them.

Chapter 15

August, 1941

Marnie and Sally followed the line of people heading towards the brightness. Grey, dust-filled daylight greeted them as they climbed the stairs and left the cellar's safety. Marnie didn't know what time it was, but guessed they must have been underground for over twelve hours.

Sally pulled out a handkerchief and rubbed the dust from her eyes. Marnie blinked as her eyes adjusted to the morning light.

"Everything seems as we left it," said Sally, looking up and down the street.

"Listen," said Marnie. She held Sally's arm, standing still as people moved around them, keen to get home after a long night. A siren could be heard, men's shouts, and the distant sound of waves reaching the shore.

"Something's happened," said Marnie. "You go home and see if Roy has made it back yet. I'll find out what's going on."

Marnie ran across the road and began striding toward the harbour. She hadn't been walking long when she noticed smoke twisting its way up against the grey sky. It was coming from an all-too-familiar direction. Marnie increased her pace until she was half running, half walking toward the smoke. At Fishery Street she stopped, clutching a lamppost to steady herself as she took in the bricks spilling into the road, shattered glass covering pavements, and burnt pieces of debris floating around, caught on the wind.

A group of firemen were working hard to contain a stubborn blaze. Men and women walked around as if in a trance, released from the darkness only to find they had lost everything to the bomb.

Marnie ran on, turning down Strand Street, relieved to see that other than pieces of debris it had escaped the worst of the blast. Her steps slowed as she drew closer to East Street. As much as she needed to know her house was still standing, Marnie wondered if it would be best not to know. A woman was scuttling along the street, carrying a basket.

"Excuse me," said Marnie. "I've just seen the damage to Fishery Street. Do you know if any other streets have been hit?"

The woman shook her head slowly. "It's bad alright. Eight bombs is what I've heard. East Street's badly hit, and Nelson Road."

"East Street," said Marnie, more to herself than the woman. "Thank you."

The woman nodded and continued on her way. Marnie walked on, an acrid smell of burning filling her nostrils. Smoke stung her eyes. At least the gas works hadn't been hit. She'd not dared to ask Sally what would happen if it were, for the consequences didn't bear thinking about.

Marnie reached East Street and turned toward her former home. Before she'd reached it, she knew what she would find. The area was partially sealed off, men with shirtsleeves rolled up heaving lumps of rubble in search of survivors. Another fire crew was attempting to put out a burning roof. Her roof.

Marnie crossed the road, and only as she drew level with her house did she collapse to the ground. Bricks and rubble lay strewn across the road, a gaping hole where her home had once stood. At the back of the house, a single curtain flapped against a glassless window frame. Marnie pictured herself singing her daughter to sleep in that very room.

All that remained of the upstairs landing was a zigzag of plaster and wood, the carpet she and Tom had saved so hard for blackened to soot. The bomb had reached its evil hand into the house and scooped beyond even the ground floor, dirt and earth exposed around the edges of the crater.

No tears came, for Marnie couldn't think past the shock of what she was witnessing. It was an ending. The end of her old life, all memories of her life with Tom wiped out in one fell swoop. *It's your punishment*, Marnie told herself. *You betrayed Tom's memory, and now there's nothing left.*

Marnie straightened up and stumbled back along the road, blindly making her way towards her in-laws' home, praying she might feel some presence of Tom inside its familiar walls.

"Marnie?"

Marnie closed the door behind her and walked through to the kitchen. She found Sally and Roy sitting at the table, a pot of tea between them. The relief of seeing Roy alive and well gave a momentary reprieve, and Marnie ran across the room, flinging her arms around her father-in-law.

"You're safe."

Roy laughed. "Of... of course I'm safe. I may be a doddery old fool, b... but I've still got it in me to find my way to a shelter."

"Which way did you walk back?"

"You mean h... have I seen what's happened?"

Marnie slumped down in a chair. "It's all gone," she said. "They've taken it all. Everything Tom worked so hard to build." Tears began rolling down Marnie's cheeks. "It's what I deserve. I should be punished."

Sally stood suddenly, her chair falling to the floor behind her. "You stop talk like that right now, young lady."

"Sally, you don't understand what I've done..." If Sally hadn't interrupted her, Marnie would have spilled out her sorry tale there and then. But Sally was in no mood for self-pity.

"As I told you in the shelter, we can't let what's happening defeat us. We're Gritsters, we're stronger than that. Anyway, what is a house? Nothing but bricks and mortar."

"But Tom..."

Sally surprised Marnie with a laugh. "Tom isn't in that house, Marnie. He's there." She pointed to Marnie's chest. "And he's in the daughter you created together. He's here too." Sally placed a hand on her own chest.

"And here," said Roy, holding a hand to his heart.

"No one's saying living through this war is easy. Hell, grieving's no fun either, but you have so much life ahead of you, Marnie. It's about time you decide what Annie's going to come home to. A mother who hides herself in work, slowly losing any fight or hope for the future, or a mother who's built a new life despite Hitler's best efforts to derail it."

"I don't understand."

"You need to live with the past. It's been two years since you lost Tom, and I know being away from Annie is hard, but you have to find moments of joy when you can. How do you think Roy and me have carried on despite all we've lost?"

"There doesn't seem much joy around at the minute," said Marnie.

"Perhaps you've not been looking hard enough. Now, I don't know about you, but I didn't sleep a wink down in that damp cellar last night.

How about we all try to catch forty winks and then see how the land lies?"

"At least all our precious belongings were already stored here," said Marnie.

"There, see, there's always light to be found in the darkness. Between us, we'll work hard to make sure Annie has something to come home to. For now, though, up the wooden hill with you."

Marnie stood, kissed Sally's cheek, and did as she was told.

Chapter 16

August, 1941

"I wish you didn't have to go."

"Come on now," said Bobby, prising Kitty's fingers from his shirtsleeves. "You know there isn't a choice."

Kitty sniffed and turned her head away from her husband. "What if you don't come back this time?"

"What's brought this on?" asked Bobby, cupping Kitty's chin and forcing her to look into his eyes. "I thought you would have been used to it by now."

How could Kitty explain that the past few weeks had been like getting her husband back? The man who'd been broken by the death of his best friend, and then his eldest son, had been inching his way home. It was news of Stevie's imminent return that had brought on the change, Kitty was sure of it. It was the first piece of good news they'd had for a long time, and seemed to give Bobby a reason to get up in the morning, to survive.

"I don't know," said Kitty. "Perhaps it was last night…"

Bobby pulled Kitty into his broad chest and stroked her hair. Her heart swelled with love and threatened to break with fear. The previous night, Bobby had pulled her close to him and made love to her for the first time in months. It had been like the early days when all they had was each other and a bright future ahead of them.

"They'll be plenty more nights like last night," said Bobby, planting a kiss on Kitty's head. "You won't be getting rid of me that easily."

"But the mines..."

"I've survived them so far, haven't I?"

"Yes, but..."

"I've a good crew with me on the *Sally Ann*. They're sensible chaps and none of us take unnecessary risks. I can't promise nothing bad will happen, but I can promise we do all we can to avoid it."

"I know you do."

"Good. Now I really have to get going. I'll be home in a few days." Bobby leaned down and gave Kitty a firm kiss on the lips. He picked up his holdall and slung it over his shoulder. "I'll see you soon."

"You'd better had."

Kitty stood in the doorway, watching until Bobby disappeared into the fading light. She knew her job was to be strong for her family, but being the one stuck at home waiting and worrying was unbearable. Deciding she needed to do something other than stare at the same four walls, Kitty pulled on her coat and let herself out of the house.

The light was fading fast, but Kitty knew the streets well enough to find her way despite the lack of streetlights to guide her. She reached Sally's house and shuddered at the sight of the gas works looming large at the end of the street. If that was hit, no one nearby would stand a chance. Kitty shook the thought from her head and knocked on the door.

"Kitty," said Marnie, opening the door and peering out. "Is everything alright?"

"Aye, Bobby got called out again, and I didn't fancy another evening by myself. Do you mind me calling round unannounced?"

"Of course not. So far there are no signs of any planes, so we might get a peaceful evening for once. We've just finished supper, but I can pull together some leftovers if you're hungry?"

"No, I'm fine, thanks. I ate with Bobby before he got the call out." Kitty followed Marnie through to the kitchen to where Sally and Roy were sitting at the table finishing cups of tea.

"Have you heard our news?" asked Sally.

"I don't think so?"

"We're getting a sailor as a lodger, someone from up at *HMS Europa*."

"Oh, that is exciting news."

"It will b... balance things up a bit," said Roy. "I'm not keen on being outnumbered by the f... fairer sex."

Sally slapped her husband's arm and shook her head. "Take no notice of him, Kitty. How are all your brood? I hear you've had good news about Stevie."

"Aye, he's coming home. And I've had letters from the others. They're having a grand old time up north on a farm. Every day I send up a prayer of thanks, as I know other kiddies haven't been as fortunate. I think the biggest problem I'll have at the end of the war is persuading my lads to come home."

"I feel the same about Annie," said Marnie. "Helen and Richard are such lovely folk, and she's been so happy there. Coming home may not seem like such an adventure."

"Ah, you're both talking rot," said Sally. "You just wait, in a few months' time all this will be over, The Grit will be filled with the sound of kiddies playing, and you'll both be dead on your feet wondering if you can send your kiddies away again for a short break."

They all laughed, happy to humour Sally, while all very much doubting her assumption that the war would be over soon.

"Shall we take our tea through to the sitting room and play cards?"

"That sounds a good idea," said Marnie. "Perhaps we could even break into the sherry?"

"Why not?" said Sally. "Best eat, drink and be merry while we still can."

"If y... you don't mind, ladies, I'll leave you to it. I'm due at the mission first thing and need a good rest before I go."

"Of course not," said Kitty. "It was good to see you, Roy."

"You too, love. Night night."

Sally walked over and kissed her husband's cheek. "Night, dear."

As the three women settled themselves in the sitting room, Sally glanced back towards the door to check Roy wasn't in earshot. "You know, I think it will do Roy the world of good having another man about the house. He was only joking about being surrounded by females, but, I don't know, with a man around he might need to..."

"Up his game?" asked Marnie. "Not that there's any need to, but when he's at home, he spends a lot of time brooding upstairs. His speech is definitely improving and perhaps with another chap around he may be tempted into conversation more?"

"Yes, just what I was thinking," said Sally. "But in the meantime, let's enjoy our chap-free evening. Who wants to deal?"

Chapter 17

August, 1941

"I'd forgotten all about this," said Roy, pulling a framed photograph from a box. He held it up to show Sally and Marnie.

"Oh my," said Sally, taking the photograph and stroking her fingers across it. They left trails through many years of dust, and tears swam in her eyes. Marnie leaned over her shoulder. A group of boys sat in rows, most serious, but with the occasional one unable to contain a grin. The boy front and centre held a trophy, a football at his feet.

"That was the year our D... David's team won the league. They all came back here for tea and sandwiches after. Do y... you remember, Sally?"

"I'll never forget the amount of mud they trailed across my carpet," said Sally. She smiled at Roy, who leaned forward and pulled her into his arms.

"Happy memories," he whispered.

"Yes. Yes, they are."

"W... what else have we got in here?" Roy pulled back from Sally, rummaging through the cardboard box which was so old and tattered, it was a miracle it hadn't yet fallen apart. "Well, well, well," he said, pulling out another photograph, this time worn yellow and fraying around the edges. "Look at this, Marnie."

Marnie took the outstretched photograph and squinted at it. "Is that you?"

Sally leaned over and pointed a misshapen finger at the photograph. "Me, Roy, his parents and mine. Taken on our wedding day."

"They look rather fierce," said Marnie. "The parents, I mean."

Roy let out a hearty laugh, which set off his cough. When he'd recovered, his eyes were twinkling. "They were furious with us, w... weren't they, Sal? Both sets of parents were against the marriage, but in the end, we left them little choice."

"Marnie doesn't need to hear about all that," said Sally, her cheeks turning pink.

"Now I'm really intrigued. What did you do? And why didn't they want you marrying?"

"Sal's parents were t... t... townies. Her father worked in sh... ship building over in Oulton Broad. Thought themselves a cut above us Gritsters. They w... wanted their daughter to marry up, not down in the world."

"And his parents wanted him marrying a Grit girl. They didn't trust town-folk, much like today, but the feeling was even stronger in those days."

"How did you meet?"

"At a dance." Sally reached across and squeezed Roy's hand. "He was the most handsome man in the room."

"After the dance, we used to meet in s... secret. In summer we'd sneak out of the h...house and meet at the beach. In winter, we'd go to my dad's shed on the beach."

"Did your parents find out?"

"They had to once we realised Sal was expecting."

Marnie looked at Sally with wide eyes. "Expecting? You mean..."

"I know, terrible, terrible behaviour. But I can't say I regret it. We may not have had David in our lives as long as we should, but to have him at all was a blessing."

"The wedding had to be arranged at lightning s... speed as Sal was starting to show."

"My parents tried to persuade me to give the baby up for adoption, but I couldn't do that. I don't know how any woman could ever do that."

Marnie tried to swallow the lump in her throat. If she'd ever wavered about telling the truth about Grace, Sally's last comment had set her straight.

"I hope you don't think too badly of us," said Sally, mistaking Marnie's silence for judgment.

"What? No, of course not!"

"That's a relief," said Sally. "I think I'm too old to still be worrying about my reputation. A year after David came along, we had Albert."

"And then a gap before having Tom?"

Sally nodded. "I struggled a lot after having Bert. I was very low, couldn't get out of bed some days. Those were hard times. We were living with Roy's parents and his mother had no time for my *foolish nonsense,* as she liked to call it. After I'd recovered, we decided not to have any more children. Then seven years later Tom came along, my surprise baby."

"Speaking of which," said Roy. He pulled out a faded blue photograph album and laid it on the floor. As he turned the pages, both he and Sally fell silent, absorbing the images of their children as they smiled from the page.

"We don't have to go through any more boxes if this is too much for you," said Marnie.

Roy wiped his sleeve against his eyes. Sally pulled a handkerchief from her pocket and blew her nose.

"Of course it's difficult, love, but it also reminds me of what a rich life we've led. We've had more than our fair share of loss, but so much love, too. We mustn't ever forget that. But you're right, we should save these boxes for later, or we'll never get this room spick and span ready for our young navy man."

On Roy's instructions, Marnie carried the boxes of photographs and letters through to her in-laws' bedroom, to be opened at a quiet moment when they could sink into their memories undisturbed. Never had she met such resilient folk, and she hoped by living with them some of that strength would rub off on her. If nothing else, Sally and Roy deserved some happiness, and to survive long enough to be reunited with their granddaughter. Marnie didn't have any sway over where or when the Germans dropped their bombs, but she could make sure Sally and Roy were taken care of in other ways. Standing surrounded by her in-laws' memories, Marnie made a silent promise that, however hard it proved to be, she would get them through the war unscathed. When Annie arrived back in Lowestoft, hopefully sooner rather than later, three generations would be reunited.

Chapter 18

September, 1941

"Blimey. You said this place was posh, but I never thought it would be like this."

Bobby and Kitty stared up at the sprawling stately home, its many windows glinting in the sun. Several ambulances were parked in the driveway, and nurses rushed in and out, assisting the Red Cross workers in admitting the latest batch of patients.

"It's more like a hospital inside," said Kitty. "Smells like one, too. Apparently, the family who own the place weren't too happy at having it requisitioned for a hospital."

"I can't blame them. If I lived in a palace like this, I'd never want to leave."

"Come on," said Kitty, taking Bobby's hand. "He'll be waiting for us."

It felt as though she were dragging Bobby towards the entrance, his steps slowing the closer they got. As they reached the threshold, a nurse ushered them out of the way as a stretcher was carried in. Bobby turned his head from the bandaged young man lying on it and took a few steps back. Kitty gripped his hand tighter.

"Bobby, you don't need to be anxious about seeing Stevie. He's the same boy you've always known."

"I know, but his injuries…"

"He's the same boy," said Kitty, her voice firm. She led Bobby inside the hospital and up the grand staircase towards Stevie's ward.

"I'm not sure I can go in," said Bobby as they reached the ward.

"You can and you will," said Kitty, pushing her knuckles into the small of Bobby's back to move him forward.

They found Stevie sitting in a wheelchair beside his hospital bed. He was dressed and holding a canvas bag. One trouser leg had been tied just below the knee and when he looked up and saw them, his mouth was set in a thin line.

"Alright, son," said Bobby, looking everywhere but at Stevie.

"I'm so glad we finally get to take you home," said Kitty, leaning over and hugging her son.

"I expect you'll be pleased to get back to your mum's cooking," said Bobby.

Kitty had to admit that Bobby was trying, but his awkwardness had not gone unnoticed by Stevie, who gave a quick nod of the head before looking away. A nurse walked over to Stevie's cubicle and smiled at the family.

"This young man is ready to be released from our care," she said. "Make sure you arrange for the district nurse to check in on him regularly. His stump will need careful monitoring. Here," she said, handing Kitty a brown bottle. "Give him a spoonful of this if the pain gets too bad."

Kitty took the bottle of medicine. "Thank you, nurse, and please thank all the staff here for taking such good care of him."

"I'll pass that on. I've arranged for two of our porters to help you with the stairs. They should be waiting for you now."

"Thank you very much," said Bobby, walking behind the wheelchair and taking hold of the handles. "Homeward bound, son. Homeward bound."

Stevie's hands tightened around the bag in his lap. Kitty wished he'd thank the nurse, but he sat quiet and still in the chair, his jaw clenched as Bobby wheeled him through the ward.

As they passed through the front door and onto the driveway, Stevie took a deep breath, filling his lungs with country air.

"Smells better out here than in there, doesn't it?" said Kitty, squeezing Stevie's shoulder as Bobby pushed the wheelchair across the gravel. The thin tires protested as Bobby forced them against the small stones, and he cursed several times as the chair dug in.

"Sorry for the bumpy ride, son," said Bobby, giving a tight laugh. "It will be smoother once we get to the road."

"It's alright," said Stevie, his voice quiet, his eyes downcast.

Kitty looked from her son to her husband, feeling as though they had a mountain to climb before life returned to anything resembling normal. As they passed by the two stone pillars that marked the entrance to the driveway, Kitty felt a weight lift from her shoulders. They might have a long road ahead, but getting Stevie out of the hospital was an important first step. And it would be a relief not to have to make the journey again, both for financial reasons and given the logistics of travelling anywhere during wartime.

The walk to the nearest railway station was mostly in silence, peppered by occasional titbits of small talk Kitty attempted to lighten the atmosphere. What she had looked forward to as a joyous moment felt as though the air had been sucked from it, like a football deflating in the middle of a game.

"Here we are."

Kitty pointed to the small rural platform, and Bobby pushed Stevie's wheelchair up a slope.

"What time's the next train?" asked Bobby.

"Hmm, let me see." Kitty ran her finger along the timetable pinned to a notice board. "It says here there should be a train any minute, but this timetable looks as though it's been here for quite some time. Things may have changed since the war."

"Let's hope not," said Bobby, pulling a handkerchief from his pocket and mopping his brow. He stretched his arms above his head and moved his hips from side to side.

"Is your back hurting?"

"No, it's fine. I'm hot and bothered, that's all."

Kitty watched as Bobby kneaded the small of his back with his knuckles. It must've been a job pushing Stevie all that way, but she knew Bobby had kept quiet for Stevie's sake. In the distance, a cloud of smoke rose into the clear summer sky.

"It's coming," said Stevie, pointing toward the treetops. "You'll have to help me out, Dad. You won't be able to lift the chair through the door with me in it."

Kitty held Stevie's crutches at the ready as Bobby moved around the wheelchair. It was the first time father and son had touched, and by the looks on their faces, neither was relishing the moment. Stevie wrapped his arms around Bobby's neck as Bobby placed his arms around Stevie and heaved him out of the chair. A flicker of pain crossed Bobby's face and Kitty prayed he'd not done any lasting damage to his back.

With Stevie upright, Kitty handed him his crutches. Although it was hidden by trees, the noise of the train was growing louder, the chug of the engine and squeal of metal as it prepared to slow. Kitty sent up a prayer of thanks as the train drew level with them, revealing mercifully empty carriages.

Kitty climbed onto the train, taking hold of Stevie's crutches and preparing to steady him should he fall. He grabbed hold of the handrails and heaved himself up, hopping on his one remaining foot. Kitty handed back the crutches and noticed his face had become white and sweaty with the effort.

"Find yourself a seat, love. Me and Dad will get the chair up for you."

Bobby lifted the chair up, and between them, they tried to manoeuver it through the doorway. It was easier said than done, Bobby muttering unrepeatable words to the guard, who paced the platform in impatience without offering to assist them.

After much heaving and panting, they had squeezed the cumbersome chair through the narrow opening and were ready to depart.

"Lowestoft, here we come," said Bobby, reaching across and squeezing Kitty's hand.

"Aye, time to go home."

Chapter 19

September, 1941

*D*ear Annie,

How are you? Are you enjoying school? I expect you are pleased to get back. Nanny and Granddad Hearn send their love. We all miss you, and pray every night that this blasted war will be over soon. I've begun making camouflage nets for the army, and I'm happy to tell you I'm much better at making nets than I am making socks! I have also found work in Chadds, the department store I worked in before I had you. They only need me once or twice a week, but it stops me missing my work in Uncle Richard's shop too much.

Uncle Jimmy sent me a letter last week. He's still up north teaching children like you, who are living away from home. He said he can't wait to see you and give you a big hug. Kitty sends her love too. Sam, Mark, Peter and Chrissy are still up in Derbyshire, living on a farm. From the letters Kitty received, they seem to be getting on well. She says Sam asks after you in every letter and misses you.

Sam's not the only one to miss you. I miss you, my darling girl, so very much, but hopefully it won't be long until we see each other again. All my love, Mummy.

Dear Helen,

Thank you for your most recent letter. It is an enormous relief to know that Annie has settled and is happily back at school. Every day I thank

God she is safe in Padstow with you. Things here are frightening, the air raid siren sounding most days. There are a few children who didn't settle as evacuees and have returned to their parents. What a worry it must be for their mothers, having their children in harm's way day after day.

In my last letter, I told you about the condition I'd found our house in. Well, if there was even a glimmer of hope we may one day return, that was stolen when a bomb flattened our house and those either side the other week. It's probably best Annie doesn't know about the house for now, and whilst I still miss him every day, part of me is glad Tom didn't live to see it

.

Kitty's son Stevie is due to be discharged from hospital any day now and both he and Kitty will be back in Lowestoft for good. It sounds as though the poor lad is finding it hard to adjust to his disability, but hopefully things will get easier once he's home.

You'll remember me talking about Kitty's husband, Bobby. At the start of the war, they drafted him in to help with minesweeping. He's just received orders to go to Queenborough, a port south of London, and will probably be away for several months at least.

Sally and Roy are both fine. Neither is in the best of health, but I think my being here helps. I'm not sure if I told you, but we're due to take in a sailor from HMS Europa *any day now. Sally's in a lather about getting the house ready. I'm hoping having a young man around the house will be good for her and not bring up too many painful memories of her sons.*

As for me, I'm keeping busy. Between making camouflage nets, caring for Sally and Roy and my shifts at Chadds, there's not much time for brooding, which is just as well. I've enclosed a letter for Annie, and please tell her Roy and Sally miss her and send their love. We're all hoping it won't be too long before we're reunited.

Send my love to Richard and Jack, Marnie

Marnie folded the paper and slipped it into an envelope. Should she have asked about Grace? No, it was best to keep a safe distance from the feelings that thoughts of her youngest daughter dredged up. A couple of weeks previously, Helen had sent a photograph of Grace. Marnie had almost torn it up, so painful was it to look at. Instead, she had pushed it to the back of a drawer, unable to throw it away or look at it. It had been a kind gesture of Helen's sending the photograph, but Marnie wished she hadn't. In order for all of them to move on, it was best to keep things as separate as possible.

With the letters in their envelope, Marnie picked up her pen and pulled out a fresh piece of paper.

Dear Jimmy,

Thank you for your last letter. I've settled back into life here, although it feels strange to be back in Lowestoft without you, Annie, or Tom. Sally's arthritis is much the same as ever and Roy puts on a brave face, although I can tell he's struggling. He's determined to get himself out to the Seamen's Mission several times a week, but it tires him out something rotten.

Stevie is due home any day now, which will be such a relief for the whole family. It's bound to take him a while to get used to his disability, but at least he'll be home and not out on the battlefield. Kitty's other bairns are doing well up north. I'm not sure if you ever come across them, but they're on a farm somewhere having a whale of a time if the letters she gets are anything to go by.

How is the teaching going? I've been surprised how many children have come back here already. I honestly don't know why their mothers would bring them home. The bombings are incessant, and if it's not an actual bomb, there's a false alarm that sees us underground for hours at a time.

On cheerier news, we should get a new lodger any day now. I've been to HMS Europa *and they're arranging for one of their sailors to move in here. I'm not sure how long they'll be with us, but it will be a useful income, and I think it will do Roy and Sally good to have someone new in the house.*

Anyway, I must dash. Lots of love to you and please pass on my love to Clara. Marnie

Chapter 20

September, 1941

"Welcome home." Even to her own ears, Marnie's words sounded feeble as a thin, pale Stevie drew closer in his wheelchair. Bobby was pushing the contraption along and Kitty followed close behind, carrying her bag in one hand and a pair of wooden crutches in the other.

"It's good to be home, isn't it, Stevie?" she said, giving Marnie a hug as they reached the front gate. Stevie kept his eyes to the ground, giving only the slightest nod of the head to show he had heard.

"Come on then," said Marnie. "There's a pot of tea waiting for you inside."

Kitty squeezed Marnie's arm and Bobby pushed Stevie up the newly added ramp by the front door. Whilst the bulky wheelchair could squeeze through the front door, navigating the cramped sitting room proved harder.

"Why don't we have our tea in here?" suggested Marnie.

"Thank you," said Kitty, throwing Marnie a grateful look before turning her attention back to her son.

When Marnie returned with a tray of cups and saucers, she found Stevie gazing out of the window, Bobby staring at the wall and Kitty perched on the edge of an armchair, wringing her hands in her lap.

"Tea, Stevie?" asked Marnie.

"No, I'd like to go for a lie down."

"I thought we could make you up a bed in here," said Kitty. "That way you won't have to bother with the stairs."

"I'll sleep in my old room, thank you very much," muttered Stevie, groping for the crutches which were lying on the ground.

"Here," said Kitty, rushing forward and handing them to him. "Let me help you."

"No!" The shout startled Marnie, tea spilling in a pool on the tray. "I can manage myself," said Stevie. He didn't apologise for the tears he'd brought to Kitty's eyes, but the lowering of his voice was as good as.

"Alright," said Kitty. "But I'll be down here if you need me."

Stevie leaned forward on the crutches. Despite still having the use of one leg, it took him several attempts to get out of the chair, and all Marnie and Kitty's restraint not to jump up and assist him. He hobbled across the room, and the two friends sat in silence, listening to his frustrated grunts as he tried to pull himself up the stairs.

"Bobby," whispered Kitty, "Why don't you try to help? Stevie may be more willing to accept help from another man."

"You heard what he said. He doesn't want us fussing."

"Any word on when you're being sent out to Queenborough?" asked Marnie.

"No." Bobby let out a loud sigh, stood up and made his way through to the kitchen.

"Right." Marnie turned to Kitty, hoping her friend would be more communicative than either of the men in the house. "I hope you don't mind, but I told Clara about Stevie."

"Of course not. I was hoping you would have. I couldn't bear having to put it down on paper yet again."

"She sends her love to you all, and she also made a suggestion I think has a lot of merit."

"Go on." Kitty took a sip of her tea.

"You remember Joe?"

"Clara's brother-in-law? The one injured in the last war?"

"That's the one."

"Wasn't he hit while out sweeping for mines?"

"Aye. He was the only crew member to survive, but he lost his sight and has been blind ever since. Clara wondered if he'd be a good person for Stevie to talk to. How much do you know about Joe's family?"

"Only the little Clara has told me."

"Well, he has adapted extremely well to his injuries and works making rope from his shed in the garden. But even more than living with his disability, he's learned to live with the guilt."

"What's my Stevie got to feel guilty about? He's done nothing wrong."

"I'm not suggesting he has. But guilt comes in all shapes and sizes." *And I should know*, thought Marnie. "With Joe, it was guilt that he was the only survivor from the boat. It's possible Stevie may feel frustrated he can't go back and fight, or guilty to be relieved he doesn't have to. He may feel none of those things and cope perfectly well with what's happened to him, but I can't see how talking to Joe would hurt, can you?"

"No, and I'm very grateful to Clara for having thought of it. These men have a tendency to keep things bottled up." Kitty glanced towards the kitchen, where they could hear Bobby moving around. "I'm not sure how keen Stevie will get on talking with a stranger."

"He doesn't have to talk at all if he doesn't want to. Just being with someone who knows something about what he's going through may help?"

"Perhaps. It can't hurt to try." Kitty sighed. "I wish he'd sleep down here. He'll wear himself out dragging up and down those stairs all the time."

"You never know, staying active may help. It strikes me he's trying very hard to maintain some independence."

Kitty flopped back into her armchair.

"Are you alright?"

"Just tired and, if I'm honest, feeling a bit at sea. First, I had to get used to the house being deathly quiet without the kiddies here, in a few days Bobby's being sent miles away, and now I've got Stevie back and I haven't the first idea how to help him."

"Kitty, you are the most wonderful mother I know. Stevie's your son, part of you. You'll work out how to help him in a way that works for the both of you. Just give him time to settle in, and you know I'm always here if you need me."

"Thank you."

"That's what friends are for."

Chapter 21

September, 1941

Marnie yawned, took a deep breath, and opened the cubicle door. Marjorie, her supervisor, walked into the ladies' toilets and frowned at her.

"I hope you're not wasting time in here. You've had all your breaks for the day."

"No, of course not," said Marnie, washing her hands quickly and drying them on a towel. It was hard, taking orders from a woman in a position she'd once held. But Marnie bit her tongue. She was lucky to have a job at all, especially so soon after arriving back in Lowestoft.

Being back in the department store brought both relief and a sense of déjà vu. Sometimes Marnie would forget her age and almost convince herself she was back in her carefree youth. It would surprise her to catch a glimpse in a mirror and see the newly acquired lines on her face, and the white hairs which had appeared in tandem with the outbreak of war.

Despite the exhaustion of juggling two jobs and her caring duties, every time Marnie walked into the store it felt like being wrapped in a familiar blanket. The shop had witnessed some of the most important moments of her life; the time she'd bumped into Clara after years of separation, Tom's regular visits to woo her, and the place her waters had broken at the start of welcoming Annie into the world. It brought a sense of normality that was difficult to find elsewhere in the rapidly changing world.

The afternoon passed quickly. There weren't as many customers as there once were, but there were enough to keep Marnie distracted from the gaping wound in her soul, that caused tears to spring to her eyes when she was least expecting it.

Whereas she'd once advised women on dresses for dances and parties, now she helped them select the most hard-wearing coats, utilitarian headscarves and drab but functional dresses.

The women of Lowestoft had lost none of their spirit, but their sparkle had dimmed. How many times in the last week had she watched women twirling wedding rings on their fingers, their minds distracted by the thought of menfolk far from home? How many times had she watched women count out coins, making sure they left enough in their purses to last them the week?

The conversation among the shop girls revolved around the war; ration cards, news from the front, dangers at home. There seemed no room left for banal conversation about the latest fashions or men who had caught their eye.

But Marnie was grateful to be back. She felt as if she'd come home, slotting into the role as though it had been made for her. There were only a few familiar faces from before, but she rubbed along with her new colleagues well enough, asking them enough questions to draw attention away from her own situation. She'd told them she'd lost her husband, and they assumed this was the reason she avoided talk of Padstow, and left her be.

At the end of her shift, Marnie collected her coat and bag from the staff room and straightened a selection of sweaters on a shelf before turning to head home.

"Excuse me, but I don't think those shelves are stacked neatly enough."

Marnie spun around, her mouth falling open.

"Close your mouth, dear, you're gaping like a fish."

"Mrs Sinclair. What are you doing here?" Marnie stared at her old boss, who'd finally retired.

"I like to monitor the place, make sure it's being run to my high standards."

Marnie smiled, thinking regular inspections from Mrs Sinclair would be the last thing the new managers wanted. "And is it up to your specifications?"

"Well, standards have slipped, but I'm sure they'll improve now you've returned. Now, dear, I know it's nearly closing time, so I wondered if you'd like to join me at my flat for a cup of tea?"

Marnie glanced at the clock on the wall. "Aye, I reckon I could. I'll need to get back to make supper for my in-laws, but a cup of tea would be nice."

"Wonderful. I'll wait outside for you."

Marnie wondered why Mrs Sinclair was showing a sudden display of friendship. As her boss, Mrs Sinclair had been a hard taskmaster, increasingly morose as her retirement slipped nearer. Offering Marnie a cup of tea was so unusual, she couldn't help but satisfy her curiosity about the older woman.

Marnie said her goodbyes to her colleagues and found Mrs Sinclair waiting outside.

"It's not far to my flat," said Mrs Sinclair.

Marnie realised she had no idea where Mrs Sinclair lived, and was surprised to find she lived only a few minutes' walk away, above a shop on the high street. Mrs Sinclair unlocked a side door and led Marnie up a narrow flight of stairs.

As they walked into the flat, a cat sidled up, leaning against Mrs Sinclair's legs and purring loudly. "This daft creature only shows me affection when he's hungry, don't you, Oscar?" She bent down and stroked the cat's fur. "Make yourself at home."

Marnie sat herself down in an armchair facing a kitchenette that spanned the far wall. The flat was both tidy and simple, a few books perched beside ornaments on a shelf, the furniture utilitarian rather than handsome.

"I'm surprised to find you still living in Lowestoft," said Marnie. "I assumed you would have moved somewhere safer."

Mrs Sinclair filled a kettle. "Yes, I probably should have. I thought about it, but decided to take my chances here. There have been many times I've regretted that decision. It can get rather lonely, with so many of my friends having left the town."

Marnie felt herself relax now she understood Mrs Sinclair's need for company.

"The last I heard, you'd moved with your family to Padstow?"

"Aye, that's right. My husband, Tom, died shortly after we arrived in a fishing accident."

"Oh no, that's terrible news. I'm so sorry to hear that."

"Thank you."

"So that's why you came back?"

"No. My in-laws need help as their health is failing, but with the outbreak of war, everyone who had been helping them moved away. I couldn't see any option but to come back. My daughter has stayed in Padstow with friends of mine."

"That must be difficult for you."

"It is."

"Here," said Mrs Sinclair, handing Marnie a cup of tea. "If you don't mind me saying, Marnie, you seem to have lost some of your get-up-and-go. To be expected, I suppose, what with all the loss you've suffered and this blasted war."

Marnie took a sip of her tea, wondering what to say in response. Before she could summon the words, Mrs Sinclair continued.

"I've had a lot of time to think since I retired. If I had my time again, there's plenty I would have done differently. You know, I always saw you as something of a kindred spirit."

"You did?" Marnie looked up in surprise, unsure this was a compliment given Mrs Sinclair's spiky demeanour during the years they'd known each other.

"Yes. I was like you as a young woman; independent, always trying to better myself. Unlike you, though, I never married. I couldn't bear the thought of being trapped by marriage, unable to do as I wished, when I wished. But now look at me. No husband, no children, no wider family to speak of."

Once more, Marnie was lost for words. Mrs Sinclair waved a hand in the air.

"Sorry, my dear, I'm rather babbling, aren't I? I suppose what I'm trying to say is although the loss you've suffered is great, don't let it close you off to the world. In my experience, that's the path to loneliness."

"Right, I'll bear that in mind," said Marnie, unsure of what Mrs Sinclair was trying to tell her.

The rest of the encounter passed with mild small talk. Several times Marnie tried to leave, but each time Mrs Sinclair asked her another question, as though trying to keep Marnie with her for as long as possible. Eventually, Marnie insisted that she really must be getting home, and thanked Mrs Sinclair for the tea, promising to return the following week. As she walked away towards her own home, Marnie thought of her visit to Mrs Sinclair as a cautionary tale. However the rest of her life played out, she hoped it wouldn't result in seeing out her winter years with only a cat for company.

Chapter 22

September, 1941

"What are we doing here again?"

Marnie laughed, linking arms with Kitty and heading towards the beach. "Sally told me I need to stop moping around and look for joy where I can find it. Even my old boss seems to think seeking fun is the best course of action."

"So we're heading to a barbed-wire-covered beach to find joy?"

"We're going to look at the sea and sky and remember the beauty is still there, even if it is covered in barbed wire."

"Don't forget about the mines. They're hidden all over the beach."

"I wasn't suggesting we go onto the beach to build sandcastles. We'll stay well clear of any mines."

A breeze teased their hair as they walked. Marnie felt a tingle inside her and realised it was as close to happiness as she had come for a long time. If Sally could see past her grief, so could she. Marnie didn't believe she deserved happiness for her own sake, but she would try to find it for the sake of Sally and Roy. She might be caring for them and helping around the house, but if she acted like a wet weekend, it would only make things harder for them.

The two women reached Ness point before they stopped walking. "The most easterly point of England," said Kitty with a smile.

Marnie leaned into her friend, resting her head on Kitty's shoulder. They stared out to the horizon, ignoring the barbed wire and soldiers walking along the seafront. Marnie closed her eyes and imagined Tom beside her.

"He'd be proud of you," said Kitty.

"Who?"

"Tom. You were thinking about Tom?"

"How did you know?"

Kitty shrugged. "Lucky guess. But he would, be proud of you, I mean."

"I'm not sure he would."

"Marnie, you've sacrificed so much to come here and take care of Sally and Roy. They're not your blood, but you did it anyway. And you've left Annie in the care of good, kind folk. I'd say all that's something to be proud of."

Marnie smiled a tight smile, thinking of all she'd kept from Kitty. She hoped Tom couldn't see the mess she'd made of everything.

"You're not doing too badly yourself," said Marnie. "You're an amazing mother, Kitty."

"I couldn't protect them all," said Kitty, her voice quiet.

"You did all you could. What happened to Al wasn't your fault."

Kitty rolled her shoulders and shook her head, as though trying to rid herself of the sadness. Her face creased into a small smile. "I still miss the songs of the herring girls. It almost feels like a completely different town without them."

"It's only temporary. Before we know it, the navy will be gone and the herring girls will have returned."

"You think so? I'm not sure. You know how things were going before war broke out."

"Aye, but people will still want fish on their plates, and someone has to catch it. Your Bobby will be back out chasing silver darlings rather than mines soon enough."

"I hope so. Have you thought about what you'll do once the war ends?"

Marnie shook her head. "I've not thought beyond bringing Annie back. I suppose I'll keep doing much the same, mending nets, working at Chadds."

"And love? Have you given any thought to love?"

"With a man?"

"That's usually the way these things work," said Kitty with a smile.

"No, my days of romance are long behind me. Men only bring trouble."

Kitty raised an eyebrow, but Marnie looked away. "What aren't you telling me?"

"Nothing. How about we get a penny of chips?"

"That sounds like an excellent idea."

Once they'd each got a packet of chips, they perched on a low wall beside the Denes and ate in silence, both mulling over their thoughts. The net drying racks were still standing, but rather than the hustle and bustle of the herring industry, the area was empty, and it was *HMS Europa* providing the area with a welcome hubbub.

"How's Stevie getting on?" asked Marnie, popping her last chip into her mouth and scrunching the newspaper into a ball.

Kitty sighed. "Up and down. To be honest, it's all been much harder than I expected."

"Has Stevie met with Joe?"

"Aye, he has, and I think it helped. I spoke to Joe too, and he advised me to encourage Stevie to be as independent as possible. I'm thinking of volunteering for some war work just to get out of the house more. I'm not sure it's helping Stevie to have me fussing over him day in, day out."

"What kind of work are you thinking? Aren't you already doing your bit with the camouflage nets?"

"Aye, but I could do more. I'm thinking of joining the Red Cross on the ambulances. With Bobby and the bairns away, it would be good to be busier. Working on the nets gives me too much time to think."

"I understand that," said Marnie. "I'm so grateful for my work at Chadds. Did I tell you I saw Mrs Sinclair the other day?"

"Wasn't she the old battle-axe you used to work for?"

"Aye, but she's not that bad. Actually, I think she's rather lonely. I've decided I'll call in on her once or twice a week. I think she'd appreciate the company."

"Crikey, you're getting quite the collection of elderly and infirm to care for. You'd better be careful you don't grow old before your time."

"Don't be so rude," said Kitty with a laugh. "In case you hadn't noticed, there's not that many young folk around these days, and anyway, we're not spring chickens ourselves."

"We should go to a dance," said Kitty, "or watch a film. Anything to remind us of our youth."

"That's not a bad idea," said Marnie. "If we went to watch a film, perhaps we could take Stevie with us? It might do him good to get out of the house?"

"I can ask him, but I'm not sure he'll say yes. Perhaps you could invite your new lodger?"

"Not likely. He hasn't even moved in yet and goodness knows what sort of fellow he'll be. A nice one, hopefully, but it's all a bit of a gamble. All I know about him so far is his name."

"Which is?"

"Frank Merton."

"Frank Merton, hmm, a nice name. I predict a handsome blond young man with a pleasant temperament."

"You can get all that from his name? Well, I hope you're right. He arrives tomorrow, so we'll soon find out."

Chapter 23

September, 1941

"Is everything ready?"

"Aye," said Marnie, struggling to keep the frustration from her voice. She'd been up since six getting the house ready for their guest and had reassured Sally more times than she could count.

"I hope this won't be too much work for you."

"It will be fine," said Marnie. "He'll be out all day every day and probably evenings too. All he'll need is a daily hot meal and a change of bedding once a week. Besides, I'm sure this house will be a big step up from whatever shared digs he's been in so far."

Before Sally could fret any further, there was a knock at the door.

"I'll get it," said Sally, hobbling her way along the hallway.

Marnie didn't want the young man to feel as though he were being ambushed, so hung back in the kitchen. She heard Sally greet their guest in what Tom used to refer to as her *visitor voice*, somewhere between her usual thick Lowestoft accent and the kind you heard newsreaders use on the wireless.

"This is my daughter-in-law, Mrs Hearn," said Sally, walking into the kitchen. She was followed by a tall, slim-shouldered man, with greying hair and a ready smile.

"Call me Marnie. Two Mrs Hearns in one house could get very confusing." She held out her hand, and the man took it.

"Frank Merton. Very pleased to meet you, Mrs Hearn."

"Marnie, please."

"Very pleased to meet you, Marnie." Frank's hazel eyes twinkled, and he dipped his head in a bow. "Is it just the two of you living here?"

"Oh no," said Sally. "My husband Roy lives here as well, but he's off down at the Seamen's Mission as often as he can. He's there now."

"Doing important work, I'm sure."

"Yes," said Sally, her face flushing with pride.

Marnie considered that, if nothing else, Frank Merton was a charmer. He had Sally wrapped around his little finger and he'd not been in the house for five minutes.

"Can I get you a cup of tea?"

"That would be lovely, thank you."

"I'll put the kettle on, and while it's boiling, how about I show you to your room?"

"I can do that," said Sally. Marnie wondered if she were keen to maintain her position as matriarch of the house.

Frank and Sally reappeared five minutes later, Frank announcing he was more than satisfied with his new accommodation.

"What is it you do at *HMS Europa*, or is that top secret?" asked Sally as Marnie poured the tea.

Frank grinned. "I assure you, my job isn't that exciting. And I'm not actually based at *HMS Europa*. My base is *HMS Minos*, down at the port. We work in harbour defence, escorting craft in and out, that sort of thing. My specific role is in logistics, and I'm sometimes called on to help train the new recruits. I may not have youth on my side, but at least I have experience."

"We're very grateful for all the work you and the other lads do to keep us safe," said Marnie, taking a seat opposite Frank and Sally. "The enemy seems to have their sights firmly set on the town."

"Yes, it's not much surprise. Aside from being so close to Europe, the shipbuilding that goes on here makes it a prime target, not to mention all the other industry."

"Do you think the war will end soon?" asked Sally, a hint of hope in her voice.

Frank shrugged and took a sip of his tea.

"Where are you from?" asked Marnie.

"Lincolnshire. A lot of the training was carried out at the Butlin's holiday camp in Skegness, so it was very convenient for me. We had little time off, but when we did, I could pop home and visit my mother."

"She must worry about you."

"Oh yes, always. I'm her only son, but I have two sisters. They're married with young families but have both signed up to the WVS. Charlotte is an Air Raid Warden and Catherine helps distribute clothing and supplies as part of the Welfare Service."

Marnie felt a pang of guilt. Making camouflage nets seemed paltry compared to Frank's sisters' war efforts.

"How about you, Mrs Hearn?"

"Me?"

"Do you have sons or daughters, or both? If you have daughters and they take after their mother, they're bound to be beautiful." Frank's mouth was spread in a wide grin, which soon slipped as he took in Sally's reaction.

Marnie watched Sally visibly wince. Frank turned to Marnie, his furrowed brow moving from confusion to concern.

"I've three boys," said Sally, standing up so quickly Marnie had to grab her chair to stop it falling. "If you'll excuse me, there's something I must see to outside. I'll be back in a tick."

The door closed behind Sally, and Frank turned to Marnie. "Dear God, what have I said?"

"Please don't worry, you weren't to know. All of Sally's sons are dead."

"Oh, good Lord." Frank leaned his head against his hands and scrubbed his hair. "Mother always says I should learn to think before I speak. I should know better now. It's not as if I'm some young lad."

Marnie tried to guess how young or old Frank was. Aside from his greying hair, there was evidence of crow's feet around his eyes, but Frank's demeanour was that of a young man, and a cocky one at that. "Really, Frank, you had no way of knowing. It was a perfectly reasonable question. Most of the time Sally and Roy hide their grief well, but I think having a man around the house has the potential to bring up some sad memories. I'll keep a close eye on them, though. Don't worry."

"Did they lose their sons recently?"

"Sally's two eldest sons died some time ago during the last war. Their youngest, Tom, my husband, died in a fishing accident two years back."

"What rotten luck they've had."

"I know. Life's been cruel to Sally and Roy. It's deeply unfair. They're such good people, but war doesn't discriminate, does it?"

"I'm surprised they can carry on at all, given what they've been through."

"They're tough folk. Besides, they've got a granddaughter to live for now."

"Your daughter?"

"Aye." Marnie smiled at Frank. "Annie, she's down in Padstow. Perhaps one day you'll meet her."

"What's she like?" asked Frank, looking relieved the conversation had moved on to safer topics.

"Hmm, well, she's bright, sharp as a pin, in fact. She's got a stubborn streak and can be a right little madam, but I've only got myself to blame for that. Folk say we're peas in a pod."

"You don't strike me as a stubborn little madam," said Frank with a grin.

"Perhaps I've mellowed with age."

"You don't strike me as old, either."

Marnie felt her cheeks heat. Worried the conversation had taken on too personal a tone, she stood up and announced she had better check on Sally. As Marnie let herself out of the back door, she decided she'd need to keep her wits about her around Frank Merton. He might think he could charm the birds from the trees, but he'd met his match with her.

Chapter 24

October, 1941

"I'm off, love."

Kitty peered up the staircase, waiting, hoping for a response. None came, so with a sigh she buttoned up her coat and pulled on her gloves. Whilst Stevie continued to improve physically, and had more good days than when he'd first arrived, the black clouds which filled his mind still appeared indiscriminately and Kitty was at her wits' end to know how to help him. She prayed that by removing herself from the house, he would feel more able to test out his independence. After all, he was now confident getting around on crutches and would soon be fitted for a wooden leg.

As she opened the front door, a sharp blast of freezing air hit Kitty's body. Winter had come early this year. She'd been knitting furiously and had sent a parcel full of socks and mittens to Derbyshire in the hope they would keep her absent children warm. From her own experience she knew the harshness of winters in the north, and hated to think of her offspring struggling with the cold.

The door slammed behind her and Kitty bent her head into the wind, setting off along the road to the local Red Cross office. She hoped her services would be needed, and she hadn't missed the boat. Perhaps she should have volunteered earlier in the war, but with the death of Al and the uncertainty around Stevie's condition, it hadn't felt possible to add any more to her plate.

The area around the Red Cross headquarters was quiet, the bad weather forcing all but the hardiest of souls inside. Kitty pushed a wooden door open with a loud creak and smiled at the receptionist, who looked up at her.

"Good afternoon. I'm here to inquire about volunteering with the Red Cross."

"Then we're much obliged to you."

"I know I'm a bit late to be volunteering now, but it's only recently I've had more time on my hands."

The receptionist smiled at Kitty. "It's never too late to volunteer and we're always grateful for new recruits. Do you have any area you'd like to volunteer for? We're always welcoming of any fund-raising ideas."

"Oh, well, I hadn't really thought about fund-raising. I was thinking something a bit more hands on, perhaps with the ambulances?"

"Do you have any experience in nursing?"

"Only of my own children, and believe me, between the seven of them, they've had their fair share of injuries. But nothing formal, no. I had a go at driving one of those new-fangled steam tractors back in the day when a neighbour bought one for his farm. I wasn't too bad at it."

"You're from the Highlands?"

"Originally, aye, but I've been down here more years than I can count."

"You came with the herring?"

"Aye."

"My mother did the same, then met my dad and never left. I'm Jane, by the way."

"Kitty, nice to meet you, Jane. So, do you think you can make use of me?"

"No question. With all the bombings we're being subjected to, we can always use more volunteers, and it sounds like you have some skills we're after. We'll provide first aid training and put you on an experienced team. When can you begin your training?"

Kitty looked at the receptionist in surprise. "Really? You'll accept me, just like that?"

"You'll have to pass through training, so it's not a done deal, but we'll happily give any volunteer a try. As I said, we need all hands on deck at a time like this."

"Goodness, well, that's wonderful. I can fit my work on the nets in around any training I need to do."

"A can-do attitude, just what we like to see here." Jane flicked through a large book, which Kitty assumed was a diary. "Right, so it's Thursday today, and I can see we're running a training session at ten Monday morning. How does that sound?"

"That sounds wonderful."

"Excellent. Well, it was lovely to meet you, Kitty, and we'll look forward to seeing you Monday morning."

Kitty said her goodbyes and had to restrain herself from skipping all the way home. When she arrived back at her house, she found Stevie leaning on a crutch, making himself a cup of tea.

"Where've you been?"

"Didn't you hear me call to you earlier? I went to see about volunteering for the Red Cross."

"Really? How did it go?"

"Very well. They've invited me for training on Monday morning."

"That's great, Mum. I didn't know you were thinking of joining up."

"I suppose I felt you could do without me hovering around you all the time, and I could do with taking my mind off your dad, Simon, and all that's going on here. Besides, it's about time I did something to help."

"You've been making camo nets ever since war broke out. And you've been helping me."

"Aye, I know, but this feels bigger somehow, like I could really make a difference. Do you mind I won't be around so much?"

Stevie smiled at Kitty. "Mum, as much as I love you, I've got to learn to stand on my own one foot sometime."

"I'm pleased to hear it. What's brought on this change of heart?"

"Clara's friend Joe called around again while you were out."

"Brother-in-law, not friend. Don't ask," said Kitty, as Stevie's face crumpled in confusion.

"Well, whoever he is, he talks a good deal of sense. Poor chap, I reckon losing your sight is worse than losing one leg, but I didn't hear him complaining. Seems like he's doing really well for himself. Did you know he's pals with Lady Somerleyton?"

"No, I didn't. I'm so pleased you're sounding more cheerful. I know these past few months have been very hard for you."

"I'm not promising it will be easy, but talking to Joe, I've realised my life isn't over. I'm far luckier than some. After all, I still have one leg and both my arms. I'm sure someone can put me to use somehow, somewhere."

"We should hear about getting you a wooden leg soon."

Stevie smiled and took a swig of tea. There was a long road ahead of them, but Kitty felt as though they'd just turned an important corner.

Chapter 25

October, 1941

"Good morning, Marnie."

"Good morning, Frank. How did you sleep?"

"Like a log. It's such a comfortable bed, and such a comfortable home. I'm thrilled to have ended up here. I've still not got used to it."

"It's about time you did. You've been here three weeks now. And we're very happy to have you."

Frank smiled, and Marnie returned it. Although at first it felt strange having a man other than Roy around, Marnie was enjoying the company of someone closer to her own age. With half the people she loved spread in all directions around the country, a loneliness had crept into her life. She loved Sally and Roy, but there was something refreshing about having someone around who didn't know her from before. Being around Frank was like having a fresh start.

"Do you have a busy day ahead?"

Marnie turned to face Frank and smiled. "No more than usual. Once I've seen to breakfast, I'm off for my shift at the shop, then home to make dinner, then starting work on the nets."

"It may be the men who get credited as heroes, but it's the women of this country who'll win the war for us," said Frank with a laugh. "Even hearing about your day makes me feel tired."

"Get on with you," said Marnie. "You may play down your work at the harbour, but you'll be putting yourself in harm's way day in day out."

"Perhaps, but not as much as the sailors who are in direct conflict with the enemy. Or those out minesweeping."

"You're not likely to be sent overseas?"

"It's unlikely. I'm rather long in the tooth these days. In fact, they only accepted me back into the navy, as they were so desperate for men."

"Sorry, I don't understand. How old are you, exactly?"

"Fifty-two next week."

"Fifty-two? Blimey."

"I know, ancient, isn't it?"

"Actually, I thought you were far younger."

"I'll choose to take that as a compliment and not an insult over my immaturity." Frank laughed, the skin around his eyes creasing and hinting at his true age.

"Do you have a wife and children?"

"I had a wife, but no children. My wife died five years ago."

"I'm sorry to hear that."

"Thank you, but in truth, it was a relief. My poor Felicity had had more than her fair share of suffering. She'd been ill for a very long time before she died. I spent a lot of time caring for her, so when I see all you do to help your in-laws, I know it's not easy."

Marnie leaned against the kitchen counter, regarding Frank in a new light. Her first impression of him had been completely off the mark. Any cockiness or charm was a cover for someone far more thoughtful than she'd given him credit for.

"Do you need any help to get breakfast ready?"

"You could cut the bread for toasting, if you like?"

Frank gave Marnie a salute and reached for the chopping board.

"So, were you in the navy before?"

"Yes, I joined up during the last war. See, I told you I was old. This time around, I didn't think they'd want oldies like me, but they bit my hand off the second I offered. You're probably too young to remember much about the last war."

"I remember enough. I'd moved to Lowestoft just before war broke out, but I was in the countryside at my brother's school, so mostly out of harm's way."

"Is your brother still teaching?"

"Aye, but he's up in Derbyshire with the evacuees. He hurt his leg years ago so couldn't join up even if he wanted to."

"It sounds like he's doing his bit in the classroom."

"Aye, I'm so proud of him. One day, I'll have to tell you all about how he got into teaching. That's quite a tale. You'd like Jimmy if you met him. I've yet to meet anyone who doesn't get on with him."

"Hopefully, I'll still be around when he returns home."

"There's talk he might be sent back here, but it all depends on this blasted war. At the moment, it's not safe for bairns to be back here."

"You must miss your daughter."

"More than I thought possible. But she's thriving down in Cornwall, so that brings some relief. Anyway, I'd best get on. Roy had another bad night, so I've told him and Sally to have a quiet morning. I'll take their breakfast up to them on a tray, give them a bit of a treat."

"They're lucky to have you."

"It works both ways. My family is up north, so Sally and Roy have become like parents to me. What time does your shift start?"

"Not for another couple of hours. How about you?"

"Same."

"If I help you with breakfast, do you fancy going for a stroll with me?"

"Oh," said Marnie, flustered. "Well, I..."

"Sorry," said Frank, "it's a silly idea. I haven't had much chance to get my bearings around town since I've been here, so I thought a walk with a local might help."

Marnie smiled, inwardly cursing her foolishness. Frank was being friendly, nothing more. "I'd be delighted to give you a tour," said Marnie, "although you'll have seen more than you think, the town isn't all that big."

"Wonderful. Now how about I make a pot of tea while you see to the toast?"

Frank and Marnie pottered around the kitchen in companionable silence, the wireless bumbling in the background with all the latest news. When breakfast was ready and on the tray, Frank turned to Marnie. "Good teamwork," he said.

"Right, well, I'll take this lot upstairs then meet you for a stroll." Marnie couldn't help smiling as she climbed the stairs. Frank was right, they made a good team.

Chapter 26

October, 1941

The cold bit through their clothes, and Marnie tightened her coat around her. Sally fumbled with a hat that threatened to blow off, but the cold was disastrous for her joints and her clawed fingers couldn't catch the fabric.

"Here," said Marnie. She stepped in front of Sally and adjusted her hat. "Are you sure you're alright to be out in this weather? It's a fair walk."

"We'll b... be fine," said Roy. "Frank told me the boys at *HMS Minos* have been working on something special ready for the parade. Has he let on to either of you what it is?"

"No, I've no idea," said Marnie, looking at Sally, who shook her head.

"Right, well, we'd better get done there and find out, hadn't we?" said Roy. He set off ahead, hobbling along the path with the aid of his stick. Marnie's heart swelled at the sight of him, an older version of Tom, or what Tom would have grown into had he lived. Sally linked an arm through Marnie's and patted her with a gloved hand.

"He'll get there through sheer stubbornness. You just watch."

Marnie smiled at Sally, admiring the resilience her in-laws displayed. "We could stay this side of the bridge. It would mean less of a walk?"

"He's determined to get all the way to Marine Parade and there'll be no stopping him." Sally smiled, shaking her head as Roy pushed forward thanks to sheer willpower rather than physical ability.

"Come on then," said Marnie.

The two women caught up with Roy, who greeted them with a grin that took ten years off his appearance. The feeling of celebration was something to be grasped with both hands, a beacon of hope in the long, dark days of war. War Weapons Week had taken on a festive feel, giving locals a chance to forget their troubles and come out to support their protectors.

The crowds grew more tightly packed the closer they drew to the harbour. Roy checked his watch. "We're in g... good time. The lads shouldn't be reaching here for another half hour." He had to shout over the joyful sound of one of many service bands turned out for the occasion.

The surrounding air filled with the blue, red and white of Union Jack flags held aloft in preparation for the spectacle to come. Marnie wondered if such a celebration were appropriate, given the battering British forces were receiving on the Continent, but pushed the thought away. Why not have a little fun while they still could?

They passed the Harbour Hotel and Marnie and Sally followed Roy as he crossed the swing bridge, naval ships packed into the water below on either side, as far as the eye could see.

"Will Kitty be meeting us?" asked Sally.

"No. She's hoping to get Stevie out to watch, but said it could be a hard task getting him down here with all the crowds, so told me not to wait for her. I offered to help, but Stevie doesn't like fussing."

"That poor lad. At least he kept hold of his life, I suppose."

"Aye, I think he's slowly coming to terms with what some would see as good fortune. Where's Roy gone?"

The two women scanned the crowd, searching for Roy among the mass of flat caps and winter coats. Uniformed police officers marshalled the edges of the spectators, ensuring the sailors would have a clear path when they arrived.

"There he is," said Sally, pointing further along the bridge. She leaned heavily on Marnie as they scurried along to catch up.

"At last," said Roy when they reached him. "I was wondering if you'd gone home. Come on, we're almost there and look, I've found the secret project Frank and his pals from *HMS Minos* have been working on." Marnie and Sally looked down from the bridge and across to the harbourside. "It's a model of the *Victory*," said Roy. "Not seaworthy, of course, but such an impressive piece of work, don't you think?"

"It really is," said Marnie. "What a talented bunch of lads they are."

"Come on, let's keep going. We can get a closer look at the model when they parade it later."

"Let's just see how we get on, shall we?" said Sally, casting a doubtful glance at Marnie. Would Roy be able to stand in the cold long enough to see the model? "He'll need several days in bed after all this excitement," Sally whispered to Marnie as they crossed the bridge.

When they reached Marine Parade, Roy secured them a splendid position near the front of the crowd by making a show of leaning on his stick and panting, playing the old age card. Marnie and Sally squished in beside him.

"Are you alright, love?" asked Sally, when Roy's panting showed no signs of easing. Perhaps he hadn't been putting it on after all?

"I'm fine now we're here. That walk wasn't the best for my old chest or hips. No mind, we're here and in a prime spot. Look, that's the saluting base just there."

Roy pointed across the path to a small stage which had been dressed in Union Jacks. A uniformed man who Marnie assumed must be one of the top brass was waiting in position on the stage. Behind him, two women stood straight-backed.

They heard the sailors before they saw them, hundreds of pairs of boots pounding out a drumbeat on the road. It felt primal, like a heartbeat resounding deep inside their bodies. Marnie noticed Roy pull out a handkerchief and dab his eyes. Sally was blinking rapidly, and Marnie had to swallow the lump in her throat.

The noise of boots grew louder and Marnie stood on tiptoes, trying to see above the heads of taller onlookers. It came as a shock to realise she was seeking one sailor in particular. But that was to be expected, wasn't it? Of course, she'd look out for a member of their own household above all others.

The sailors marched four abreast, in perfect synchronicity. They turned toward the stage to receive their salute, making it hard to distinguish one sailor from the next. Marnie kept searching, but to no avail.

"I can't see him either," whispered Sally with a wink.

Marnie flushed and turned back to the crowd, pretending she hadn't heard.

Chapter 27

October, 1941

"Room for two more?"

"Kitty! How wonderful," said Sally, kissing Kitty's cheek. "And, Stevie, good to see you out and about."

"It's good to be out and about," said Stevie with a smile. "Hello, Roy. How are you?"

Roy reached out a hand to shake, but realising Stevie couldn't take his hands off his crutches, turned it into a salute. "G... good to see you, lad. I'm alright, just m... my old joints playing up."

Marnie frowned at Roy. The droop on one side of his face was becoming more pronounced, as it always did when he was tired. His words were slightly slurred too, as though he'd sneaked a hip flask in his pocket and been swigging all morning.

"Was the walk down here alright?" asked Sally.

"I thought I was a sturdy chap until I started using these," said Stevie, waving one crutch in the air. "But my arms have turned to jelly."

"Well, my legs are like jelly, so we're a fine pair," said Roy.

"Did you catch the parade?" asked Marnie.

"Aye, we saw it from the other side of the bridge. The WRENs were my favourites. Don't you love their uniform? So smart. Makes me wish I'd joined them rather than the Red Cross."

"How is your training going?"

"Sorry to interrupt, ladies, but perhaps me and Stevie could find a bench somewhere to nurse our wounds. It's likely to be a while until the model ships come along."

"Good idea," said Kitty. "There's a bench over there. We'll call you if we see the models coming." Kitty waited for Roy and Stevie to hobble off, then turned back to Marnie. "In answer to your question, the training's going well. It's a lot to learn, but I think I'm getting the hang of it. Turns out driving an ambulance isn't as hard as it looks, so I think I'll mostly be doing that, although I'll still need to know my first aid, so none of the training will be wasted."

"I think it's wonderful what you're doing. And with you both making those nets, well, I couldn't be prouder." Sally beamed at the two women.

"Stevie seems brighter," said Marnie, brushing off the compliment she didn't feel she deserved.

"He has good days and bad, but the good are winning out. Clara's idea of sending Joe round was a stroke of genius. They've already met several times and Stevie's started looking into getting work. I must write to Clara to thank her. Joe's told Stevie all about your island, so I think we may all be keen for a visit once this war's over."

"Well, Clara has room for us all at least," said Marnie. "I'm pleased he's getting there."

"The next challenge will be getting used to walking on a false leg. I'm worried it will feel like going back to square one."

The sound of a brass band interrupted their conversation. Marnie leaned forward, trying to see past the crowds. "I think they're coming."

Sally held their place in the crowd while Kitty and Marnie ran over to the bench and helped the men make their unsteady way back.

"We've not missed Frank, have we?" asked Roy, struggling to get his breath and leaning against Sally.

"Not that I've seen. Goodness me, just look at that."

They laughed, oohed and ahhed as a model of Britannia made by the sailors of *HMS Europa* rolled past. Behind them was a model of a sleek white vessel.

"Blimey, it's an M.T.B," said Roy, letting out a whistle. "How the heck did they get it looking so realistic?"

"M.T.B?" asked Marnie.

"Motor Torpedo Boat," explained Roy. "They're so nimble, I'd love to have had the chance to sail one of them."

"I for one am pleased you haven't," said Sally. "I'd much rather have you safe and sound with me than darting around the sea in a killing machine."

Roy tutted and shook his head. Stevie tried not to laugh.

"Is this what you've been waiting for?" Stevie asked, picking up his crutch and pointing further down the parade.

"Aye, it's them," said Marnie, standing on tiptoes as the model of the *Victory* was wheeled along.

"Can you see Frank?"

"There he is!"

Unlike in the earlier parade, this time there was no mistaking Frank as he walked beside the model he had helped create. He cut a fine figure in his uniform, his eyes fixed straight ahead as he marched. As he drew level, Marnie noticed the tiniest flick of his eyes as they scanned the crowd, then an almost imperceptible curl in the corner of his mouth. Had he seen her? Perhaps it was Roy he had spotted.

As the final model boat rolled past, Marnie could see Roy had had enough. His eyelids were drooping and air rattled in his chest.

"I think it's time we got you home," said Sally.

"For once I won't argue," said Roy. "All this standing around has left me feeling done in."

"You and me both," said Stevie, hiding a yawn as he turned his head into his shoulder.

"I was going to suggest heading up to Pakefield as Lady Somerleyton's organised a fundraiser for the Red Cross," said Kitty.

"Why don't you and Marnie head up there?" said Sally.

As much as Marnie would have liked to, she couldn't see how Sally could get Roy back to the house by herself. "If it's alright with you, Kitty, I'll save that treat for another day. I'm pretty jiggered myself after all the excitement."

"Aye, you're probably right," said Kitty. "Besides, I'm on my first shift this evening. Only as an observer, but it's best I'm not worn out before I even get going."

"I don't need babysitting," said Stevie, a hint of surliness creeping into his voice.

"I'm not thinking about you. It's me I'm worried about," said Kitty. As the group turned to make their way home, Kitty winked at Marnie, who winked back. Best let their menfolk keep hold of their pride. There'd be plenty more fundraisers to go to before the war was done.

Chapter 28

November, 1941

"Sorry I'm late," said Kitty, running up to Marnie and kissing her cheek.

"Were you working?"

"No, my shift's not till this evening. Stevie had a fall, nothing too serious, but I needed to check he was alright before coming out."

"We can do this another day if you need to be at home?"

"Oh no," said Kitty, dismissing the idea with a wave of her hand. "It's all part of him getting used to his new leg. He'll get the hang of it, and he'll feel much better about things if he can get out and about more. I think it's hard because he was getting used to his crutches, and although the new leg is a good thing, to him it feels like it's set him back in his recovery."

"Hopefully, he'll get used to it sooner rather than later. Any word from Bobby?"

Kitty's face clouded over. "No, nothing. I've no idea if he'll be home for Christmas. I'll not be putting any decorations up this year, it wouldn't feel right with only me and Stevie in the house."

"Why don't you come to ours for Christmas lunch? It won't be up to much what with rationing, but at least the pair of you will have company. Can Stevie walk as far as ours?"

"By then he should be able to, but are you sure Sally and Roy won't mind?"

"They'll be delighted to have you. And if Bobby's home, he can come too. Frank doesn't know if he'll get leave to go home for Christmas so it could be a houseful, but that's part of the festive season, isn't it? Besides, it would help me have some distractions from missing Annie."

Kitty linked arms with Marnie, and they began walking down the street. "And how are things going with the lovely Frank?"

"I don't like your tone, Mrs Thorne."

Kitty laughed, choosing not to mention how pink Marnie's cheeks had turned, and not through the cold. "I've not met the man yet, but you've had more of a spring in your step since he arrived."

"That has nothing to do with Frank and everything to do with feeling more settled here. Annie is doing well down in Padstow, so that's another weight off my mind."

"Could you ask her to write to my Sam again? I don't think he's had a letter yet and I think he's pining for her."

"Pining? At seven years old? What is the world coming to?"

The two friends were still laughing as they pushed open the door to Waller's restaurant. They were hit by a wall of warmth that saw them hastily removing layers as a young waitress showed them to a table.

"I've not been here in years," said Kitty, choosing a seat at the table and picking up a menu.

"Me neither. Tom brought me here a few times once we were married, but that feels like a lifetime ago."

Kitty reached across the table and squeezed Marnie's hand. Marnie smiled.

"It's alright, I don't mind talking about Tom. In fact, I want to. Since coming back to Lowestoft, I've felt so much closer to him."

A young waitress came over to take their order. "We'll have a pot of tea for two and two buns, please."

The young girl scurried off and Marnie studied the menu again. "It looks like we were lucky to get our buns. Half the things on this menu have been scrubbed out."

"Well, I for one am looking forward to the taste of something sweet on my tongue," said Kitty. "Between rationing and all the worry over my boys, I've had to take in most of my clothes. There'll be nothing left of me by the time the war's over at this rate."

"Who would've thought, all those times we worried about our weight and all we needed was a war to come along and hey presto! Problem solved!"

"If only our men were around to witness our new slim physiques," said Kitty with a sad smile.

Now it was Marnie's turn to reach across the table. "Kitty, Bobby's a survivor. You only have to think back to the storm that claimed Tom's life to know that. If Bobby survived that, he can survive the bloody Jerrys and their bloody mines."

"Shh," said Kitty. "Mind your language. We're in a posh establishment, don't you know?"

Marnie laughed and gave Kitty's hand a playful slap. The waitress arrived with their order and the two women took grateful bites of their buns.

"Not quite up to pre-war standards," said Kitty, dabbing a napkin to her lips to catch crumbs, "but it's marvellous to taste sugar again."

"Aye," said Marnie, taking tiny bites of her bun in order to savour it.

"This was such a lovely idea to come here," said Kitty.

"Think of it as your Christmas present. You've more than earned a treat."

"Thanks. Have you taken Sally and Roy to the British Restaurant yet?"

Marnie shook her head.

"You should do, it would give you a break from cooking. You know you can get a three-course meal for ninepence?"

"Blimey, that's not bad."

"I know, that's what I thought. Once Stevie's got the hang of walking on his new leg, I'm going to take him there for a treat. I thought it might take business away from here, but it doesn't seem like it."

"This place is a local institution," said Marnie. "It would take more than a bit of competition to close it down."

"We'll have to bring all the kiddies here for afternoon tea once they're home safe and sound."

"Cheers to that," said Marnie, clinking her teacup against Kitty's.

Chapter 29

December, 1941

"**M**arnie!"

The shout made Marnie drop the pile of stockings she was stacking on the display. She spun around, her mouth falling open as Frank stood grinning in his uniform.

"Frank, whatever are you doing here? What's happened?"

"It's the Americans. They've joined the war. You know what I told you about Pearl Harbour? Well, that clinched it."

"This does sound like good news, but I'm surprised you rushed all the way up here to tell me."

"Don't you see, Marnie? This changes everything. Now the Yanks are on board our chances of winning this thing have shot up." Frank lunged forward, grabbed Marnie by the waist, and spun her around three times before setting her back down.

"Frank! Whatever has gotten into you?" Marnie looked around the shop, red-faced. Thankfully, there were few customers in, but the other shop girls had noticed Frank's outburst and stared at Marnie with raised eyebrows, hiding sniggers behind their hands.

"Sorry, that was very inappropriate of me. We heard the news, and you were the first person I wanted to tell. I'm sorry for getting carried away."

"Don't worry," said Marnie, smiling at Frank's infectious enthusiasm. "I'm as pleased as you are, but do you really think it will make that much of a difference to our chances?"

"Oh yes, you mark my words, this is the beginning of the end as far as old Hitler's concerned. I'd like to celebrate."

"Isn't that a little premature? We were still in the middle of this blasted war the last time I checked."

"There's so little to celebrate these days, and yes, it might tempt fate, but I don't care. Let me take you out for a drink at the end of your shift. What time do you finish?"

"Five, but..."

"Wonderful, I'll see you then." Frank turned on his heel and left before Marnie could protest. It looked as if she'd be off to the pub later, whether she liked it or not. As she watched Frank stride out of the shop, the thought struck Marnie that she'd be quite happy for Frank Merton to buy her a drink. Besides, it was nearly Christmas, so what harm was a drink between two friends?

Later that day, as she stepped out from the warmth of the department store, Marnie found Frank already waiting for her. He stood rubbing his gloved hands together, hopping from foot to foot.

"Sorry," said Marnie, "my supervisor asked me to cash up, or I'd have been out sooner. Have you been waiting long?"

"No, not too long," said Frank, the pink tip of his nose and blue tinge to his lips giving him away.

"Hmm," said Marnie, "you look to me like you're about to get frostbite. Let's find somewhere warm, and quick."

Frank offered a hooked elbow, and Marnie linked her arm with his. They hurried along the high street, a north-easterly wind clawing at them as they went.

"Here," said Frank, holding open a door to the welcome sight of a bar and fire.

"Thank you," said Marnie, walking in and removing her gloves.

"Why don't you take a seat over there and I'll get us some drinks? What would you like?"

"I'll have a half pint of whatever you're drinking, if that's alright?"

"Coming right up."

Marnie settled herself at a table beside a roaring fire. A cat lay curled on a rug beside it, the occasional twitch of its whiskers the only sign it was alive. Marnie hung her coat on the back of a chair and glanced over to where Frank leaned against the bar. All her life she'd striven for independence, but she couldn't deny how nice it was to have someone look after her for a change.

"Thank you," said Marnie, as Frank laid two glasses down on the small round table.

"You're welcome," he said, taking a seat. "Let's have a toast." Frank picked up his glass and Marnie did the same.

"What are we toasting?"

"How about hope?"

"To hope," said Marnie. "And to friendship."

"To hope and friendship," said Frank. After clinking his glass against Marnie's, he took a sip of beer, wiped froth from his moustache and placed his glass back down. "I'm sorry about rushing into the shop earlier and disturbing you at work. I'd just gone on my break when we got the news about the Americans, and you were the first person I wanted to share the news with."

"Then I'm honoured," said Marnie. "How do the other chaps feel about it?"

"Same as I do, that we need all the help we can get and no one's going to sniff at a good deal of extra manpower."

"It certainly is a piece of good news and a very festive time of year to receive it. Do you know your plans for Christmas yet? Will you get leave to go home and visit your mother?"

"No, I'm afraid I shan't. So I'm sorry to say that means you'll be stuck with me over the festive period. I won't get under your feet, though. I'll be working most days, including Christmas Day itself."

"That's a shame, that you'll be working, I mean, not that you'll be spending Christmas with us."

"I'm pleased to hear it," said Frank with a chuckle.

"We'll save you some Christmas dinner, although it may not be up to much. Depends what we're able to cobble together with our rations."

"I'll finish work by the evening, so won't miss all the fun. It must be a difficult time of year for you, being away from your daughter."

Marnie took a sip of her drink. "Aye, it is. But I know the couple she's living with will give her the best Christmas they can. That brings me a lot of comfort. What about you? Will you miss your mother and sisters?"

"Not especially. For years now my mother has gone to my eldest sister for Christmas, so it's been years since I spent a Christmas in my childhood home. Last year, I was working through all the festivities. It's easier in a way. I've no children, so it makes sense for me to be on duty. Let the other chaps get back to their families."

"That's thoughtful of you."

Frank shrugged. "They'd do the same for me if the boot was on the other foot. Do you fancy another?"

Marnie looked at her glass, surprised to find it already empty. "Why not," she said. "It's my round this time."

Chapter 30

January, 1942

*D*ear Marnie,

    Happy New Year! At least I hope it has been, and the bombers left you alone over the festive period. Thank you for the presents you sent down for us. Annie was delighted with her books and Grace won't stop chewing the ragdoll which I'm taking as a sign she likes it!

Were you able to celebrate Christmas? We managed a small celebration and gave the girls as good a Christmas as rationing would allow. Annie made a big fuss of Grace, keen to mark the fact it was her first Christmas. She's as free-spirited as ever, but each day I see Annie's kind streak growing stronger. She really is a credit to you, Marnie.

There are still plenty of reminders of war here with the air base so close, but the town has remained unharmed since the bombings you were here for. I'm aware it's a very different picture up with you. It must be so hard to carry on with normal life with that wretched air raid siren going off day and night!

Richard still grumbles about missing you in the shop. I tell him our loss is your department store's gain, and it was a waste of your talents selling groceries when you could sell silk and lace gowns. He doesn't like that argument, as you can well imagine!

How are Sally and Roy? Send them my love, and season's greetings. I've attached two letters from Annie, one for you and one for her grandparents. All my love, Helen.

"Helen sends her love," Marnie told Roy as he shuffled into the kitchen.

"That's kind of her. How's my granddaughter getting on?"

"Very well, by all accounts. What are you doing up? You know I'd happily bring your breakfast up to you."

"I'll go mad if I stay up there any longer."

"The doctor said you had to rest."

"Sod the doctor, I know my body."

"At least sit down here at the table and let me cook you some porridge."

"Yes, ma'am," said Roy, sitting heavily in a chair.

Roy chattered on about how he couldn't wait to return to the Seamen's Mission, but Marnie wasn't listening. She was thinking of how to respond to Helen's letter. At least someone had had a nice Christmas. Worry and doctor's visits had marred their own after Roy suffered what turned out to be another minor stroke on Christmas Eve. At least Frank had been there, helping Marnie clean Roy's soiled sheets and clothes, and taking charge of the doctor's visit. Sally had been in no fit state to deal with anything, so terrified was she by the thought of losing Roy. But as the doc said, Roy should make a decent recovery even if not quite back to his old self.

"I was thinking I might try to get down the mission today."

"What?"

"If I take it slow..."

"You'll be doing nothing of the sort. Not until the doctor gives you the all-clear."

"*Humph*," said Roy, scowling as Marnie placed a bowl of porridge down in front of him.

"Here," she said, handing him a newspaper. "This will keep you busy until you can go gadding about again."

"Now this is enough to cheer a fellow up," said Roy, folding his paper in half. "Look, the Yanks have arrived already. I doubt they'll have the spirit of our lads, but the more the merrier I say when it comes to defeating Mr Hitler."

"I couldn't agree more. Frank was delighted when he heard the Americans were joining in the war."

"He's a good chap, is Frank."

"Aye, he is."

"And fond of you, too."

"He's fond of us all."

Marnie turned her back on Roy and began scrubbing out the porridge pan.

"Of all the things wrong with my body, there's nothing wrong with my eyes," muttered Roy, before chuckling quietly to himself.

Marnie continued her scrubbing, pretending she hadn't heard. Before Roy had had the chance to finish his porridge or comment further on Frank, Sally rushed into the room, all in a lather over Roy being out of bed.

"Don't worry, Sally. He'd be off to the Seamen's Mission if I hadn't put a stop to his plans."

"When will you learn, Roy? You're a daft, stubborn old fool." Sally cuffed Roy around the side of the head and he looked up at her like a mischievous schoolboy.

"Sorry, my love."

"You will be if you keep disobeying the doctor's orders. I want you straight back upstairs the moment you've finished your breakfast."

"Alright, alright. Now, can you please leave a chap in peace to finish his breakfast?"

Later, with Roy safely ensconced upstairs and Marnie working on the nets, Sally sat down beside Marnie with a loud sigh. "I worry about that man."

"Aye, so do I. He's his own worst enemy."

"I know it's silly, but... I..."

"You won't lose him anytime soon," said Marnie, laying down her net and wrapping an arm around Sally.

"I don't think I could go on if I did."

Marnie placed a hand on each of Sally's shoulders and looked into her eyes. "Number one, you're not going to lose Roy. Number two, you've survived far too much to be giving up now. Number three, before you know it, this war will be done and dusted and you'll have a granddaughter here needing her grandmother. Alright?"

Sally nodded. Marnie pulled Sally close and hugged her. She prayed her words were true and Roy had plenty more fight left in him. The whole reason for coming back had been to care for Roy and Sally, and she didn't intend to fail at that anytime soon.

Chapter 31

January 1942

"Do you mind if I head off early today? Only, I'm worried the roads will be closed at this rate."

Marnie joined her manager, Marjorie, who was staring out of the large glass window to where snowflakes tripped and danced their way to the ground. "No, you head off. It looks as though it's laying."

The street beyond the window was quiet other than a few locals bundled up in coats, scarves and hats, hurrying home.

"At least we'll be safe from bombs. Surely no planes will fly in this weather?"

"Aye, I expect you're right. It's certainly been quiet today, both in the sky and in the shop."

"And you don't mind closing up?"

"Not at all. You've further to get home than me."

"Alright. If you're sure."

"Away with you, go on."

Marjorie took one more uncertain glance out of the window, then, with a sigh, went through to the staff room to collect her coat. Marnie was more than happy to close up on her own. She didn't mind Marjorie, but would be glad to be out from under her scrutiny. The younger woman seemed to have a point to prove, expecting higher standards from Marnie than the other girls. Despite her earlier misgivings, it suited Marnie to be a simple shop girl without the responsibility she'd once relished. Between keeping home, caring for Sally and Roy and making nets, she was happy for Marjorie to carry the weight of supervisor. If only the younger woman could see that, she might stop feeling the need to assert herself, as though Marnie would snatch her job from under her given the opportunity.

"Right then, I'll see you tomorrow." Marjorie walked through the shop, buttoning up her coat and pulling on her gloves.

"Take care on the walk back. I'm not rostered on tomorrow, but if any of the girls are stuck and can't get in, I'll be happy to cover."

"Thank you, Marnie. I appreciate all the work you do."

"Oh, well, ta very much." Perhaps Marjorie was growing used to Marnie's presence, after all.

The bell chimed as Marjorie let herself out of the shop. The door closed with a click and Marnie turned back towards the counter. There had been no customers for the past hour. The only remaining staff member in the women's department besides her was down in the stockroom, and as the snow outside blanketed any sound, the shop felt eerily quiet.

The till's bell chimed out as Marnie opened it and began cashing up the day's takings. She had just picked up a pile of paper notes when the air raid siren rang out loud and clear. Marnie jumped, and the money she had been holding flew up into the air like confetti.

Marnie ran out from behind the counter, trying to gather up the dropped takings. Before she could bend down to collect money from the floor, a loud cracking sound caused her hands to fly to her ears. The surrounding air turned into a mass of sparkling jewels as her body was flung several feet into the air before being plunged back down. Marnie's scream was buried beneath a thunderous bang.

Her ears ringing, Marnie's eyelids fluttered, and she lifted her head an inch. The shop looked as it always did, but some hangers had fallen off the display stands, and a handful of dresses lay crumpled on the floor. But, if the shop hadn't been hit, why was she splayed out on the floor?

Another bang. More glass, the walls shaking, the ringing in her ears growing louder. The sound of footsteps on the stairwell. Two pairs of polished shoes running towards her. Strong hands gripping beneath her arms and pulling her upright.

"We've got to get down to the stockroom, miss. There's no time to check you over now. Come on."

Time seemed to slow. The two men half dragged, half carried Marnie towards the stock room. Brief introductions were made, and she now knew her rescuers to be Stan and Roger from the electrical department. Workers Marnie recognised from other departments were rushing in the same direction. Before they turned the corner, Marnie glanced back. The front windows had shattered, spraying glass across the room, but there was no fire that Marnie could see, no twisted metal or torn apart brickwork.

Another explosion.

"Get down here, quick, everyone."

Shoes of all shapes and sizes thundered down the wooden staircase into the stockroom, and Marnie was pulled into the scrum.

"What's happened?" Marnie asked one of the men holding her up.

"Can't say for sure, but it seems like a bomb's landed very close to us. More than one, three or four, I think. There'll be H.E.s, you know, high explosives?" Marnie nodded. "That's why we've felt the impact up here. I'd guess they've landed within half a mile of us, but I can't be sure."

As Roger spoke his last words, the surrounding walls shook with the force of another blast.

"Quick."

Workers pushed and shoved their way down to the stockroom, which, although providing some shelter, would do little in the face of a direct hit. Marnie was carried to the far end of the room, where towers of stacked shoe-boxes surrounded her.

"Vera, can you come here and check this lady over, please?"

Roger and Stan were joined by a lady who Marnie guessed must be in her fifties. "What happened to you then, dear?"

"I was thrown down when the windows blew out. There might be a bit of glass stuck to me somewhere, I can't be sure."

"You're from the women's department?"

"Aye."

"And was anyone else with you when the windows blew?"

"No, it was just me, my supervisor Marjorie... my... my supervisor Marjorie..."

"She was with you?"

"No... she... she'd... she'd left only moments before." Marnie stared at the woman. "I have to check she's alright."

"No," said Stan, placing a hand firmly on Marnie's shoulder. "It's too dangerous to go anywhere at the moment. I'm sure Marjorie will be fine."

His voice sounded convincing, but Marnie noticed the grimace that passed between her rescuers. The woman gave Marnie a thorough check over, pulling the odd piece of glass from her skin with a pair of tweezers.

Another rumble sounded even louder, its force cutting off electricity and plunging the storeroom into darkness. Of the twenty odd folk down there, all were quiet, listening intently, trying to work out how close the enemy was. Had a bomb hit the building? Should someone check? Marnie looked around, wanting answers, but knowing she'd not find them.

"I don't understand why the air raid siren didn't go off?"

"It did, don't you remember?" said Roger.

"It's all a bit of a blur."

"Well, it went off, but not quick enough, I fear. We've had so many false alarms lately, I just hope folk didn't think this would be another. I dread to think what we'll find when we get out of here."

"You think we're here for a long haul?"

"I'd say make yourself as comfortable as you can, for I doubt we'll be leaving here till morning."

Chapter 32

January, 1942

"Come on, Kit, you can do this."

"Bloody machine," said Kitty, dropping the clutch and pushing the stick to first gear. She applied the lightest of pressure to the accelerator, dipping and releasing her right foot. The ambulance wheels spun, churning slush beneath them but not creeping forward even an inch.

"Carol, nip out and put something under the wheels. I can't get any traction and we need to get to the bomb site pronto."

With a sigh, Carol opened the door, a freezing blast of snow-filled air sweeping into the ambulance cab. Kitty shivered, rubbing her hands together and blowing on them.

"Give it another try," shouted Carol.

"Alright, but climb back in. If we get moving, I won't risk stopping on your account."

Carol heaved herself up into the cab and Kitty turned the key in the ignition.

"I hope you've got everything crossed?"

Carol held up two crossed fingers in response.

"Come on, girl," said Kitty, stroking a hand across the dashboard. She moved the gearstick to first and began pumping gently on the accelerator. With a jolt, the ambulance lurched forward, its wheels skidding on the cardboard Carol had laid down. "Come on, come on."

The two women cheered as the ambulance picked up pace, jolting its way onto the road before settling into its usual rhythm. As they drew closer to the main street, their earlier enthusiasm waned. Smoke and dust rose high into the air, mixing with the falling snow.

"I counted at least four dropped. You?"

"Same," said Kitty. She manoeuvred the ambulance around debris strewn across the road. "I'm not sure I can get much further. I'll park up here and we can find out the lay of the land."

Kitty drew the ambulance as close as she could get to where a row of shops had once stood, and turned off the engine. The smoke, snow and chaos made for a disorienting scene, but as Kitty squinted into the darkness, she knew all too well where she was. "Waller's," she whispered under her breath. She started running towards the rescue teams.

"No one goes past this cordon, miss."

"I'm Red Cross," said Kitty, opening her coat enough to reveal her uniform. "How many casualties?"

"Too many."

The chap guarding the perimeter of the disaster was wearing a Home Guard uniform and looked to be around sixty. Kitty wondered if he'd expected to see so much action when he volunteered.

"Any we can take now? I've parked the ambulance as close as I could get her."

"Best ask those chaps down there," said the man, pointing to where a group of men were trying to douse the flames before making their way into the ruined carcasses of buildings.

Kitty shielded her eyes and used a handkerchief to cover her mouth and nose as she drew closer to the bomb site. Despite the freezing weather, the flames all around her gave off a heat which felt unnatural rather than comforting. The cold evening filled with the shouts of men and screams coming from somewhere among the ruins.

A woman stumbled through the smoke, her hair black and tangled with soot, her blouse torn and bloody. She clutched her arm, which, from the colour of her hand, was bleeding profusely. "Here," said Kitty, rushing over to the woman. "Come with me, I'll get you to hospital."

"I can't leave without Pearl," wailed the woman.

"Who's Pearl?"

"My sister. We were out for tea when the bomb fell."

"You were in Waller's?"

"Yes." The woman fell into Kitty's arms, sobbing into her shoulder.

"Listen," said Kitty. "All these chaps you see around you are doing everything they can to get survivors free. The best thing we can do is leave them to their work. Let's get you over to the ambulance where my friend Carol can look at your arm. While she's seeing to you, I'll come back here and see if I can't find some news about your sister."

"Thank you," said the woman with a sniff.

"Here," said Kitty. She pulled off her coat and draped it over the woman's shoulders. "What's your name, love?"

"Lily."

"Right then, Lily, let's get you away from here."

Back at the ambulance, Carol was preparing a stretcher and looked up as Kitty staggered towards her with a bleeding woman.

"See to this poor lass, would you?" asked Kitty. "Then once she's patched up, come and find me, as there'll be plenty of others. It looks like the other crews have arrived, which is just as well as we'll need all hands on deck tonight."

"That bad?"

"Worse." Kitty was going to say more, but remembered her patient's earlier tears and kept quiet. "I'm heading back over. See you there?"

"Won't be a tick," said Carol, easing the woman's blouse down so she could get a look at the wound.

"Don't forget to ask about Pearl," called the woman as Kitty walked away.

"It's the first thing I'll do," said Kitty.

More men had gathered, crowds of them tearing at the smouldering ruins, searching desperately for survivors. Kitty tripped over something and looked down to see a charred high-heeled shoe lying on the pavement. She shuddered, kicking it away with her boot and scanning the surrounding ground.

The timing of the bomb couldn't have been worse. Kitty pictured the inside of the restaurant, filled with women chatting and soldiers and sailors taking some much-needed respite. Was nowhere safe anymore? Would this destruction and uncertainty never end? A couple of months earlier and it would have been her and Marnie caught in the blast.

"There's a man here needing urgent attention!"

Kitty jumped, becoming aware once more of the noise around her and the smell of soot creeping from her nose down to her lungs. "Sorry, sorry," she said, scrubbing a tear from her eye and starting to run. "I'm coming."

Chapter 33

January, 1942

Marnie and her colleagues emerged bleary-eyed out onto the street. Snow swirled around them, sticking to Marnie's eyelashes and settling a white blanket across her coat. In contrast to the crisp white all around them, lines of black smoke pierced through the air, and as they moved further down the street, black and white met in slippery, grey slush.

What hours before had been an ordinary shopping street was now a scene of devastation, unrecognisable from its previous form as men and women stumbled and tripped their way through the rubble as though blindfolded. The walking wounded sat propped against undamaged walls. Some lay in the street screaming or groaning, while men poured in to help with the rescue effort.

"Oh Lord," said a man at the front of the group. "Waller's restaurant has been hit."

"What?" Marnie pushed forward, her feet skidding against the frozen ground. Stan reached out an arm and caught Marnie before she fell. "Ta," she said. She closed her eyes to get her bearings. She pictured the street as it was, opened her eyes and tried to reconcile the mental image with the new reality.

"Don't rush down there," said Stan. "It looks like it's been a bad hit. Boots has gone too, and Hepworth & Sons, not to mention the five flats above Hepworths'. Bloody hell." Stan scrubbed his head with his hands and looked around. "It's hard to tell, but I reckon there could be ten shops gone. I just pray to God they weren't full of customers."

The gathering crowd brushed snow from their eyes. The men went ahead to see how they could help with the rescue. Marnie tried to get closer and offer to help tend to the wounded, but was blocked by a man from the Home Guard.

"Best not, missy. We're trying to keep the area clear until we know it's safe."

"Bit late for that, isn't it?" asked Marnie, peering through the half-light to the ruins of buildings, as if a god had reached down from the sky and punched a series of holes along London Road North.

"There are parts of those buildings that could yet collapse. The Red Cross has set up over there. You can offer them your services if you like?"

"Thank you, I will."

Marnie walked in the direction the man had shown her, to where a group of women were tending to the walking wounded, while carrying away others on stretchers.

"Kitty? Is that you?"

"Marnie? Oh, thank God you're alright. When we got the call and they said London Road North, I feared the worst."

"I got away with a few scratches, thankfully. The glass blew out of the windows, but those of us still in the shop made it down to the stockroom and waited it out. Anyway, I'm here to offer my services. I'm no trained nurse, but have plenty of experience of cuts and bruises."

"Thank you." Kitty raised her hand to cover a yawn. "Sorry, we've been here all night, so could do with the help. We've sent a fair few casualties over to the hospital, but with casualty numbers still so uncertain it's been suggested we use the Odeon cinema as a temporary treatment area... and mortuary," she added with a shudder. "This group over here has been assessed and mainly need wounds dressing, and some have minor burns. Could you see them over to the cinema and dress their wounds? There's a medical pack you can take, and Carol will be over shortly to help you."

"Of course. Kitty, before I go, you haven't come across my supervisor, Marjorie, have you? Marjorie Ruthers."

Kitty shook her head. "No, sorry, I don't think so. Why? Was she not at work?"

"She left about five minutes before the bombs hit. Let's just pray she walked in the opposite direction."

"Aye, let's."

Marnie introduced herself to the walking wounded, helped them to their feet and led a procession over to the cinema which, although damaged, was still structurally sound. Rather than set up in the entrance lobby in full view of where the corpses would be brought in, Marnie found a staff room complete with a sink and a handful of chairs.

The patients Marnie had been left to care for were in a state of shock. Several were visibly shaking, some were blank-eyed, confused, staring into space, and several had tears running down their cheeks.

Marnie went around the injured one by one, cleaning wounds, patching them up, waiting for the professionals to arrive. When Kitty's colleague Carol came, it was with a further group of wounded.

"How's it going out there?" asked Marnie.

"Hang on," said Carol. She made sure the injured were comfortable before taking Marnie by the elbow and pulling her out of the patients' earshot. "It's bloody awful over there. These folk in here are the lucky ones. There're men come from all over to help with the rescue, and some of the naval lads have got involved, but it doesn't look very hopeful for finding many survivors. Most of the folk we've got in here have loved ones or friends who are missing, so let's keep upbeat for them, hey?"

"Of course. I can't imagine how worried they all must be. Do you want to check over the dressings I've done?"

"Yes, I will once I've seen to this lot. They're going to bring the dead in here soon, so let's pull down the blinds and try to keep this area as calm as we can."

"How long do you think the rescue will go on for?"

"Days most likely, if not weeks. There's so much rubble to sift through, but these first few hours are crucial if any rescues are to take place. Anyway, that's enough nattering. Let's get to work."

Chapter 34

January, 1942

The front door banged against the wall, the force of it taking out a chunk of plaster. Frank ran through to the kitchen, skidding to a stop when he saw Marnie sitting at the table, cup of tea in her hands.

"You're here. You're safe. When those bombs fell, I thought... I mean. Well. I..."

"I'm fine, as you can see."

Frank rushed around the table and flung his arms around Marnie. "I'm so glad. So very, very glad."

"Alright," said Marnie, attempting to laugh off her embarrassment. Frank smelled of smoke and as his hair tickled her cheek, she could feel the roughness of soot and dust clinging to it. "There's no need to go all soppy on me."

"Sorry," said Frank, straightening up and brushing off his uniform. "Well, now I know everything's well, I'll return to my duties."

"Really? But you've been out all night, according to Sally."

"A group of us from *HMS Minos* have been released to assist with the Waller's rescue effort, but they gave me a brief reprieve to come and check you were all alright."

"That's kind of you, but as you can see, we're fine," said Marnie, realising Frank hadn't actually asked after Sally and Roy. "I saw out the attack in the stockroom at work, and Roy and Sally were in the brewery cellar. I helped Kitty and her pals tend to the walking wounded, but by now," Marnie glanced at the clock, "any injuries coming out will be well beyond my skill level. Given how close the bombs fell to Chadds, I feel very fortunate to have walked away unharmed."

"And thank goodness you did."

Marnie smiled at Frank. His face was streaked with soot, his hair sticking up in dirty tufts. The arm of his uniform was torn and, aside from looking dishevelled, he seemed exhausted. "When did you last sleep, Frank? You left first thing yesterday morning, which by my reckoning is over twenty-four hours ago."

"I'm in no worse position than the other men."

"But you still need to rest. You'll be no good to the rescue otherwise."

"I really can't, Marnie."

"Half an hour, that's all I ask. Come on." Marnie took Frank's hand and led him through to the sitting room, ignoring the way her cheeks had reddened with his touch. "I'm not sending you to bed in your pyjamas with a hot cup of cocoa. All I ask is that you have half an hour of snoozing in an armchair. It will do you the world of good, I promise."

"Alright," said Frank with a yawn. "But please come and wake me up. Time is of the essence in the rescue effort. It's still possible there are survivors buried in the rubble."

"I promise to wake you in half an hour."

Frank sat in an armchair and Marnie fussed around him, placing a cushion behind his head and covering his knees with a blanket. Marnie was about to leave Frank in peace when he took hold of her hand, lifted it to his lips and kissed it. Before Marnie could wonder what was going on, Frank had let go of her hand and closed his eyes.

Marnie closed the sitting-room door and crept up the stairs, poking her head around Sally and Roy's door. Both were still asleep, exhausted after a night in the shelter. Some folk had left for their own beds in the early hours, but Sally and Roy had stuck it out all night, worried another raid would only send them back down there should they attempt to leave.

Marnie crossed the landing to her own bedroom and perched on the end of the bed. What she really wanted was to lie down and sleep, but she'd promised to wake Frank in half an hour and couldn't do that if she too was dead to the world. Instead, to keep herself from dozing off, Marnie pulled her writing implements from a drawer and sat herself at her dresser.

Dear Annie,

Thank you for your last letter, I received it yesterday. I'm so pleased to hear you are enjoying school. Well done for helping Richard in the shop and Helen with Grace.

Marnie paused her writing. Aside from a brief mention of school, Annie's last letter had mainly comprised of musings on how wonderful it was to be living with Helen, Richard and Grace, particularly Grace. Marnie felt a knot of dread surface in her stomach. What would happen when the time came to bring Annie home?

"Stop it," Marnie said, talking to her own reflection in the mirror. "There's enough to worry about in the here and now." She picked up her pen and returned to her letter.

We were taken by surprise yesterday afternoon by a German bomber. He destroyed an entire row of shops on London Road North. I'm not telling you this to worry you (me and your grandparents are fine!) but because I wanted to tell you about Aunt Kitty. I think I mentioned that she's now volunteering for the Red Cross. Well, you should have seen her last night. She looked so smart in her uniform and did such a wonderful job of caring for the injured.

Unsure how much to tell Annie about the raid, Marnie set aside her letter to return to later. She went downstairs and listened at the sitting-room door. The occasional snore and snuffle reached her ears and Marnie smiled. It seemed cruel, only allowing Frank half an hour to rest when he was clearly exhausted. With fifteen minutes until his thirty were up, Marnie made herself a cup of tea and picked up Roy's newspaper.

After checking the clock, Marnie poured a fresh cup of tea and went to wake Frank. She found him sprawled against the armchair, arms and legs flung out, his head tilted back, and his mouth wide open, explaining the earlier snoring she'd heard.

"Frank? Frank? It's time to wake up."

Frank shifted his position, but his eyes remained firmly shut. Marnie put down the cup of tea and gave his shoulder a gentle shake. "Frank? It's time to wake up."

"Huh?" Frank's eyelids flickered, and he looked around in confusion. "Where am I?"

"You're in the sitting room. Remember, you said you'd only rest for a little while before going back to help the rescue effort?"

"Rescue…" Suddenly Frank was alert, sitting up straight, rubbing his eyes, then reaching down to pull on his boots.

"Hold on," said Marnie. "Drink this up first. There's no use rushing off before you're fully awake. Besides, the snow's not letting up, so you may as well warm yourself up properly before heading out into the cold."

"You're an angel," said Frank, taking the cup from Marnie with a smile.

"Frank, before you go, I don't suppose you know casualty numbers? Only, my colleague left work but a minute before the first H.E. hit and I was wondering…"

"It's too early to tell for certain," said Frank, "but the casualty list is growing. The restaurant was full of civilians and service people. I'd best get back and see where I'm needed."

"Of course. And, Frank?"

"Yes."

"Take care of yourself out there."

Chapter 35

March, 1942

Kitty stood absentmindedly stirring a pot of stew. Ever since the Waller's raid, she'd been able to think of little else. At least Marnie's manager had escaped the blast, so that was something. But all those other poor, poor families, torn apart. It made Kitty's head and heart ache to think about it. She'd never found Pearl, the sister of the first casualty she'd come across, and although rationally Kitty knew it wasn't her fault, it felt like a personal failure. Another life cut off in its prime, without even a body to bury. Kitty chewed on her lip to keep threatening tears at bay.

A loud knock on the door made Kitty jump. "Oh, for goodness' sake," she said, rubbing her hands on her apron and giving the pot on the stove a quick stir. She rushed through to the sitting room and opened the front door. "Roy," said Kitty, "this is a surprise."

"I hope you don't mind me turning up uninvited," said Roy.

"Of course I don't, but you shouldn't have walked all that way."

"I didn't," said Roy, gesturing with his thumb to a small van parked up beside him. From the driver's seat, Frank smiled and waved at Kitty.

"You're not going to leave your chauffeur sitting out in the cold, are you?" asked Kitty, shaking her head. "I've no idea what all this is about, but the pair of you had better come in."

Roy signalled to Frank, who jumped out of the van and followed Roy into Kitty's house.

"Can I get you chaps a cup of tea?" asked Kitty.

"Oh no, don't go to any trouble on our account," said Roy. His hands played with the woollen hat in his hands.

Kitty looked at Roy and narrowed her eyes. "Roy Hearn, what are you up to?"

"Nothing really, it's just Frank and me, well, we had an idea that might help young Stevie."

"Stevie? What do you want with Stevie? Shall I call him for you? He's only up in his room, hard to get him anywhere else these days." Kitty didn't mention how the cold winter weather gnawed at Stevie's stump, or how difficult he'd found getting a company to take him on.

"We will speak to Stevie," said Frank, "but not yet. We want to run our idea past you first."

"And what idea is this?" Kitty looked from Roy to Frank, thinking what an unlikely pair they seemed. Frank, in his smart navy uniform with his airs and graces, and Roy, his thick Lowestoft drawl, pipe hanging from his mouth and faint aroma of fish that still hadn't left him despite it being years since he'd been at sea.

"We'll completely understand if you think it's a terrible idea," said Frank. "Only when Roy told me about the puppy, it just seemed the logical course of action."

"Puppy?"

"She's been turning up at the Seamen's Mission," said Roy. "I think her home must have been bombed out as, although she has a collar, no one seems to be missing her."

"I'm very confused," said Kitty. "What has this dog got to do with me or my son?"

"Marnie told me that learning to walk on his new leg has knocked Stevie's confidence a bit."

"Did she now?"

"She wasn't gossiping," said Frank, "she was telling me because she cares."

Kitty kept her thoughts to herself. "Go on."

Frank sighed. "This was a bad idea. Roy, I think we should go."

"For goodness' sake," said Kitty. "The two of you are like a pair of naughty schoolboys. Just spit it out why you're here and what any of this has to do with a dog, then I can get back to cooking my supper."

"We thought a dog might help Stevie," said Roy. "She needs a loving home."

"How would a dog help?"

"I had a dog growing up," explained Frank. "She was my best friend and a wonderful companion and comfort after my father died. We thought not only might she be company for Stevie, but taking her out for walks would build his confidence in moving around."

"I really don't know about this. I'll need to think about it, and talk to Stevie about it, of course."

"Ah, right..." said Frank.

Roy cleared his throat. "The thing is, Kitty, we've... well, we've brought the dog with us. She can't come home with me thanks to Sally being allergic, and it seems an awful shame to put her out on the streets again."

"Back in a tick," said Frank, letting himself out of the house.

"He'd better not be going where I think he's going," said Kitty.

When Frank appeared a few minutes later, it was with a large-eyed puppy at his heels. "As you can see, she's been well trained," said Roy.

"We've named her Missy as none of us knew what to call her at first and in the end the name just stuck."

"But... what... I mean..."

Before Kitty could continue, Stevie poked his head around the door. "I thought I heard voices. Oh, you've brought a dog with you."

Frank let go of the lead and Missy trotted over to Stevie, licking his outstretched hand.

"Is she your dog?" Stevie asked.

"Actually, we were hoping..."

"They've come to see if we'd like her, given Sally's allergies," said Kitty, "but as I was about to say, the last thing we need is an animal to care for on top of everything else going on."

"What happened to her owners?" asked Stevie.

"We can't be sure," said Roy, "but we think they may have fallen victim to one of the raids. We've put posters up around town, but no one's come forward for her."

"We can't see her on the streets, Mum."

"But she'll need walking," said Kitty, "and I've too much else to be getting on with."

"I can walk her."

"You? But you're still getting used to your new leg."

"And this will spur me on, won't you, pup?" Stevie lowered himself awkwardly down onto the floor and began scratching Missy beneath her chin. "You like that, don't you? See, Mum, she's already feeling at home."

Kitty sighed. "You can tell Marnie I'll be wanting a word with her for this. And if I find out the animal's not house-trained, then woe betide you, Roy, and you, Frank."

Kitty looked down at Stevie. Taking on a dog was a ridiculous notion, but she had to admit Missy had ignited something in Stevie she'd not seen in a long time. He was laughing, a sound Kitty had almost forgotten the sound of. Her eyes filled with tears and she turned away to the kitchen. "I'll leave you all to it," she called over her shoulder. "Shout if any of you want tea."

"Thanks, Mum, but I think I might take Missy out for her first walk."

"You do that," said Kitty with a smile.

Chapter 36

March, 1942

"How did it go?" asked Marnie when Frank and Roy arrived home.

Roy grinned. "You should have seen the lad. It was love at first sight, wasn't it, Frank?"

"It certainly was. Though you might get a flea in your ear from Kitty. She's convinced you're behind the scheme, despite our best efforts to dissuade her from the notion."

"Well, as long as it does the trick and doesn't give Kitty more to worry about."

"The hair-brained scheme went well, did it?" asked Sally, carrying a basket of shopping into the room.

"Told you it would," said Roy.

Sally shook her head and tutted. "You're both as bad as each other. I should tell you off for encouraging him, Frank."

"My apologies, Mrs Hearn, but your husband is a man who knows his own mind. Speaking of which, do you fancy a quick pint, Roy, to celebrate our success?"

"Oh, no you don't," said Sally. "He's had enough excitement for one day. It's an early night for you, Roy."

Marnie expected Roy to protest, but Sally knew her husband well and it appeared the scheme with the dog had tired him out as he shook Frank's hand, made his apologies, and headed for the stairs.

"Why don't the two of you go out?" asked Sally.

"I don't really fancy squeezing into a pub full of sailors," said Marnie. "Besides, I've still got plenty of nets to work on."

"They'll still be here when you get back," said Sally. "Why don't you go for a stroll if you don't fancy the pub?"

Marnie regarded Sally through narrowed eyes, trying to work out why her mother-in-law was so keen to get them out of the house. Did she need to have a private word with Roy? "Alright," said Marnie, "but I can't stay out long. These nets won't make and mend themselves."

"Sally seemed very keen to get rid of us," said Marnie as she and Frank left the house.

"I'd put money on her wanting to scold poor Roy over the dog," said Frank.

"Hmm, yes, she didn't seem best pleased. Oh well, whatever the reason, let's enjoy a dose of fresh air before heading back into the warm."

"Shall we walk along the seafront? There should be a convoy passing this evening, and it will be an impressive sight."

"Lead the way." Without thinking, Marnie slipped her arm through Frank's, enjoying their shared warmth as they headed towards the sea. "I hope you're here long enough to see the beach when it's not covered by barbed wire," said Marnie. "Have they said how long you'll stay here?"

"Till the war's over from what I've been told, and possibly longer, as decommissioning the fishing vessels and crews will take some doing, not to mention clearing mines. They won't disappear overnight just because the fighting's stopped."

"Goodness me, don't let Kitty hear you say that. She's banking on getting Bobby home once the war ends. I'm not sure she'd cope with the thought of him minesweeping long after guns have been laid down."

"I'll keep quiet. What with the worry over her sons, Kitty's got enough on her plate by the sound of things."

"Have you heard from your mother recently?"

"Last week. She seems very well. Luckily my sisters' children have been able to stay with them so Mother is enjoying her grandparent duties."

"You never fancied having children?"

"As I've told you, Felicity's illness was a long one. Even before we knew she was ill, she struggled to conceive. Not that I regret it now. Although it would be nice to have some of her passed down in a child, I wouldn't have done a very good job of raising a child singlehanded."

"I think you would have made a wonderful father."

"Thank you."

Embarrassed by the compliment, Frank strode on. He stopped a safe distance from the barbed wire and pointed into the distance. "See the ships out there?"

"They'd be hard to miss." They both stared out to the large convoy of Merchant Navy vessels, dark against the pastel sky. The flashing lights of escort vessels could be seen drifting along the horizon. "Where are they heading?"

"Often south towards London, but these look to be heading north. They'll be going to one of the northern ports, though I couldn't tell you which one."

"Such dangerous work."

"It certainly is."

Right on cue, through the still air came the distant whine of an engine and suddenly the sky filled with vibrant colours shooting up into the sky.

"Tracer bullets," explained Frank. "It sounds like there's an enemy aircraft above them, so they'll be doing their best to defend themselves."

A bright light filled the sky above the convoy as a searchlight tried to expose the hidden enemy plane. The droning of the engine grew louder, and the explosion of bullets met with sparks of enemy fire raining down from the sky. Marnie grabbed Frank's arm and held it tight. They waited for signs of fire, but after a few minutes of back and forth, the engine's drone faded and Frank let out a long breath.

"It seems they live to sail another night," said Frank.

Marnie shivered, and Frank removed his coat and draped it over her shoulders. "Don't make yourself cold," she said, trying to hand it back.

"You need it more than me," said Frank. "How about we head home and get you in the warm?"

As they turned their backs on the beach, an air raid siren pierced the air. "Quick," said Frank, grabbing hold of Marnie's hand and pulling her toward the town. "We have to find cover now!"

Chapter 37

March, 1942

F rank and Marnie had only been running for a minute when the unmistakable whine of several aircraft reached them. "There's no time to get to the brewery," said Frank. "Let's try in here." He clicked open a garden gate and pulled Marnie down the side of an end of terrace house.

"Thank God," said Marnie as they reached the garden to find a less than sturdy-looking Nissan hut. "It's not the best shelter I've seen, but it's better than nothing."

Frank hammered on the closed metal door, but there was no answer. He lifted the sheet of aluminium and peered into the darkness. "No one here. Come on, quick, get inside."

Marnie ducked her head and entered the shelter. Frank pulled the door closed, and they found themselves surrounded by thick, pitch-black air.

"Have you got any matches?" whispered Marnie.

"Yes, in my pocket. Why are you whispering?"

"It feels like we're trespassing," said Marnie, letting out a giggle, despite her shaking limbs and racing heart.

Frank struck a match against its box and cupped his palm around the flame. "It doesn't look like anyone's used this shelter for a while."

"No," said Marnie, shivering and stepping away from a very large cobweb. "Look at this newspaper. It's dated December 1940. What do you think happened to the folk who this shelter belonged to?"

"As their house is still standing, I think we can assume they're still alive. They probably hung around for a while when war broke out, then thought better of it once things heated up."

"Let's see if they left anything. Can you bring the light back here a bit? It looks as though there's something on this shelf."

"Hold on, this match is about to burn out." Frank blew out the flame and lit a fresh match. He held it closer to the shelf.

"Well, this is handy," said Marnie, picking up a paraffin lamp and shaking it. "And there's still fuel inside. Here." She held the lamp up for Frank to light.

"Now we can see the wood for the trees."

The shelves were bare apart from a few tins of food and two blankets. When Marnie put her hands on the blankets, they were damp to the touch and she whipped her hand back. "We shan't be using those," she said, wrinkling her nose. "But there's a can of corned beef and a tin of peaches."

"Given we don't know how long we'll be here, let's save them for later. Here, take a seat." Frank brushed off an old camp bed with no mattress.

"It's not as uncomfortable as it looks," said Marnie, shuffling against the exposed springs, "but I wouldn't want to sleep on it."

Just as Frank was about to reply, the walls of the shelter shook and they heard an explosion in the distance. "It doesn't sound too close," said Frank. "I'd say about half a mile."

"That's close enough."

Another explosion sounded, then another and another. "How many's that?" asked Marnie.

"Four, five, maybe six? Sound like H.E.s but it's hard to tell."

Marnie put her head in her hands. "I'd hoped after what happened in the Waller's raid the Jerries would've left us be for a while. This is the sixth raid since then, and things show no sign of letting up. And that last one, landing in the sea near the gas works?" Marnie shuddered. "It doesn't bear thinking about what might have happened. Honestly, I'm sick to the back teeth of this blasted war."

"You're not the only one."

Marnie and Frank sat side by side on the camp bed, listening out for any further explosions.

"I think that's it," said Frank after ten minutes of waiting.

"It's certainly enough to keep Kitty busy tonight."

"She's doing a grand job on the ambulance. As are you with your nets."

Marnie laughed. "Making camouflage nets hardly compares with driving an ambulance, Frank."

"It all contributes to the war effort."

"Aye, maybe."

Frank took hold of Marnie's hand. She hid her surprise by staring straight ahead, telling herself it was only one friend comforting another during a frightening episode. Marnie tried to ignore how her hand seemed made to fit within Frank's, how the feeling of his skin warmed not only her hand but her whole body. With a start, Marnie stood, Frank's hand dropping into his lap. She stamped her feet and rubbed her hands together.

"What are you doing?"

"Keeping warm." *Avoiding touching you. I don't deserve to feel those things.*

"Sit back down."

"I'm best off standing." *I don't trust myself to be close to you.*

"Very well." Frank stood up and began stamping his feet in time to Marnie's.

"What are you doing?"

"Keeping warm, just like you."

"That looks suspiciously like dancing, Frank Merton."

"Dancing? Of course not." Frank did a little skip.

"That's from the foxtrot."

"Is it?" Frank looked at Marnie. Lamplight accentuated his features, creating pools of darkness around his eyes while his smile was brought into focus. "You know, Mrs Hearn, there are worse things to do during a raid than dance."

"So you *were* dancing?"

"Maybe I was, maybe I wasn't." Frank stepped forward and pulled Marnie close to him. She tried to wriggle free, but he held on tight, slipping one arm around her waist and taking her hand in his. "It's only to keep us warm," he said, rocking back and forth.

Marnie rested her head on Frank's chest. "And what dance is this?"

"The warming-up waltz."

"That's a new one to me," said Marnie with a laugh.

"It's a special dance for tight spider-filled spaces. I'm surprised you've not heard of it before." Frank hummed as they rocked back and forth on the spot in their ballroom hold. He bent his head lower until Marnie could feel his warm breath on her cheek.

"The last dance I went to was in Padstow." Silence stretched out between them and Marnie knew Frank was waiting for her to elaborate.

"You never talk about Padstow," he said eventually.

"Aye, well, it wasn't a happy time."

"Of course, I'm sorry. That was insensitive of me. Losing your husband must have overshadowed your whole time there."

"Something like that." Marnie felt her eyes fill with tears, partly at the reminder of Tom, but partly from the guilt of knowing she could say no more. She didn't deserve to be held in a man's arms, to feel safe, loved, even. Those feelings were for other, more deserving women, not her.

"Marnie..." Frank's voice had become husky, his mouth brushing against her ear.

The all-clear siren sounded and Marnie stepped away from Frank, pulling off the jacket he had lent her. "Here you go."

"Marnie..."

"We'd best get back now we've had the all-clear. I know it sounded as though the bombs were far off, but I'd like to check on Sally and Roy, anyway. I don't suppose they made it to a shelter."

"Yes, of course," said Frank, straightening his clothes and pulling on his jacket. Before he could say any more, Marnie was moving the sheet of corrugated iron from the entrance.

"Come on," she said, "let's go home."

Chapter 38

June, 1942

Marnie rubbed her eyes and checked the clock beside her. She checked again. Surely it couldn't be midnight already? She placed down the net she'd been working on and stretched her arms above her head, letting out a long, loud yawn. There'd been so many air raid scares over the past few weeks she'd fallen behind on her work and was struggling to catch up.

The click of the front door made Marnie jump. "Hello?" she whispered. The sound of footsteps heading towards her caused Marnie to grab a knife from the draining board just in case.

"Oh, it's you."

"Good evening to you too," said Frank. He checked his watch. "Actually, I rather think that should be good morning. What are you doing up so late and why do you have a knife in your hand?"

"I thought you might be an intruder. And the reason I'm up so late is that thanks to the bloody air raids, I've spent most of the past few weeks underground unable to do my work."

"Is there anything I can do to help?"

Marnie gave an incredulous laugh. "With the nets?"

"I was thinking more about making tea. I'm afraid I can barely tie my shoelaces, never mind all those complex knots you seem so skilled at."

"It's not that hard. But aye, tea would be lovely, thank you."

Frank turned his back on Marnie and began filling the kettle. "Mother trained me well," he said.

"Really? You mean you didn't have a maid tending to your every need?"

"Hah! You think I had a maid?" Frank spun around, the kettle clasped between his hands.

"Aye, you seem the type."

"And why is that, then?"

"Your posh voice and confidence."

"My voice isn't posh."

"Well-spoken then."

"Fine. And what's confidence got to do with anything?"

"It's your manner, the way you try to charm everyone around you. I've not come across that before so assumed it must be an upper-class mannerism."

Frank placed the kettle on the stove, shaking his head and laughing softly to himself. He said nothing else until the kettle had boiled, and the tea was brewing in its pot.

"Here," he said, placing the teapot and two mugs on the table. "As I said before, I grew up in Lincolnshire. I'm curious. What kind of house do you think I grew up in?"

"A big one."

"Try a flat above a corner shop."

"Really?"

Frank laughed. "It's true." He held his hands aloft, palms facing Marnie. "I may be a lot of things, but a liar isn't one of them."

"Where did you learn to talk like that, then?"

"Elocution lessons. My father died when I was eleven. Mother needed me to take over running the shop. I was an early developer, so had the stature of a man, but not the presence. She was worried we'd be ripped off by suppliers, so set about training me up. Once a week, she sent me to one Clive Rotherfield Esquire. He was a stuck-up former butler, and I didn't like him much, but he did a good job. Taught me a lot about how to carry myself and the way to speak to different types of people."

"I see. And did it work? With the suppliers and customers, I mean?"

Frank grinned. "It did. I had to leave school young, but I was a quick learner and, with Clive's help, I soon had command of the business. It may only have been a corner shop, but I increased our turnover enough to take care of my mother and sisters."

"What happened to the shop?"

"Mother runs it now. She's in her seventies but still fit as a fiddle. My sisters help when they have leave."

"You must miss them."

"I do." Frank twirled his mug against the table. "Mother was worried that growing up in a house full of females would make me soft. She was terribly worried when I joined up."

"You don't seem soft to me."

"Really?" Frank held Marnie's gaze, and she turned her eyes back to the net in front of her, grateful for the half-light that hid her blush. "I hope it's not making too much extra work for you, my being here."

"No, not especially. What are a few more sheets to wash when I'm already doing a full load?"

"I've seen how hard you work to care for Roy and Sally. I hope you're taking care of yourself, too."

"I enjoy being busy. It takes my mind off missing my girls... girl. Annie, I mean."

"Speaking of keeping busy, I've been thinking. There's a show being put on at *HMS Europa* next week. Part of the navy's efforts to keep our spirits up. They've told us we can invite our landladies. I reckon I can get tickets for you, Sally and Roy if you'd like to come?"

"What kind of show is it?"

"Does it matter?"

"No, I suppose not. It's not like we have a bustling social life these days."

"You'd be surprised how much goes on at the base. They often have visiting musicians. Would it help you decide if I told you that the next visiting musicians are the London Symphony Orchestra? It should be a good evening's entertainment."

"The London Symphony Orchestra? My goodness, that is something. Hmm, well, thank you for the offer, it's very kind of you. If you don't mind, I'll see where I'm up to with my work and decide closer to the time."

"Marnie, there'll always be more nets to make and mend. Come on, you deserve a bit of fun, and how many times do you think you'll be able to see the London Symphony in concert?"

"We'll see."

Chapter 39

June, 1942

"This is jolly good of you," said Roy, pulling on his jacket.

"Not at all," said Frank. "I'm pleased to be able to thank you for your hospitality."

Roy laughed. "You know the navy are paying us?"

"Yes, but I still consider myself fortunate."

"Oh, Roy," said Sally. "You've got your tie all squiffy. We can't have you looking like that among all those smart sailors."

Marnie caught Frank's eye and smiled. It had been a long time since she'd seen Sally so excited, and Marnie couldn't remember the last time she'd seen her mother-in-law dressed so smartly. Sally had chosen a burnt orange two-piece with a cream blouse under the jacket. She'd swiped colour across her lips and either pinched her cheeks or added a touch of rouge.

With his tie straightened, standing there in his suit, Roy looked younger than he had in a long time. There was colour in his cheeks and less of a stoop to his back. Marnie made a mental note to thank Frank for bringing out the improvement in his hosts.

Frank came over and stood beside Marnie. "You look lovely," he muttered under his breath.

"Thank you," said Marnie, fumbling in her purse to hide her blush. Had she misjudged the occasion and gone overboard? The tea dress she was wearing was old and patched in several places, but she'd opted for her brightest red lipstick, and hoped it didn't send out the wrong signal.

"Now I've been mollycoddled to within an inch of my life, I think we're ready to go," said Roy.

Frank placed one hand on Marnie's back and pointed to the door with the other. "After you, madam."

Marnie smiled and led the group out onto the street. "What a lovely afternoon."

"Isn't it just," said Frank, tilting his head to the cloudless sky. "And thank goodness, for an outdoor concert is never so appealing in the pouring rain."

"Would it not have been wise to hold the concert indoors?" asked Sally.

"I think they wanted as many people as possible to attend. You can fit far more people on the lawn outside *HMS Europa* than in any room in that building. It's such a treat getting the symphony orchestra here, it would be a shame to place a limit on numbers."

Roy's walking stick clicked against the pavement as he attempted a head start on the rest of his party. Marnie watched him favour his right side, his left foot dragging against the pavement before being thrust forward. She wished Roy would relent and let her get hold of a wheelchair, but he wouldn't entertain the idea.

"Did you say Kitty's coming?" asked Sally.

"Aye, and Stevie. When he's wearing trousers, you'd never know there wasn't a real leg under there. He's done a wonderful job of mastering walking on his wooden leg. Having to take that old stray for walks has really spurred him on."

"Less of the old stray," said Frank. "Missy's a thoroughbred."

"A thoroughbred what?"

"That we'll never know," laughed Frank. "Alright, she may have been a stray of indeterminate origin, but she's definitely a puppy."

"And a lively one at that," said Roy. He turned back to the women. "Stevie seems brighter as well as walking better. He popped in the mission last week with Missy. Cheered the lads up to have a young 'un around the place, and he seemed in good spirits. It must be a weight off Kitty's mind."

"It is, although there's still no word from Simon."

"Simon is Kitty's son?" asked Frank.

"Aye, he joined up at the same time as Stevie and her eldest, Al, but she hasn't heard from him for a very long time. After what happened to Al, it's no wonder poor Kitty is worried."

"He'll be alright. And Bobby should be home soon."

As they drew closer to the entrance to *HMS Europa*, the streets grew busier, sailors side by side with landladies and friends as they queued to show their tickets and gain entrance to this most special of concerts.

After making it into the grounds, Frank helped Roy reach the allocated seats. He made sure Roy was on the end of the row so able to stretch out if need be. Marnie and Sally moved further along the row. Only five rows from the front, they had an excellent view of the bandstand where the orchestra would perform. Marnie looked around until she spotted the familiar shape of Kitty's favourite smart hat.

"Kitty, over here."

Kitty turned and spotted Marnie. She said something to Stevie, who turned and waved before the two of them made their way over.

"Isn't this rather special?" said Kitty as she reached them. "And so kind of you to invite us, Frank."

"You're most welcome, Kitty."

"I was worried we'd be late, what with Stevie fussing over that blasted dog."

"We couldn't leave without giving Missy her dinner," said Stevie. Leaning closer to Frank and Roy, Stevie added under his breath, "don't be fooled. Mum loves Missy even more than I do."

"I heard that," said Kitty, batting Stevie with her programme. "It's all lies, Roy. That dog has been nothing but a nuisance since the moment she darkened our door."

"That's why you let her sleep in bed with you, is it?" asked Stevie with a grin, earning himself another whack from Kitty's programme.

"I'm glad it's working out for you," said Roy. "You walking her alright?"

"I certainly am," said Stevie, knocking his knuckles against his wooden leg.

They all shuffled into their seats, Marnie finding herself between Sally and Frank. Sally flicked through her programme, oohing and aahing at photographs of musicians she had never heard of but admired nonetheless. "And look at their gowns," she said, holding out the programme for Marnie to see.

"Very smart, and the chaps' suits."

"Isn't this just wonderful?" asked Sally, beaming as she looked around at all the locals taking their seats.

"It is, especially after such a rotten start to the year, this is just what the town needed."

"They have plenty more performances lined up for the coming months. From what I read, the sailors will also be putting on a show. It's wonderful for morale and to be applauded if you ask me."

"I agree. Oh, look, the musicians are taking to the stage."

A hush descended on the audience. People closed their mouths mid conversation, bodies were held still in anticipation, the only noise the occasional rustle of a programme. Black-clad musicians filed into seats, holding a selection of instruments that caught the low sun and sparkled like distant jewels. The air crackled with excitement, and it was as though the entire audience were holding their breath.

As the music washed over them, Marnie felt as close to at peace as she'd felt in a very long time. The only blot in her serenity was the closeness of Frank and her unresolved feelings. Since their night in the air raid shelter, there'd been a heaviness to their encounters, as though there was something left unsaid or unacknowledged. Marnie closed her eyes. She tried to push misgivings about her new friendship out of her mind and let the orchestra soothe her, for if the London Symphony Orchestra couldn't salve her mind, nothing could.

PART TWO

1943-1944

Chapter 40

August, 1943

"B last," said Sally. "Whoever can that be? You're not expecting anyone, are you, Marnie?"

"No, perhaps it's Kitty. I'll see."

"Would you mind? Only if I put this down now, I'll lose track of where I am in the pattern and will have to unpick this entire row."

"It's looking good," said Marnie, glancing at the pile of knitting in Sally's lap before heading to the door.

Marnie opened the door and screamed. "Is it really you?"

Jimmy dropped his bag to the ground and caught Marnie as she threw herself into his arms. "What a lovely welcome," he said, holding her to him just like he'd done when she was a baby.

"Is everything alright, Marnie?"

"Everything's fine, Sally," Marnie called, grinning at Jimmy. "We've had a special delivery. I'll bring it through to you."

"It?" whispered Jimmy.

"Come on," said Marnie, taking her brother's hand. "Let's surprise Sally."

When Marnie walked into the kitchen empty-handed, Sally sighed. "I thought you said we'd had a delivery? And what was all that shrieking about?"

"Surprise," said Jimmy, walking into the kitchen with a big grin spread across his face.

Sally dropped her knitting to the ground, her hands holding her cheeks as she stared at Jimmy. "Did you know about this, Marnie?"

"No," said Marnie, "why do you think I screamed? Jimmy was the last person I expected to turn up on the doorstep."

"Apologies," said Jimmy. "I should have written, but my return was so last-minute and I didn't want to raise your hopes only for something to go wrong."

"So, why are you back?"

"I was asked to come back due to the number of children who've returned to the village. They need to be in school, and it made sense for me to come back and teach them rather than send one of the female teachers back down here."

"I don't understand why they're bringing kiddies back," said Sally.

"Some have had an awful time away," said Jimmy. "Not all the host families have been kind, and not all the evacuees have been well behaved. Some placements have broken down because of the evacuees becoming unmanageable, whether that's because of bad behaviour or homesickness. I'm sure Marnie will testify that the evacuation process isn't an easy one for the child or their parents."

"I'm more worried Annie won't want to come home," said Marnie. She laughed to hide the truth in her words.

"Of course she will," said Jimmy. "And although she'll miss Richard and Helen, it's not as if she'll never see them again."

Marnie swallowed. How could she let Annie maintain a relationship with Richard and Helen without having to see Grace? It wouldn't be fair for Helen or Grace to have Marnie frequently popping up.

"How's that lovely Clara?" asked Sally.

"Very well, thank you, Sally. We could see a fair bit of each other while I was up north, which was lovely. It's given me a lot of food for thought…"

Marnie waited for Jimmy to expand but he stared out of the window, lost in his thoughts.

"Roy will be very pleased to see you," said Sally. "You'll stay for dinner?"

"Hmm." Jimmy glanced at his watch. "I'm not sure I can. The schoolhouse has been sat empty for so long, I fear it will be quite the job to get it habitable again."

"When do you start back at the school?" asked Marnie.

"Next week."

"How about you stay here tonight, then I'll come over with you tomorrow and give the schoolhouse a good spruce up? I've got a day off tomorrow, so I'll be at a loose end."

"*Pah*," said Sally, "don't be fooled, Jimmy. Poor Marnie here is never at a loose end. She's either working in the shop, working on the nets, looking after us, or cooking and cleaning. Tied in knots would be more accurate than at a loose end."

"You know me," said Marnie. "I like to be busy."

"I suppose staying here for one night couldn't hurt," said Jimmy. "But don't feel you need to come over to the schoolhouse with me. I can manage by myself."

"And what if I'm making excuses to spend time with my favourite brother?"

"Only brother, you mean," said Jimmy with a chuckle. "All right then, we'll go over to the schoolhouse together tomorrow."

Later that evening, after everyone had shared their news, Marnie went up to her bedroom and made up a bed on the floor beside hers.

"Need a hand?" asked Jimmy, poking his head around the door.

"No, almost done. Are you sure you don't mind sleeping down there? I'd be happy to give up my bed."

"Don't be daft. I'll be fine down there. I'll say goodnight to Sally and Roy, then I'll be up."

By the time Jimmy reappeared, Marnie was snuggled down beneath her covers. Jimmy climbed into his makeshift bed and chuckled to himself.

"What's so funny?" asked Marnie, turning on her side to look down at her brother.

"Nothing. It's just this reminds me of when we were bairns, all tied up in knots on the floor together. Now here we are, sharing a room again in our forties and fifties."

"Don't get too comfortable," said Marnie, "it's only for a night. And besides, this is nothing like our old cottage. Here we've got carpet, mattresses, warmth."

"And no Da ranting and raving."

"Precisely. Isn't it strange how far we've come from those days?"

"Yes, and to have lived through two world wars, I don't think anyone could have predicted that all those years ago on our island."

"I'd love to go back."

"To the island?"

"Aye. I was thinking I could take Annie up there once this damn war's over. Me and Tom always planned to, but never got the chance. I don't know if you ever met Joe, Clara's former brother-in-law, but he's befriended Stevie and told him all about the island. Now both Stevie and Kitty fancy a holiday there, too. Also, it's been so long since I saw Mam. We got on well the last time I saw her and I know she's not been in the best of health."

"I might be able to give you a reason to visit," said Jimmy.

"Oh?"

Jimmy sat up and leaned against the bedside cabinet. "This war's given me a lot to think about, and being up north closer to Clara even more so. I've been wondering for a while now whether it's time I went home."

"Home for a visit?"

"Home for good."

"Oh."

"Don't be sad," said Jimmy. "I won't do anything until the war's over."

"I'm not sad," said Marnie, "although I'll miss you. I'm actually surprised it's taken you so long to come to this decision."

"Please don't breathe a word of this," said Jimmy, "but I'm going to ask Clara to marry me."

"About time too," said Marnie, laughing. "Jimmy, you've been a married couple in all but name for donkey's years. It's about time you made it official."

"My thoughts exactly. But please, Marnie, don't breathe a word to anyone. I want my return to be a surprise, and like I said, it could be years till this war is over, anyway."

Marnie groaned. "Don't say that. I've had enough of air raid sirens, rationing and all the loss that goes hand in hand with war. No, let's talk no more about it, and instead dream of how wonderful your wedding will be. Goodnight, Jimmy."

"Goodnight, Marnie. Sleep tight."

Chapter 41

August, 1943

F rank stepped past Marnie to reach the sink and placed a hand on
the small of her back. She smiled at him, briefly leaning her head
against his shoulder before moving away. For over a year now, they'd
been living in some sort of limbo, not stepping out, but with something
between them which amounted to greater than friendship.

Any opaqueness about the state of their relationship was not for lack
of Frank trying to pin Marnie down. She'd lost count of the times he'd
tried to bring it up. But, just like each time he'd tried to kiss her, she'd
ducked the issue, pretending she had somewhere urgent to get to, or a
headache, any excuse to avoid cementing their feelings.

Of course, when in the company of Sally, Roy or Kitty there was
nothing between them but polite friendliness, and certainly no quick
squeeze of fingers, or hand grazing a back. They were careful not to even
hold a gaze.

Marnie dreaded the moment their strange state of being was forced
into the open or choked through confusion and frustration. For the
time being, it suited her to keep things as they were. She and Frank
provided each other a level of comfort, without the need for honesty
that a kiss would warrant, or a formal acknowledgment that there was
more than friendship between them.

As soon as she stepped deeper into a commitment with Frank, all sorts of thorny issues would be thrust into the light. How would Roy and Sally take the news? How would Frank respond to the truth about Grace? As kind as he was, knowing Marnie had borne an illegitimate child conceived in a moment of madness was bound to lessen his opinion of her.

"Morning," said Jimmy, running a hand through his greying curls.

"How did you sleep?"

"Like a log. I think the journey must have tired me out."

"Jimmy, this is our lodger, Frank Merton."

Jimmy held out his hand. "Very pleased to meet you, Frank."

"Likewise. I'm sorry I wasn't able to get home in time to meet you last night. It was gone midnight before I made it home."

"No need to apologise. Marnie's told me about the important work you do down at the port."

"I do my best. Would you like a cup of tea, Jimmy?"

"Yes please. Are you off to the harbour this morning?"

"Yes, but not till lunchtime. Twelve till midnight are my hours today."

"That's a long shift."

"I've had worse. And if we're talking about demanding jobs, I couldn't stand in front of a class of children in a million years."

Jimmy laughed and accepted the mug Frank handed him.

"What time do you want to head over to Somerleyton?" asked Marnie.

"That depends on when the trains are running."

"It shouldn't be too different from what you're used to. Thankfully, the bombers have avoided hitting the station and the bridge."

"Lowestoft's really had it rough these past few years."

"You're telling me. I couldn't believe it when I arrived back from Padstow and saw what had befallen the town. And now with Waller's gone and all those other shops... Have you been into town yet, Jimmy?"

"No, I came straight here from the station. It was an awful shock seeing what's happened to The Grit, never mind the rest of town. And such a shame about your house."

"Aye, I know. At least we've got this place to call home. There're many families not as fortunate as we are."

"Speaking of family, how's my niece getting on down in Cornwall?"

"Very well, according to Helen's latest letter. I can't believe she'll be ten years old next summer. I'm worried I'll not recognise her."

"Of course you will," said Frank, placing a hand on Marnie's arm. As quickly as it landed, Frank whipped his hand away, but not before Jimmy had seen the look that passed between his sister and her lodger.

"I'll take Sally and Roy a tea up, then get myself ready and we'll head for the station. That sound alright to you?"

"Yes," said Jimmy. "I'll have a wash and make sure I'm ready."

Marnie found Sally and Roy both still snoozing when she entered their room with a tray. Sally stirred and smiled when she spotted Marnie. She rubbed her eyes, pulling herself up against the pillows. "Thank you," she whispered.

"Sorry to have woken you."

"We need to be getting up. I'll let Roy sleep a little longer. He's not used to staying up late anymore, but there wasn't any point trying to drag him away from Jimmy. You must be so pleased he's back."

"I really am. I'll go over to the schoolhouse with him today to help get it shipshape. Is that alright?"

"Yes, you go. I'm going to leave Roy to sleep and convince him to have a leisurely day."

"There's no need for you to rush out of bed either," said Marnie. "Enjoy your tea and a moment of peace."

"If you insist," said Sally with a smile. "If you insist."

Chapter 42

August, 1943

Kitty woke screaming, kicking at sheets which were tangled around her legs and twisted tight across her body.

"Mum, it's alright, everything's alright."

Kitty rubbed her eyes, trying to calm her breathing as Stevie pulled her shaking body towards him.

"Was it the same nightmare?"

"Aye." Kitty found it hard to speak, fear still tearing through her.

Stevie said nothing, just rubbed Kitty's back and shushed her until her body stopped trembling.

"Thank you," she said. "I'm sorry to have woken you yet again."

"I'm sure I've given you plenty of sleepless nights over the years," said Stevie. "It's about time I returned the favour. Shall I make you a cup of tea?"

"Thank you," said Kitty, "but I can see to that myself. You go on back to bed. Now you're a working man, you'll be needing your sleep."

"Sure?"

"Sure, off you go."

Stevie picked up his crutches and hopped back towards his bedroom. Kitty heard his bed creaking as he climbed into it. She swung her legs over the edge of her bed, pushed her feet into a pair of slippers, and pulled on her quilted dressing gown. Kitty let out a loud yawn, then left the warmth of her bedroom and headed downstairs.

With the kettle on the stove, Kitty sat at the kitchen table and closed her eyes, snapping them open as unwanted images played against her lids. She slapped her cheeks, startling her tired body away from the horrors that filled her mind. After coming out of the Waller's raid and its aftermath unscathed, Kitty had wrongly assumed she was strong enough to withstand the horrific sights she witnessed during her Red Cross shifts. How wrong she'd been.

The kettle screeched and Kitty rushed to take it off the stove, not wanting to wake Stevie for a second time that night. She poured boiling water into a cup, but her hands were shaking so much she spilled more on the worktop. Kitty set down the kettle and clutched the wood. The tears took her by surprise, her body lurching up and down as sobs wracked her tiny frame.

"Mum."

Kitty turned as Stevie turned on the kitchen light and clicked across the room on his crutches.

"I told you to go back to bed," she said.

"I heard you crying. Sit down, I'll make the tea."

Kitty did as she was told, her body shuddering with phantom sobs even once she'd brought the tears themselves under control.

"I know you don't want to, but you need to tell me about your nightmare. It may or may not help, but it certainly can't make things any worse."

"Sharing my doom and gloom won't help anyone."

"You may be surprised. By my calculation, the nightmares started in the spring. Was it the May raids that triggered it?"

Kitty pulled a handkerchief from her sleeve and blew her nose. She folded the soiled cloth and slipped it back in her pocket. "Aye. It was the May raids."

"Go on."

"I'd seen plenty of death and destruction by then, not least with Waller's. I should have been used to it."

"What changed?"

"I think it was because it was so unexpected. We'd had a couple of close shaves earlier in the year, but no casualties. By the time May rolled around, there was a feeling we may be through the worst, like we'd turned a corner. That's why what happened that night in May was so shocking."

"I remember it well."

Kitty nodded. "I wasn't even supposed to be on shift that night, but my friend Carol had come down with a nasty cold, so I said I'd cover for her. The shift started quiet. We were even playing cards back at base, so sure were we there'd be no call out. Then, just before nine, the bombers came. Twenty-three H.E.s they dropped in total. Thirty-seven killed and God knows how many injured. It was carnage. A low-level fighter-bomber taking out targets from Milton Road right up to Belle Vue Park and Corton Road. We were running round like headless chickens, trying to tend to the injured. The sights I saw... I don't know... it's like that night seared itself in my brain and I can't get rid of it."

"No wonder it's causing you nightmares."

"Aye, but worse than that, in my dreams you're all caught up in it. I turn a badly burned man around only to find its Al, or there's a bairn trapped in a collapsed building screaming and I run to them to find it's little Sam. And as hard as I try, I can't help any of you. You're all there, in my dream, and I lose you all."

"Mum, you have to remember it's only a dream. I'm here, the boys are safe up in Derbyshire, Dad will be home soon."

"But Al's never coming back, and as for Simon, well, I fear the worst."

"It will be alright," said Stevie, wrapping an arm across Kitty and giving her a squeeze.

"Aye, maybe, but I worry I've damaged something in here." Kitty tapped the side of her head with a finger. "One minute I'm fine, then the next I'm flying into a rage for no reason."

"That's most likely down to the lack of sleep."

"Aye, you're probably right. I just long for the day we're all back together again and I can go back to my favourite job of being a mam to you all."

"That day is coming, I can feel it in my bones. There've been no more raids since that night, have there?"

"No."

"Exactly. The tide is turning, Mum. We just have to hold strong for a little longer."

"I hope you're right."

"I am. Now, drink your tea before it goes cold."

Chapter 43

August, 1943

"Good Lord," said Jimmy, stepping into his old bedroom. "I think it must be a leak." He pulled a chair into the middle of the room, climbed up, and inspected the ceiling.

"It's definitely coming from up there," said Marnie, staring at the black circle which stained most of the ceiling. "You'll need a new mattress, the bed's ruined. Do you reckon the floor's sound?"

"Let's hope so, or I'll be down in the kitchen before I know it." Jimmy looked down at Marnie and grinned at her shocked expression. "I think the floor is fine. I gave it a prod before putting any weight on it. It looks as though the bed soaked up most of the leak."

"Can the roof be repaired?"

"I'll get John Barnaby the local thatcher to take a look. He's in his sixties, so won't have been called up. If I seek him out, do you mind tackling some of the mould on the walls?"

"Of course not, I came here to help you clean, whether it's mould or dust makes no difference to me."

"I've been worried about bombs getting the schoolhouse, but as it turns out, the good old British weather is enough of a foe."

"Don't worry, I'm sure it's an easy enough fix. We'll need to sort you out with a new bed and bedding, though. It looks like some of the wood in the frame is rotting. Stay at Sally's with me for a few more nights till we get you sorted."

"I don't want to impose on them when they've already got a house full."

"You know they love having you there as much as I do. Now, stop your dithering and find old John. I'll make a start here."

By the time Jimmy returned, Marnie had scrubbed one wall free of mould and was starting work on the next.

"Any luck?" asked Marnie.

"Yes, he's fetching his ladder. You've been busy in here."

"It's not too bad once you get going. There are a lot of happy memories in this place. Things were so much simpler when we were living here together."

"Yes, perhaps, but life was less rich."

"What do you mean?"

"Well, when we first arrived here, I'd not found Clara again. You hadn't met Tom. Our ties to the island had been severed. All we had was each other. I know you lost Tom, but you now have Annie, Sally and Roy, and I have Clara. Our lives may be more complicated these days, but I wouldn't swap them."

"No, maybe not."

"Marnie, is everything alright with you?"

"I... it's just..." Marnie looked into Jimmy's eyes. Was she ready to tell her brother about Jack? About Grace? About the no man's land she'd entered with Frank? She opened her mouth to speak just as John Barnaby arrived on the landing.

"Mr Watson?"

"Through here," said Jimmy. "John, I'm not sure you've met my sister, Marnie."

"A pleasure," said John, offering a hand for Marnie to shake.

"Have you been up and had a look at the roof yet?"

"Yes."

"Have you found out what's causing the leak?"

"It's a wooden spar broken in the ridge."

"Is that easy enough to repair?"

"Should be, a week, two at most, likely less."

"Will all the thatch need replacing?"

"Nah, doubt it. And you can live here while I get on with the work. It's about twelve years since I last did any maintenance on the roof so it's no wonder it needs a little care and attention. I'll start tomorrow if that suits you?"

"That sounds wonderful, thank you."

"The kiddies will be glad you're back, Mr Watson."

"Thank you, John. It's good to be back."

John tipped his cap at Jimmy and left the schoolhouse.

"Why don't we get rid of that bed," said Marnie, "then we'll have more room to work. Have you checked the other rooms?"

"Yes, your old room is fine, just a bit dusty. Downstairs has suffered no water damage. You know, I could probably camp out here until I get a new bed."

"There's really no need. And you know how much Roy will enjoy having you around."

"How does he get on with Frank?"

"Good. It's hard not to get on with Frank." Marnie rinsed her cloth in the bucket of water, allowing her hair to cover her blush.

"You seem to get on well with Frank."

"Aye, he's a nice enough chap." Marnie began frantically scrubbing a patch of mould. Jimmy walked over and took her hand, holding it still.

"It's been a long time since Tom died, Marnie. If you're ready to find happiness with someone else, no one will think the worse of you for it."

"If only things were that simple."

"Does he have a wife waiting for him?"

"No, of course not."

"Is it because you're under Sally's roof and worry about upsetting her?"

"That's one of my concerns."

"I would place money on Sally being the last person to begrudge you a little happiness."

"Do you mind if we talk about something different? Like, when are you going to propose to Clara?"

Jimmy laughed. "That really is an about turn. I'm not going to propose to her for quite some time. I'm not even going to tell her my plans to return to the island. There's so much uncertainty around, the last thing I want is to raise her hopes, then dash them. Besides, I think turning up as a surprise would be very romantic."

Now it was Marnie's turn to laugh. "It certainly will be after all these years you've made her wait."

Chapter 44

September, 1943

"It's so kind of you all to come," said Kitty, raising her mug of tea. "To friendship."

"To friendship."

"It's just what I needed."

"Is there still no more news on Simon?" asked Marnie.

"None. They say no news is good news, but in this case I can't see how it can be." Kitty's voice shook as she spoke and she clutched her hands together to stop them trembling. When she'd heard Jimmy was back in town, all she'd wanted was to gather everyone together, but now her house was full, it felt too much. She felt as though she couldn't breathe under the weight of false cheerfulness.

"He'll be fine, Mum," said Stevie.

"I hope so, but to have had no word for this long, well, it's impossible not to worry, especially after... after losing Al." Kitty sniffed, wiped a sleeve across her eyes and pulled on a smile she hoped was convincing. "I'm just so grateful to have you all here, especially with Bobby still away."

"You don't need to thank us," said Marnie. "The chance of a night away from the stove was more than enough to tempt mc." She popped a chip into her mouth and smiled at Kitty.

"The company's not bad either," said Sally, nodding her head in Jimmy's direction.

"I can't believe you're back in Lowestoft," said Kitty. She reached across and pinched Jimmy.

"Ow!"

"Just checking you're real."

"I'm definitely real," laughed Jimmy, "and very pleased to be here with you all. The village they sent me to in Derbyshire was very beautiful and on the whole folk were friendly, but it never felt like home."

"I've been thinking about going up there myself for a visit," said Kitty. "I know plenty of other mothers who've visited their bairns, but more often than not they end up coming home with them, so I've not been able to trust myself. I think I'd be alright now, though."

"It might put your mind at rest," said Jimmy. "But take it from me, your lads are thriving up there. Not that they don't miss you," he added quickly.

"They'd better do! I appreciate you keeping half an eye on them these past few years. To be separated from your children, well, it's something no mother should ever have to face."

Marnie squirmed in her seat. She'd kept her secret hidden for so long now, sometimes hours passed without her thinking of Grace and what she'd done. But the longer she put off telling those she loved the truth, the more impossible ever revealing it became. Surely they would hate her for lying by omission for so long?

"Derbyshire is a beautiful place," said Frank. "We went there on a holiday when I was little. When do you think you might go up there, Kitty?"

"Oh, it's only half an idea. I've not made any firm plans as yet."

"It must have been good to be closer to Clara while you were there," Roy said to Jimmy.

"Yes indeed. While I was grateful to come home, I feel the distance from Clara more keenly than ever."

Marnie caught Jimmy's eye and winked. She'd kept her promise and not let slip Jimmy's plan to return to the island of their childhood.

"I had a letter from Clara last week," said Kitty. "She sounded well, and the hotel seems to be bumping along nicely despite all the restrictions in place."

"Yes, if she can get the hotel through the war, she can get it through anything," said Jimmy.

"We should go up there for a visit when the war's over," Roy told Sally.

"Yes," said Sally. She glanced at Marnie, then looked away. Both were aware that Roy's health was deteriorating at an alarming rate. The thought of him travelling a few streets required meticulous planning, never mind taking a trip to the other side of the country.

Although there'd been no further strokes, Roy had never fully recovered from the last, despite the doctor's promises that the effects would be temporary. Marnie's wash day had expanded to at least three a week due to the incontinence that was never mentioned but couldn't be ignored.

Roy seemed happy to be spending the evening among friends, even more so now his visits to the Seamen's Mission had been curtailed to once a fortnight. If, or rather when, Jimmy and Clara wed, Marnie doubted Roy would be well enough to make the journey.

"Are you alright?" Frank muttered, quiet enough for only Marnie to hear.

She nodded and let her hand rest for a second on Frank's knee, before quickly bringing it back to her own lap. When Marnie looked up, she noticed Sally watching her closely. Marnie flushed. "Let me clear away these plates for you," she said, gathering up the dirty dishes.

"You don't need to do that," said Kitty. "You're here as our guest."

"It's no bother, honest," said Marnie, making her way into the kitchen. As she began piling dishes in the sink, someone tapped her on the shoulder and Marnie jumped. "Oh, goodness, Sally, you gave me a fright." Marnie clutched a hand to her chest, laughing.

"I wanted to catch you while the others were distracted."

"Oh, is everything alright?"

"I wanted to tell you I've seen how Frank looks at you, and you at him. You need to know that neither Roy nor I would have any objection if the pair of you started courting."

"Goodness... I mean..."

"Tom would never have wanted us to stand in the way of you living a happy life. He would have wanted to know you had someone to take care of you, and I think he would have approved of your choice."

"But I haven't made any choice."

"Ah, love, I know you're probably trying to protect me and Roy, but you really don't need to worry about us."

"Really, Sally, there is nothing going on between me and Frank, and there won't ever be."

"Well, that sounds like a mighty big shame. The two of you would make a good match. If it's not me and Roy stopping you, is it Annie you're worried about?"

Marnie sighed. How could she explain she didn't deserve a man like Frank, without giving away her secret? She leaned against the kitchen counter. "I suppose I don't feel ready to start a new romance, and besides, enough will have changed for Annie when she comes home without making her play happy families with a man who isn't her father."

"Then I'll say no more about it," said Sally, "except that I think you'd be a fool to ignore what's right under your nose."

Chapter 45

October, 1943

"No, no, no, no, no." Kitty tried to close the door on the official from the War Office.

"Please, miss, I need to give this to you."

"Go away. *Go away!*"

Kitty slid down against the wall beside the front door. The official opened the door and crouched beside her. He patted her knee, bowed his head, then handed her the news. Half an hour later, when Stevie returned from work, he found Kitty curled up in a ball in the middle of the living room floor.

"Mum, what is it?" Stevie lowered himself down beside Kitty and stroked her hair. "Mum, please, is it Dad?"

Kitty sniffed and shook her head.

"Simon then?"

Kitty nodded.

"Good God, please no, not now the Allies are finally getting somewhere against the enemy. That would be too cruel."

"He's not dead," said Kitty with a sniff. "They've taken him prisoner."

"Prisoner? Where?"

"Singapore."

"When?"

"Last year, they think. The army has only just located him, which is why we're only hearing about it now. All those months waiting for news, and now this."

"But it means he's alive, Mum. That's better than the alternative."

Kitty sat up, pulled her knees to her chest, and hugged her arms around herself. "It's just all too much."

"Come on now, Mum." Stevie sat beside Kitty and placed an arm across her shoulder. "It will all be alright. When did you get in last night?"

"Just after two. There were bombs dropped on Yarmouth Road, but thankfully no casualties."

"Well, that's something. Could you sleep when you got in?"

"A little."

"Nightmares again?"

Kitty nodded.

"None of this will feel manageable on little to no sleep. Come on, sit yourself in an armchair, and I'll make you a cocoa. Then I want you to catch forty winks."

Kitty managed a watery smile as Stevie used the arm of a chair to pull himself up.

"You've come such a long way these past couple of years."

"All thanks to this," said Stevie, knocking his knuckles against his wooden leg. "I always wanted to be a pirate when I was little."

"Don't they have hooks instead of hands rather than wooden legs?"

"I don't think there are any rules about which lost limb gets you into pirate club," said Stevie with a grin. "Now get yourself into that chair, and that's an order."

Kitty waited till Stevie had left the room, then pulled herself up and flopped into the armchair. The weight of worrying for her family left her limbs feeling heavy. She yawned, grateful that she had an evening off her Red Cross work. Not once had she regretted volunteering, but the work took its toll, not just in the long hours but in the things she'd seen, the destruction of homes, businesses and bodies at the hands of enemy planes.

"Here," said Stevie, walking in ten minutes later, Missy at his heels, to find Kitty curled up in her chair. "Drink this, it will make you feel better. And, Mum, what I said earlier about the difference my new leg's made? Well, it's not just the new leg, is it?"

Kitty frowned. "What do you mean?"

"I'm trying to say thank you. It's been you propping me up literally and otherwise since I came home. I know it's not been easy for you and I wanted to say thanks. That's all."

Kitty reached out and squeezed Stevie's hand. "I'm just so pleased you've come through the worst." Missy jumped up onto Kitty's lap and she stroked her ears. "I think we need to thank Missy here for your recovery. She's done as much, if not more, than me to raise your spirits and get you moving again."

"That's true," said Stevie, reaching forward and scratching Missy under her chin. "You need to take care of yourself too, Mum. Why don't you rest today, and I'll treat us to fish and chips tonight?"

"Your treat? How could I refuse?" Kitty yawned again. "Sorry, I feel so tired. I think I could sleep for a week. I'll just close my eyes and get forty winks."

When Kitty woke, she could hear the wireless playing in the kitchen and a man's voice humming along to the latest Bing Crosby hit. For a moment, she thought it was Bobby, but then she remembered Bobby was somewhere in the middle of the English Channel and the voice must belong to Stevie. Kitty reached her arms up and yawned loudly. Missy looked up at her, then jumped off her lap and went to find Stevie.

"How long have I been asleep?" asked Kitty, rubbing her eyes as she walked into the kitchen.

"Ah, you're awake. You've been out like a light for these past three hours. You must have needed your rest."

"When I heard you singing, I thought for a moment Dad was home."

"He must be due leave soon. Are you going to send word to him about Simon?"

"No, there seems little point. He can't do anything about it from all the way down there. All it would do is worry him, and we need his mind fixed firmly on his work."

"Too right."

Chapter 46

November, 1943

"Phew," said Kitty, as she and Marnie left the Seamen's Mission. "It's getting harder and harder to get poor old Roy there. I'm going to have to start driving him in my ambulance if we're not careful. You know I still have Stevie's old wheelchair if you think Roy would go for it?"

"I can imagine his response if I suggested that, and it wouldn't be pretty."

"No, you're probably right. How are things at home?"

Marnie sighed. "Difficult. Between me and Sally, we're managing, although the other evening Roy had a fall and if Frank hadn't been there, I'm not sure how we'd have got Roy off the floor."

"I'm pleased it's worked out having Frank with you."

"Aye, it's hard to believe it's been almost two years now."

"The pair of you seem to get along very well."

"Aye we do." Marnie realised Kitty had stopped walking and turned back to her friend. "What is it?"

Kitty grinned. "Are you sure there's nothing you want to tell me about you and Frank?"

"No, of course not."

"No one would mind, you know. It's been years since Tom died. You can't be expected to live like a nun. I'm sure Sally would give you her blessing."

"Maybe, but it's not just about Sally. There are other reasons I can't take up with another man just like that."

"Really? You're not worried about Annie, are you?"

"No, it's not that." Marnie strode off along the road. The day was cold, a north wind tugging at a grey sea, forming foamy white crests on top of bulging waves. Her hair whipped into her eyes, sand stinging her skin, caught up and carried on the wind from the nearby beach.

"Marnie, wait." Kitty ran to Marnie's side. "What's the matter with you today? You seem in a right old tizzy. Is there something on your mind?"

"I suppose it's the thought of another Christmas without Annie, and worry over Roy. And then there's you and God knows who else insinuating there's something going on with me and Frank. As if I could ever deserve a man like him."

"Hey," said Kitty, putting her arm around Marnie's waist and guiding her to the sea wall. "What's brought all this on? Have you been getting enough sleep?"

"Roy's been waking a lot in the night and I can't expect Sally to keep getting up. I'm beginning to suspect Roy may have had at least one more stroke. Not as big as the others, but there are signs something's not right. He won't hear of going to the doctor, of course."

"Can't you persuade Sally to take him?"

"She's not keen either. I think she's worried it will be bad news." What Marnie didn't add was that, on top of worry over her in-laws, Frank was growing impatient with the state of affairs between them. A few times recently he'd tried to kiss her, and Marnie had had to push him away. She could see the hurt in his eyes despite his attempts to brush off her rejection. In truth, she'd like nothing more than to be whisked up in his arms, but she couldn't deceive Frank, he deserved better. And she wasn't prepared to tell him the truth, either.

"What have you got planned for the rest of the day?"

"I'm working from ten in the shop." Marnie yawned.

"When did you last have a proper day off?"

"Sunday," said Marnie, suppressing another yawn.

"So you didn't work on any nets on Sunday?"

"Only for an hour or two."

Kitty sighed. "Marnie, that does not count as a day off. You need to take care of yourself or you'll be no good for anyone else."

"I'll get an early night tonight."

"You'd better had. And why don't you let me cook for you? It always feels sad just cooking for me and Stevie. I could bring a casserole over once you're home from work?"

Marnie leaned in and rested her head on Kitty's shoulder. "I'm so lucky to have a friend like you." *And I can't risk losing you by telling you the truth*. "A casserole would be lovely, but you're working just as hard as me, so it seems rather unfair."

"Then how about you cook for us next week? If we take it in turns each week at least one of us will get a night off."

"That sounds like an excellent idea. Fancy walking me up to the shop?"

"Why not? I've got a while until my shift starts."

The two women linked arms and headed inland towards the high street.

"Any news on Bobby?" asked Marnie.

"Aye, he should be home on leave at the end of the week. I just thank my lucky stars he wasn't sent further afield. You know some crews are all the way over in India, some have even been sent to the Arctic if you can believe it? I had a letter from Bobby last week saying everything's alright down there and he's looking forward to getting home."

"That's good news. And Simon? Any more news about him?"

Kitty's face clouded over. "No, nothing, and I don't expect there will be until the war's over. They're hardly going to release a prisoner before then, are they? Oh, I wish none of my boys had been old enough to join up. I should've waited longer to have children like you did."

"I don't think either of us could've predicted another war," said Marnie. "Besides, from what I remember of those days, there was no stopping you and Bobby. Every time I saw you, there was another bairn in your belly."

"Hardly," said Kitty. "I miss those days, when it was you and Tom, me and Bobby, the bairns were little and life was simpler."

"Aye, so do I, but there's little point looking back now. Right, I'll say goodbye here to save you from walking up Mariner's Score. See you later?"

"Aye, see you."

Chapter 47

November, 1943

"Well," said Marnie, dropping her bag down onto Jimmy's bed and turning around to admire the room, "this is looking so much better. You seem to have settled in nicely." She pointed to a selection of books piled up beside his bed. "Are those what I think they are?"

Jimmy laughed. "Yes, they're the books the teacher gave me when I was still at school. They're rather dog-eared, but I can't bear to part with them."

"What was she called again?"

"Mrs McKinnon."

"That's right. I never got to go to school like you did, so don't really remember her." Marnie picked up a book and began flicking through the pages. "How are things going here?"

Jimmy sighed and sat down on his bed. "In some ways, it's good to be back, but in others... I've had quite a few losses among the parents of my pupils. It's been hard on the children, hard on the mothers. All I can do is try to keep things as normal as possible."

"Aye, and I'm sure having you back here will help. Shall I make us a nice cup of tea?"

"Good idea. You make a start and I'll be down in a minute."

Marnie made her way to the kitchen and put the kettle on the stove. She leaned back against the warm Aga, wrapped her arms around herself and closed her eyes. Each time she visited the schoolhouse, it was like going back in time. She pictured Raymond, mentor and father figure, drinking brandy at the kitchen table, Clara and Jimmy laughing over breakfast on the morning of her wedding.

"Is everything alright?" asked Jimmy. "Ever since I came home, I've had the feeling there's something you want to tell me but haven't been able."

Marnie sighed. She'd been right in thinking she could keep no secrets from her brother.

"Marnie? Come on. We're too long in the tooth now for secrets, aren't we? Is this about you and Frank?"

Marnie put her head in her hands, unable to meet her brother's gaze. "It has nothing to do with Frank. Something happened in Padstow. I did something very stupid. Not just stupid, selfish."

Jimmy pulled out a chair and sat beside Marnie. He prised her hands from her cheeks and lifted her chin so he could look her in the eyes. "Have you killed someone?"

"What? No, of course not!"

"Then whatever you've done can be forgiven."

Marnie's shoulders slumped. She knew Jimmy would love her regardless, but still feared his reaction. She looked into her brother's eyes. He hadn't exactly chosen a conventional route where women were concerned. "You might hate me for it."

"I won't."

"You might."

"Goodness me, Marnie. Just spit it out."

"There was a man in Padstow."

"A man?"

"Jack."

"Helen's brother?"

Marnie nodded.

"And you and Jack had an affair?"

"No! No, it wasn't like that."

"Right, so if you didn't have an affair, and you didn't kill him..."

"It wasn't an affair, not exactly. There was a night when Padstow got bombed. Jack's cottage came off badly, but worse than that, a little lad next door died. We saw his body being brought out, saw his whole family."

"You poor thing."

"I don't deserve your sympathy. It's no excuse for what happened." Marnie gave her damp eyes an angry scrub. "Jack took it really badly. He's a good man, but the bombing seemed to break something in him. When I went to see him a few days later, my intention was only to offer comfort. But then we started arguing and the next thing I knew... well... let's just say the comforting turned into something more..." Marnie's cheeks flushed, but Jimmy's gaze didn't waver.

"You made love?"

"There wasn't any love involved," said Marnie, letting out a bitter laugh.

"And this is what you were worried about telling me?"

"There's more. A few weeks after I became ill. We'd all been poorly, only my illness never left me. I was throwing up every morning."

"You were expecting?"

Marnie nodded.

"What happened to the baby? Did you lose it?"

"No." Marnie took a deep breath. "I need you to understand, Jimmy. There was nothing romantic between me and Jack. Tom's death was still so raw and I still loved him. In fact, I probably always will. I knew I couldn't stay in Padstow as an unmarried mother, that would be too much to ask of Helen and Richard. I also knew I couldn't bring the baby back here. It wouldn't be fair to ask Sally and Roy to accept another man's child. And even if they did, how would I take care of it? It's one thing working while Annie's at school, but a baby would have needed much more attention. Can you imagine leaving Sally and Roy alone with a toddler? They're too poorly these days to manage such a responsibility."

"I would've helped you," said Jimmy. "You know that."

"I know. But think about what it would have cost you. You've said it yourself, you're ready to go back to the island, to be with Clara properly. If I'd come back to Lowestoft with a baby in tow, you'd never have felt able to leave."

"What happened to the baby?" Jimmy spoke softly, and Marnie struggled to tell if he was sad or angry.

"I left her with Helen and Richard. They'd always longed for a child. It seemed the best solution for all concerned. Jack can be part of Grace's life, as her uncle, me and Annie can start over once the war's ended."

"Grace?"

"Helen wanted me to choose the name."

Jimmy pushed his chair back and moved to the fire, his back to Marnie.

"You hate me, don't you?"

"Marnie," said Jimmy, turning to face her. "I'm going to tell you something I've told no one. Many years ago, I went to a dance. At that dance, I saw Clara, with the man who would become her husband. I was angry. I drank too much." Jimmy paused and leaned against the wall. "I ended up down on the beach with a woman. A horrible, lewd, drunk, older woman. We... we... well, you can imagine what happened. It left me feeling dirty. I hated myself. I think it ultimately led to the events which caused my accident. I wasn't in my right mind after that happened. Anyway, I'm telling you this so you know I understand. When emotions are heightened, we make choices we'd never normally contemplate."

Marnie thought back to the darkness in Jimmy's eyes in the days after his accident. She wanted to rush over and hug him, for only a man as kind, thoughtful and sensitive as her brother could let such an incident trouble him so.

"You didn't abandon a baby, though."

"Not that I know of. I never sought the woman to check, though given her age, I think it was unlikely..."

"Exactly how old was she?" asked Marnie, managing a small smile.

Jimmy let out a long breath and smiled. "Now I've said it out loud it sounds so ridiculous, so insignificant. I think it was seeing Clara that upset me more. Thankfully, we were given a second chance. And you've got a second chance too. How has Annie been with all this?"

"I'm hoping she's too young to understand fully. We kept my pregnancy a secret the best we could. I hope in time she'll forget much of what happened while we were in Padstow together. She'll have several years' worth of more recent memories by the time she finally comes home."

"You don't intend to visit the child?"

"I don't think it would be fair to Grace, or Richard and Helen. They need the time and space to be parents, and I know they'll do a wonderful job of raising her. Seeing her would be for my own selfish reasons, and I've done enough damage already."

Jimmy picked up the brandy bottle and carried it to the table. "I just wish you'd told me this sooner," he said, pouring them each a glass. "I wouldn't have judged you, but I might have been able to support you."

"I had to get things straight in my mind first," said Marnie. "Thank you for being so understanding."

"Of course," said Jimmy, raising his glass. "I know things have been hard, and will continue to be. But let's raise a toast. Here's to fresh starts, and honesty."

Chapter 48

December, 1943

K itty linked arms with Stevie as they walked down Wapload Road. The night was still, their breath pouring out like clouds of silk, then hanging listlessly around them.

"That was nice, wasn't it?" asked Stevie, his steps more uneven than usual.

"Aye, it was kind of them to invite us."

"But?"

Kitty sighed. On the one hand, spending Christmas at Roy and Sally's had been lovely, but on the other hand...

"What is it?" asked Stevie, slowing his steps and frowning at Kitty.

"It's just me being silly."

Stevie frowned, took a few steps forward, then winced, reaching down to rub his leg. "Do you mind if we stop here for a moment?" He pointed to a low wall and sat down, stretching out his legs with a grimace.

"Are you alright?"

"Yes, I will be. The leg's been rubbing on my stump and I seem to have got a bit of an infection."

"What? Why didn't you tell me?"

"Because it's Christmas, and I didn't want you worrying."

"You silly boy," said Kitty. "We need to call the doctor out."

"Tomorrow," said Stevie. "It can wait until tomorrow."

"But..."

"Mum, it can wait." Stevie's voice was firm enough to stop Kitty pressing the issue further. "Now, tell me what's the matter with you."

Kitty let out a long sigh, creamy swirls of breath filling the air around her. "I had a lovely day, but for me it highlighted all those missing."

"I know," said Stevie, taking Kitty's hand in his own.

"And worse than that, I found myself getting jealous."

"Jealous? Jealous of who?"

"Marnie." Kitty's voice was quiet, her cheeks flushed.

Stevie let out a bark of a laugh. "Jealous of Marnie? Why would you be jealous of her?"

"I don't know," said Kitty. "Just me being silly. I think it was seeing her there, surrounded by people who love her and she loves back..."

"I'm sorry, Mum, but you really are being silly. What about her losing Tom? He wasn't there, was he? And neither was her daughter; Annie's miles away. Yes, she has some family around, but that's not easy, is it? Didn't you see the bags under her eyes? Didn't you notice her hands shaking as she served up dinner? If I were you, I'd be worried about her rather than jealous."

"I'm a horrible person," said Kitty, a lone tear trickling down her nose.

"Come here," said Stevie, pulling Kitty close.

"I just miss them all so much. My little bairns all the way up north, forgetting what I look like, your dad surrounded by mines in the sea, Simon being treated in ways I can't bear to think of by the enemy, and Al... Al..." Kitty's silent tears turned into noisy sobs.

"Christmas Day can be funny like that, can't it?" said Stevie. "The one day of the year we're all supposed to be having a jolly old time, never mind what's going on the day before and the one after. There's nothing wrong with missing family, Mum, but of all the people to envy, I'd suggest Marnie isn't one of them."

"You're right," said Kitty. "Shall we head home before we catch our death?"

"Yes, good idea. Let's get home and then I think we could both do with a brandy."

"Why not? It is Christmas, after all."

Later that evening, after sharing a drink and checking over Stevie's poorly leg, Kitty lay in bed trying to sleep. Since the letter arrived a week ago, sleep was something that seemed ever further from her grasp. Measles. All four boys down with measles, and at Christmas time, too. When the letter arrived with a Derbyshire postmark, Kitty had been so excited, but the excitement quickly turned to despair as Mrs Burrage laid out the varying conditions of her four youngest sons.

Kitty had kept the bad news to herself. Why worry anyone else during the festive period? It wasn't like anyone could do anything to help the lads. Her whole body ached with a desire to cradle her boys through their illness, yet here she was, miles away. She couldn't lose another of her bairns. She couldn't.

Turning onto her front, Kitty banged a fist against her pillows, thumping out the frustration and helplessness that had cloaked her since she heard the news. Stevie was right. It was silly to be jealous of Marnie, but seeing her friend at the centre of a family, her own daughter safe and sound, Kitty found she couldn't help it. It was plain as day Frank was sweet on Marnie, yet her stubborn friend refused to see it for herself.

"Oh, Bobby. Please come home soon," whispered Kitty, her hand running over the empty side of the bed where her husband should be lying. She pulled a pillow to her chest and cradled it, trying to find comfort. Even Stevie, who she'd thought was safe, was now battling some blasted infection in his leg. Kitty squeezed her eyes shut, praying that when the New Year came, it would be better than the last.

Chapter 49

February, 1944

Marnie screamed as a figure in a white gown appeared at the end of the bed.

"It's only me," whispered Sally. "I'm sorry to have frightened you."

"Don't worry," said Marnie. "What time is it?"

"Just gone two."

"In the morning? What's wrong?"

"It's Roy. He's had another funny turn, and I need to change the sheets. I'm so sorry to wake you, but I can't do it on my own."

"Of course you can't. Don't worry about waking me, I'd rather you did that than do yourself an injury." Marnie yawned and stretched. She swung her legs over the edge of the bed and was just pulling on her dressing gown when Frank popped his head around the door.

"Is everything alright? I heard a scream."

"It's fine," said Marnie. "Roy's had a funny turn, but between me and Sally we can manage."

"Are you sure?"

"It's very kind of you to offer," said Sally, "but I don't think Roy's pride could take seeing you when he's in this state."

"Alright. But you know where I am if you need me."

"Thank you," said Sally, then turning to Marnie, "come on."

The two women crossed the corridor into Roy and Sally's room. A lamp poured out a dull orange pool of light, throwing Roy's face into shadow and making him appear almost ghoul-like.

"Sally says you've had a funny turn," said Marnie, walking across the room and perching beside Roy on the bed.

"U... I'll be... right... as rain... soon."

"I'm sure you will be, but right now, we need to get you cleaned up."

"No," said Roy, his cheeks flushing as he shook his head. "No." A single tear snaked through the lines and crevices of his cheek.

Sally stepped forward and took Roy's hand. "I'm so sorry, love. I know this is horrid for you, but I'm not strong enough to help you by myself. Besides, Marnie's helped you plenty of times before."

"Not... like this."

From the smell in the room, Marnie knew what Roy was talking about. "Don't be daft, Roy," she said. "This is no worse than any other time. Now, we'll help you into the bathroom where Sally will give you a hose-down, and then I'll come back and make you up a nice fresh bed. Alright?"

Roy nodded. His head hung low, his eyes screwing up in shame. Between them, Marnie and Sally helped him off the bed. Marnie grabbed a clean towel and wrapped it around his waist.

"It's going to be tricky getting you down the stairs, Roy. Hold on to the banister and I'll go in front in case you lose your footing."

With much grunting and swearing, Roy, with Marnie and Sally's support, made it to the top of the stairs. It took a good ten minutes to get him to the bottom of the stairs, and on each step Marnie experienced a rush of fear that he'd fall and she wouldn't be strong enough to stop him.

As they shuffled Roy through the kitchen, Marnie considered how fortunate they were that he had moved the bathroom inside a few years earlier.

"Sit here a moment," said Marnie, lowering Roy down onto the toilet seat. He did as he was told, and Marnie leaned over the bath to check the water temperature. "Perfect," she said, wiping her hand on a towel and giving him a smile.

Roy was shaking, his eyes blurred with tears he stubbornly kept contained.

"Roy, I'll step outside while Sally helps you undress. I'll pop back in to help you get in the bath, but my head will remain turned towards the door. I won't see anything you'd rather I didn't."

Roy gave a small nod, and Marnie slipped out of the bathroom. Only once Sally had called her did she re-enter, keeping her promise as she averted her eyes. Once he was settled in a freshly run bath, Marnie turned to Sally.

"Will you be alright if I see to upstairs?" said Marnie under her breath.

Sally nodded, placing a hand on Marnie's arm and squeezing gently.

In Sally and Roy's bedroom, Marnie began collecting up soiled bed-linen and clothes, bundling it into a wicker basket in the corner of the room.

"Is Roy downstairs?"

"What are you still doing up?" Marnie asked Frank, whose head was poking around the door.

"I thought with Roy out of the way, I could give you a hand."

"If you're sure, that would be wonderful. Could you fetch me clean sheets and blankets from the airing cupboard, please? I'm going to take this lot outside to soak in a bucket in the yard overnight. Once I'm done, I'll come up and make the beds."

"Alright, see you shortly."

Marnie carried the basket of laundry downstairs, filled a large bucket up with water, added a good dose of soap flakes and stirred the contents around with a stick. It would be no more pleasant a job in the morning, but at least she'd be able to see what she was doing. Marnie tipped out the water, refilled the bucket with fresh, then went back inside.

"Oh my word, look at this." Marnie walked around the bed, admiring the hospital corners and smoothness of the sheet.

"They teach us how to make beds in the navy, you know," said Frank with a grin.

"If I'd known that sooner, I'd have had you on bed making duty since you arrived."

"Why do you think I kept quiet?"

Marnie flung a pillow at Frank, who caught it and threw it back. Marnie giggled, then stopped, her face falling into a frown. "We shouldn't be messing about up here while Sally's down there with Roy. Goodness knows what we're going to do with him. He won't see a doctor, but this keeps happening and each time he seems to get worse."

"I think you're going to have to force a doctor upon him," said Frank. "You can't keep going on like this. You and Sally walk around the house like you're half dead some days."

"Oh, ta," said Marnie.

"You know what I mean. You both look so tired. I worry about you."

"Well, let's put talk of doctors aside for now and finish up this bed. Then I can help Roy back up here and we can all get some sleep. It must be almost morning by now."

"It's getting on for three," said Frank, checking his watch. "You'll be able to get a few hours' kip yet."

With the bed made, Frank went back to his room and Marnie helped Sally dress Roy.

"Did you enjoy the bath?" Marnie asked him.

Roy stared ahead as if he hadn't heard the question. Marnie looked at Sally, who shook her head. "Tomorrow," she mouthed.

Marnie nodded. Tomorrow they could sit down and work out how best to help Roy, but for now, bed was calling, and they were all in great need of some sleep.

Chapter 50

April, 1944

"Well, aren't you a sight for sore eyes?" Marnie grinned at the sight of Roy in his best suit.

Roy held his arms out and did a little bow. "Back in a tick. Just need to run a comb through my hair one last time."

Sally moved beside Marnie and they squeezed each other's hands, listening to the sound of his shuffling footsteps on the landing above. The thought of a night out with the chaps had lifted his spirits, and he'd physically rallied enough that Sally was happy to let him go.

"I can't believe he's up and about," said Sally. "The doctor was happy with his progress at the check-up yesterday and is more convinced than ever that the last funny turn resulted from some sort of virus."

"Just make sure he doesn't overdo it," said Marnie. "Although the thought of a night of playing darts with the boys seems to have put a spring in his step."

"And very thoughtful of Frank to organise it. What time is Jimmy arriving?"

Marnie checked the clock in the hall. "He should be here any minute." Right on cue, a knock came at the door. Sally opened the door to Jimmy and Stevie.

"I bumped into Stevie on my way from the station," said Jimmy.

"And I see you've brought another friend with you," said Sally, throwing a disapproving glance at Missy, who was sniffing something on the pavement.

"Don't worry, I know all about your allergies. We'll wait out here," said Stevie.

"How are you getting on with the boat building?" asked Marnie.

"Good, thank you. I've been there long enough now to feel like one of the team. It's mostly older chaps with the young fellows off at war, so I bring down the average age by quite some margin."

"I'm sure they're grateful to have a lovely chap like you working for them," said Sally. She turned her head and called up the stairs, "hurry up, Roy, they're all down here waiting."

"Coming."

Jimmy ran up the stairs to help Roy down. It was a timely reminder that, although much better, Roy's movement was still limited and they needed to keep an eye on him.

"You will take care, won't you?" said Sally. "Head straight to the shelter if you hear a siren, and don't come back too late."

"Yes, ma'am," said Roy.

"Go on, get on with you. Frank will be waiting."

The men left and Sally closed the door, leaning against it and smiling at Marnie. "Peace at last, and for a while at least."

"And now it's our turn," said Marnie, picking up her coat. "Kitty's going to meet us there."

After all the worry over Roy and the recent change they'd all noticed in Kitty, Marnie and Frank had come up with a plan to cheer everyone up. Dancing was out of the question for Roy, but he could manage a game of darts without too much trouble. Marnie fancied the idea of a dance herself, but Sally's joints were no less painful and it didn't seem fair to drag her to a dance where she'd be sitting on a chair all evening.

Marnie had failed to calculate the extra time it would take to walk with Sally, and so by the time they reached Crown Street, Kitty was pacing up and down, having clearly been waiting for quite some time.

"Sorry," said Marnie, rushing forward and kissing Kitty's cheek.

"I was worried you'd got lost," said Kitty, with a tight smile.

"Blame me and my old joints," said Sally. "Thankfully warmer weather is just around the corner and will act as a good dose of oil to my old bones."

Now Kitty offered a more fulsome smile, settling the atmosphere between the women. For months now Kitty's moods had been erratic, and those around her trod a tightrope, one wobble enough to send Kitty off in a fit of tears or anger.

"In we go," said Marnie, opening the door and holding it open for Kitty and Sally.

"My, my," said Sally as they stepped into the dining hall of the Crown Street Restaurant. "This is really quite something."

"Isn't it just," said Marnie, turning to admire the impressive mural covering the walls. "They had a lady from the Borough School of Art in to paint it."

Sally rested a hand on a picture of a fisherman standing beside his boat. "This could be Roy," she said, sniffing.

"Aye, it's a lovely reminder of the old days."

"Best not to think of how things were," said Kitty, pulling out a chair and keeping her eyes away from the depictions of old Lowestoft life.

"Well, I think it's beautiful," said Sally, sitting opposite Kitty and smiling to lift the tension.

"Stevie looked well," said Marnie, picking up a menu.

"He's doing all right."

"He's doing more than all right by the looks of things," said Sally, "though I wish he wouldn't take that mutt everywhere with him."

Kitty flashed a genuine smile at the talk of Missy. "That dog's been the best thing to happen to us for quite some time," she said.

Conversation halted as a waitress came over and took their order.

"Such reasonable prices," said Sally.

"Any news from Bobby?" asked Marnie.

"He made it home for a couple of days last month, but in his last letter, he said they have cancelled all future leave. Something's afoot, but either he doesn't know what, or isn't allowed to tell me."

"Right, well, it must have been good to have him home, however briefly."

Kitty nodded, and Sally and Marnie pretended not to notice the tear that dropped from her eye and bled into the tablecloth. On the whole, the meal was pleasant enough. Between Sally and Marnie, they kept the conversation going, but by the time they came to leave both were exhausted from the effort of trying to gee up Kitty, and burdened by worry over a friend who was very much not herself.

Later, with Roy and Sally in bed and Jimmy on a train home, Frank and Marnie compared notes on their evenings.

"It did Roy the world of good," said Frank. "His balance was a bit off, but we had a good old laugh and he seemed to enjoy himself. How was your evening?"

Marnie sighed. "I don't know. On the surface it was alright, but I'm so worried about Kitty. She's grown so thin, and her hair is almost all white. From the sagging skin around her eyes, I'd say she's surviving on very little sleep. At one point, someone dropped a fork against their plate and she leaped into the air with a scream. We smoothed over it, but something's not right there."

"I've seen that kind of behaviour before, among chaps who've witnessed terrible things in battle. It's a mistake to think war only affects the minds of those fighting. Plenty of civilians have seen sights that haunt them, and Kitty more than most with her work on the ambulance. Add to that her grief and worry over her family, and it's no wonder her nerves have been affected."

"What can I do to help her?"

"The only thing you can do is to be a good friend, and be ready and waiting if she asks for help. We can also pray this war ends sooner rather than later. Come here," said Frank, pulling Marnie into his chest. He gave her a chaste kiss on the top of her head, and she allowed his warmth to comfort her.

Chapter 51

August, 1944

"How are things at school?"

"Quiet now the holidays have arrived, but everything's been going very well, thank you," said Jimmy, linking arms with Marnie as they strolled in the warm summer sunshine. "I've been using the time to do a few repairs to the school and paint some classrooms. The children were so excited to reach the summer holidays and that excitement was infectious. Especially now so many have returned home. It will be the first time some of them have spent any meaningful time with their friends in years. They're out all hours playing on the village green, and it's lovely to see them enjoying themselves."

"Things feel like they're turning a corner," said Marnie. "What with D-Day last month and children returning home. Speaking of which, I've been wondering about Annie, and when to bring her home."

"Have you spoken to Helen about it?"

"Aye, we've been discussing it in our last few letters. She's suggested, and I'm minded to agree that it's better to be cautious and not rush things. It looks as though the tide has turned on the war and our lads are making gains, but with Hitler the man he is, who's to say he won't try to enact some revenge? We'd be first in the firing line if he did."

"So what time frame has Helen suggested?"

"She thinks we should see out the year as we are, then if things are still looking good, I could bring Annie home in the New Year."

"Not for Christmas?"

"Perhaps, we'll see. It's hard to plan anything with any certainty these days."

"How far should we walk? Is it too hot for you?"

"No, there's a lovely sea breeze. It reminds me of the island."

"Really? Look at all these houses around you, it couldn't be further from the island if you ask me."

"I'm not talking about what we can see. I'm talking about the smell of seaweed, the tang of salt on your tongue, the feel of a sea breeze on your skin. I know it's been a long time since you were on the island, but surely you've not forgotten it completely?"

"Of course not, and it's been on my mind more and more since I made my decision to return."

They continued walking until a sight ahead of them made them stop in their tracks. "Is that? Oh... Jimmy..." Marnie let out a whoop of excitement, pulled her hat off her head and began running as fast as she could towards the pier.

"Wait for me," shouted Jimmy, panting as he struggled to keep up. "I'm an old man now."

Marnie stopped on the sea wall, shielding her eyes against the sun.

"Are you laughing or crying?" asked Jimmy.

"I don't know," said Marnie. "Both?" She let out something between a laugh and a choke, her cheeks slick with tears, her mouth pulled into a wide smile. "Isn't that the most wonderful sight you've ever seen?"

Jimmy stepped forward and put his arm around Marnie's shoulders. "Yes, it's pretty special alright."

Rather than the usual barbed wire covering the creamy-gold sand, the area known as Children's Corner was packed with bodies. Groups of women lay on towels, soaking up the sun, elderly couples rested their limbs on deckchairs, sharing tea from flasks, and children ran in and out of waves, squealing in delight as cold water lapped against their bodies.

"I was losing hope of ever seeing such a sight again," said Marnie. "This gives me so much confidence I'll be able to bring Annie home sooner rather than later."

A woman walked past them, a young girl with pigtails skipping along in front of her, and a toddler with a mop of curls running behind, trying to catch her sister up. A lump formed in Marnie's throat. That could've been her, bringing her two children to the beach. But no, there would never be a family visit like that.

"Oh no, the tears are back again," said Jimmy, brushing a finger against Marnie's cheek. "Still happy tears?"

"Of course," said Marnie. "It's just such a momentous thing to have the beaches open again."

"Not all of them."

"No, but enough for the town to get back to something like normal."

"Let's hope so."

"Come on," said Marnie, pulling off her shoes and stockings.

"Oh, no, I really don't think..."

"You're not that old, Jimmy. Where's your sense of adventure? Besides, I'm not asking you to go for a swim, just dip your toes."

Jimmy sighed, sat down on a low wall, and began removing his shoes and socks. "You always were the bossiest of my sisters."

"How rude. Come on, race you there."

In the end, it wasn't just Jimmy's old leg injury slowing them down, but the number of bodies crammed onto the patch of sand. They picked their way past delighted faces, reaching the water's edge after what felt like an obstacle course.

"Three, two, one…" Marnie took Jimmy's hand, and they stepped forward into the water. After a few initial squeals, they grew used to the cold, the water caressing their toes. Around them, children kicked up water, splashing each other and yelling in delight. The sun beat down, tightening their skin.

"I wish Annie was here with us," said Marnie when they eventually made their way back up the beach.

"She'll be back soon enough. Have you thought any more about talking to Sally and Kitty about what happened in Padstow?"

Marnie shook her head. "I hate keeping it from them, but I also hate the thought of rocking the boat. Kitty's not been herself for months now and I worry that telling her will only make things worse."

"Or it might help."

"How?"

"Well, if she knows that you've also had hard choices to make, that things haven't all been plain sailing."

"She knows that already after what happened to Tom."

"Yes, but you're very good at putting on a show and pretending that everything's alright. I know how much giving up Grace cost you, and how hard it was to come back here and leave both girls behind, but you've not exactly complained, have you?"

"I'm worried she'd take my news badly."

"Perhaps, but at least your friendship would be one without secrets. You never know, being honest with her might encourage her to do the same and share how she's feeling. I know from my conversations with Stevie he's very worried about her."

"All right, I'll think about it."

"Good. Now, how about an ice cream?"

"Great minds think alike," said Marnie, following Jimmy towards the pier.

Chapter 52

September, 1944

Their usual walk along Marine Parade, past Royal Green and up to Claremont pier had been undertaken in silence. The day was warm, the sun beating down, a soft breeze brushing against their skin, but the mood between them felt glum. Marnie glanced at her friend. Kitty's skin was grey, purple crescents were under her eyes and she didn't look as though she'd brushed her hair that morning. What was it Jimmy had said about being honest and sharing their feelings? Marnie thought anything was worth a try. She placed a hand on Kitty's arm to stop her walking.

"Kitty, there's something I've been meaning to tell you ever since I came back here."

"Sounds serious."

"I suppose it is. And I'm not sure what you'll think of me once I've told you."

Kitty sighed, as though the conversation were too much effort. "Marnie, what are you talking about? There's nothing you could do that would make me think badly of you, except perhaps if you ran off with Bobby and that would be tricky given he's still miles away in Queenborough."

"Can we sit down?"

"Aye." Kitty followed Marnie to a bench overlooking the sea. The Home Guard were going about their business on the pier, but the sea was unusually blue and the view from the bench was magnificent. "Shall I fetch us a cuppa?"

Marnie nodded, and Kitty went off to a tea hut, returning a few minutes later with two steaming mugs.

"Come on then," said Kitty. "Spill the beans."

Marnie blew across the top of her cup and took a cautious sip. "Something happened while I was in Padstow. Finding out I had to come back and help Sally and Roy turned out to be rather timely as it offered a way out of a tricky position I'd found myself in."

"Did you fall out with Helen and Richard? I can't imagine it, they seemed such kind folk."

"No, that wasn't it. It's to do with Helen's brother Jack."

Kitty screwed up her eyes and tapped her fingernails against her mug. "Tall fellow with unruly red hair? Not that I'm one to talk," she added, smoothing down her curls that still held a faint hint of ginger.

"That's the one."

"I remember you complaining about him in your letters. Was it him you fell out with?"

"No, we became friends, of sorts. And then one night, about a year after Tom died, we were both in a bit of a state and one thing led to another."

"Oh, I see. But that's so out of character. I've always thought you verged on the prudish. But no matter, it doesn't change how I think of you. You should have seen the things us herring girls got up to while travelling the country on the hunt for silver darlings. The stories I could tell, good grief, they'd make you blush."

"I haven't got to the worst part yet."

"Oh, sorry, I'll stop interrupting you. Go on."

"Well, the result was that I fell pregnant. With another little girl." Marnie reached up and brushed tears from her eyes.

"Oh no," said Kitty. "Why didn't you write and tell me? Did you lose the baby early? Oh, dear God, you weren't too far gone, were you?"

"I didn't lose the baby. I gave birth to a healthy little girl and named her Grace."

Kitty stood up and took a step away from the bench. "I'm sorry, Marnie, but I'm very confused. Are you telling me you have two daughters down in Padstow? But why not just say so from the start? I know it would be a shock for Sally and Roy, but they'd get over it."

"The thing is, Kitty, I don't have two daughters in Padstow, or at least I do, but I don't."

"Stop talking in riddles, Marnie. Have you been on the brandy or something?"

Marnie took a deep breath. "I gave Grace up. I gave her away." Now she'd said it, it was as though a weight had lifted from her shoulders.

"You gave your child away?" Kitty's voice was quiet, too quiet for Marnie's liking. Kitty inspected her fingers, picking at the grime beneath a nail. When she looked up, the muscles in her face were taut and her left eyelid fluttered in spasm. "Who did you give your baby to, Marnie?"

"I gave her to Helen and Richard. They've never been able to have children of their own, so it seemed the right thing to do. Jack can still see Grace, but it avoids any scandal."

"Right." Kitty let out a long breath, kicking the toe of her shoe against the ground. "And you couldn't do what normal folk who get knocked up do and marry the father?"

"We didn't love each other. It wouldn't have been right."

"Right?" Kitty laughed. Marnie fidgeted on the bench, sensing her news wasn't going down well, but unsure what was coming next. "Right?" said Kitty again, her voice growing louder.

"Look, Kitty, I know..."

Kitty stepped forward, leaning over Marnie and pointing a finger at her chest. "You know nothing." She spat the words, her voice cold and loud. "You gave away a healthy child because, what, the father wasn't quite right for you? Didn't he live up to your high standards, Marnie? Good God, you have no idea, do you?" Kitty laughed again, the cold, brittle laugh that spoke of danger rather than mirth.

Marnie sniffed and turned her head away. Once she'd regained her composure, she asked Kitty, "no idea of what?"

"No idea what it's like to really lose a child. Not through choice, not like you did, I mean to have your son snatched away by some invisible enemy in a part of the world you've never even heard of before, to not be able to bury your firstborn, to have to go on pretending everything's right with the world when it never will be again, to carry on for your other bairns because *that's what mothers do*."

"Kitty, please stop shouting." Marnie looked around and saw that a couple of men from the Home Guard were staring. An elderly couple rushed past, as though not wanting to be tainted by whatever was going on next to them.

"Stop shouting? So convenient, wasn't it? Coming here, playing the saviour. Oh, good old Marnie, coming to care for her ailing in-laws. What a lovely, kind woman she is. *No, that is not the truth*. It suited you to come here and leave your bairns behind. I remember what you were like with Tom in those early days, always putting off having babies so you could carry on pandering to your own needs."

"It wasn't like that." Marnie's voice was not much more than a whisper. "I was scared... I..."

"Scared? Scared is having your son taken prisoner and dumped into a camp on the other side of the world to be tortured and each day you wonder whether he's survived. Scared is having your husband miles away trying to clear up bloody mines that could blow him to smithereens at any moment. You know what, Marnie? I used to think we were alike. Both from fishing villages, both from big old families that struggled by from day to day. Cut from the same cloth, I thought we were. Now I see how wrong I was. I could never give up a child willingly, and I can't be friends with any woman who could."

"Kitty, please let me explain."

"No. You've said enough."

Kitty put her mug down on the bench with such force the handle detached. Marnie watched on in horror as her friend strode off along the seafront. She had known this would be a hard conversation to have, but the last thing she'd expected was that she'd lose her best friend. For once, her wise brother had been wrong. She should have ignored Jimmy's advice and carried on hiding the truth. Her vision blurred from tears, Marnie began stumbling her way home.

Chapter 53

September, 1944

The door slammed against a wall and the group of sailors drinking at the bar looked up in surprise as Kitty stormed into the Harbour Hotel. She would happily have entered any drinking establishment, this just happened to be the first she'd reached. Kitty glared at the curious sailors and they turned their attention back to their pints.

"I need a drink," said Kitty, slapping her handbag down on the bar and climbing onto a stool.

"Right. Any in particular?" asked the barman, turning to the men propping up the bar and raising an eyebrow.

"Gin."

"Coming right up."

The barman placed a glass of gin down on a mat and Kitty slid several coins across the wood. She slung her handbag over her shoulder, climbed down from the bar, and made her way to a table in the corner. Once seated, she picked up the glass with a shaking hand and took a large glug of gin, welcoming its burn as it slid down her throat, searing a trail all the way to her stomach.

Was she going mad? Kitty couldn't remember feeling so angry in all her life. She took another swig from her glass, her eyes prickling at the liquid's heat. How could Marnie have given up her child? It wasn't right. It wasn't natural.

Kitty squeezed her eyes tight shut and took a deep breath. She couldn't decide if she was more angry about what Marnie had done, or the fact she'd lied about it ever since her return. As far as Kitty knew, they shared everything. Now, to find out Marnie had been keeping something so important from her made Kitty question their entire friendship. And besides, how dare Marnie burden her with this when she had so much of her own to deal with?

Sally and Roy had a right to know, of that Kitty was certain. And what about Annie? She was living with the baby down in Padstow. Surely she would've noticed Marnie's expanding belly? And what would happen when it came time to bring Annie home? Could Marnie really be so heartless as to leave the baby behind?

Kitty walked up to the bar, her glass landing heavily on the wood. "Another, please."

"Are you sure, miss? Bit early, isn't it?"

"Very well. If you don't want my custom, I'll take it elsewhere."

"No, don't be doing that," said the barman, reaching for Kitty's glass and refilling it. "There you go."

"Ta."

"You're Bobby's missus, aren't you?"

"Aye."

"Know how he's getting on?"

"Alright, I think."

"Must be hard, being left on your own."

"Sometimes."

"Right, well, when you next see him, tell him there's a pint waiting for him and all the other lads."

"Ta, I will do."

Kitty took her refilled glass back to the corner table. She should go home, she should be making nets, but her anger pinned her to the spot. She drank more gin. Once the burning subsided, Kitty waited for the alcohol to anesthetize some of her anger but it had the opposite effect.

Pushing her glass away, Kitty pulled on her coat and stormed out of the hotel, stomping her way towards the harbourside. She would tell Frank. He had a right to know.

Sailors moved with purpose around the harbour. Where once fishermen had landed creels jam-packed with silver darlings, now naval vessels waited to escort ships into the harbour. All the trawlers had been converted into minesweeping vessels, and standing by the harbourside, Kitty felt lost, as though she'd stepped into a different world.

"Can I help you, miss?"

Kitty looked up into the eyes of a kind-faced sailor.

"Are you alright, miss? Only, we don't like civilians hanging round this area."

"No, right, I completely understand. I'll be on my way."

Kitty turned her back on the harbour, just about managing not to break into a run. Tears rolled down her cheeks as she let the hopelessness of the situation wash over her. Perhaps if she could just get a full night's sleep, things would feel better? But Bobby and the kiddies would still be gone, Al would still be dead. Now she was cut off from Marnie and her family, too.

Kitty stuffed a fist in her mouth and bit down to stifle a scream. How could Marnie be so selfish? She must have known how Kitty would take the news. Hadn't she got enough to be dealing with already? Kitty rushed along pavements that had seen better days, concrete and stone crumbling into the road. The path in front of her sparkled intermittently with glass blown out from windows. She pushed on past Central School, empty and cold after being bombed back in '41.

By the time Kitty arrived on her street, she had calmed down enough to allow Marnie a grace period. It wasn't her place to tell Roy and Sally what Marnie had done, but if Marnie was too cowardly to do it herself, it would leave Kitty with no choice.

Chapter 54

November, 1944

I t had been a slow day at work and Marnie had even had time to nip to Mrs Sinclair's for a cup of tea at lunchtime. It was with a sigh of relief that she heard the clock strike five and she could fetch her bag and coat. She stopped on the way home at a greengrocer and butcher to pick up some ingredients for tea, but despite having plenty of tokens left in her ration book, other women had beat her to it and it was a meagre selection of mouldy veg and gristly meat that went into her basket.

As soon as Marnie opened the door to Sally's house, she felt something was wrong. Had Roy had another funny turn? The house was too quiet, and the air closed around her like an unwelcome shroud.

"Hello?" Marnie walked through to the kitchen but found it empty. Back in the hallway, she stopped and listened. The clink of a china cup against a saucer came from the sitting room. "Hello?" Marnie pushed open the door to find Kitty and Sally sitting side by side on the settee. "Is everything alright?"

"I've told her," said Kitty, standing abruptly but refusing to look Marnie in the eye.

"What?"

"I've told Sally all about what you got up to in Padstow and about abandoning your bastard there."

Marnie took a sharp intake of breath. "Bastard? How dare you use a word like that!"

"It's what she is, isn't it? You may have given her a pretty name, but it can't hide the truth."

"I can't believe you've done this," said Marnie, shaking her head.

"Me?" Kitty let out a laugh that made her sound more nervous than amused. "You're the one who's been lying to Sally these past years. Pretending to be a perfect daughter-in-law, pining for your own daughter. It was only right she hear the truth."

"Perhaps, but it wasn't your place to tell it."

Kitty still wouldn't look at her. Instead, her eyes darted around the room as if she'd only just realised what she'd done and was now looking for an escape route.

"And would you have told me?" asked Sally, looking up at Marnie for the first time. "Or would you have kept your secret hidden and carried on lying to us?"

"Part of the reason I gave Grace away was to protect you!"

"Stop lying to yourself, Marnie." Kitty spat the words, each syllable filled with abrupt anger. "You never wanted Annie, and you didn't want this latest bastard. Don't blame Sally for your failures as a mother."

"But it's not true. It's not! I was scared about having a child, but I love Annie. I always have and always will. I love Grace too, but I couldn't keep her. Please, Sally, you have to understand."

"Oh, I do," said Sally. She sounded tired, frail, and as she heard the despair in Sally's voice, Marnie hated Kitty almost as much as she hated herself. "I understand that you've tarnished my son's memory, and spent the past two years lying to us. As if we haven't been through enough."

"Sally, please." Marnie dropped to her knees in front of Sally. "Please, it's one thing I didn't tell you, and I'm so very sorry that I kept it from you. But what I did was for the sake of everyone concerned, not least Grace. I'd never deliberately deceive you if I didn't think it was absolutely necessary."

Sally turned her head away and ignored Marnie's pleas. "I'm sorry, Marnie, but this has been such a shock. I feel like we all need some time away from one another to decide what to do next for the best. As Jimmy's back now, perhaps you could stay with him for a few days?"

"You're asking me to leave?"

"Just until we've got this all straight in our minds."

"Is this what you wanted?" Marnie asked, turning to Kitty. "Do you really hate me this much? Well?"

"This isn't my doing."

"Oh, really? Frankly, I can't see what business it is of yours, anyway. You seem to have taken my actions as a personal insult, but it's me who has to live with my decision, me, not you. I'll pack a bag."

Marnie stormed out of the room, slamming the door behind her. Of course, what she'd done was wrong, but after all she'd done for Sally these past couple of years? And Kitty, how could she? Marnie's eyes burned with tears that wouldn't come. Instead, her fists clenched, and she ran up the stairs to her bedroom, throwing clothes into a suitcase with no care or thought.

Rather than leave straight away, she found a piece of paper and a pencil. Goodness knows how long she'd be in exile for and it wouldn't be right to leave without a word to Frank.

Dear Frank,

Me and Sally have had a bit of a falling out. I'd rather you hear the reason for our disagreement in person, from me, but if Sally chooses to tell you, I suppose there's nothing I can do to stop that.

I'll be staying with Jimmy until a truce is called. This might not be a bad thing, to have a bit of time away from one another. Hopefully, I'll see you soon and will explain everything in person,

Marnie

Marnie folded the letter and placed it on Frank's pillow. Then she crept downstairs, pausing outside the closed sitting-room door. Unable to trust herself not to say something she'd regret, Marnie didn't say goodbye to Sally. Instead, she let herself out onto the street and closed the door quietly behind her.

Chapter 55

November, 1944

B y the time the train pulled into Somerleyton station, the sun had set and Marnie emerged from the train onto a pitch-black platform. Where once the odd farmhouse window would have helped her get her bearings, with the blackout there were none of the usual clues.

One hand holding on to a railing, Marnie slowly made her way from the platform onto the road that would lead to the village. As long as she didn't stray off the path, she would be alright.

The first tears arrived when Marnie was halfway between the station and the village. They were triggered by a memory of walking along this same road with Jimmy and Raymond, just after Jimmy had been released from hospital. How stubborn he'd been, how proud she'd been.

So much water had passed under the bridge since that day. Marnie wiped her sleeve across her eyes. How could she have made so many mistakes? Ever since the moment she left her island home, all she'd wanted was to keep her independence. But now, all these years later, independence didn't seem to matter the same way it once had. Wasn't family more important? And friends? What was the point of freedom if you had no one to share it with?

Marnie stumbled on, the hooting of an owl causing her to jump out of her skin. When a horse sneezed on the other side of the fence, Marnie screamed and ran the final few hundred meters to the village. Once she was within the village confines, Marnie's heartbeat slowed. She'd lived there long enough to find her way to the schoolhouse without the need for light.

With no idea what time it was, or if Jimmy would still be up, Marnie knocked on the schoolhouse door. When after five minutes there was no answer, Marnie turned the handle and stepped inside. She found Jimmy in the sitting room. The fire was blazing in the heart and his socked feet were pointed towards it as he lay snoozing in a chair, a newspaper spread across his chest.

Marnie stood beside Jimmy, wondering how best to wake him. He stirred, muttered something in his sleep, then returned to his slumber.

"Jimmy," said Marnie, gently shaking his shoulder. "Jimmy, it's me, Marnie."

"Huh?" Jimmy's eyes sprang open, and he flinched.

"It's alright, it's me."

Jimmy rubbed his eyes, then rubbed them again. "I'm getting a strange sense of déjà vu," he said, grinning.

"To your hospital bed?"

"Yes. You gave me a fright then, too, turning up out of the blue. What are you doing here this evening? Is everything alright at home?"

"Roy and Sally are fine, but Sally's asked me to leave."

"What? Why?"

"I told Kitty the truth about Padstow, and about Grace. She didn't take it too well."

"Oh no, and to think it was me that told you to do it. I'm so sorry, Marnie."

"You're not to blame. It's me who created this mess."

"When I suggested you tell Kitty, I should have thought things through more. Her entire identity is tied up in motherhood. It would be very difficult for her to understand the idea of putting a child up for adoption."

"I tried to explain, but she got more and more angry. It was back in September I told her and she hasn't spoken to me since."

"Oh, Marnie, I'm so sorry."

"You've nothing to be sorry for. Dear God, Kitty was so angry. She implied that I'd never deserved to have children in the first place, that I never wanted Annie. It's true I wanted to put off being a mother, it's also true I found those early years hard, but I never didn't want her."

"I know how much you love Annie," said Jimmy, passing Marnie a handkerchief to wipe her eyes. "Kitty's under a lot of strain, what with Simon in a prison camp God knows where, and Bobby away searching for mines. Not to mention Stevie's injuries and the rest of her bairns being hundreds of miles away."

"It doesn't excuse what she did, though."

"And what was that?"

"I thought she'd forgive me in time so I've not tried to contact her, but then when I got home from work, I could tell something was wrong. Kitty was there, in our house. She'd gone and told Sally about Grace. Not for Sally's sake, just to spite me."

"Oh dear God, what a dreadful thing to do."

"I know. And now Sally doesn't want me in her home. Oh, Jimmy, I've lost everything. Absolutely everything."

"Come here," said Jimmy, guiding Marnie to a chair and stroking her hair. "You've not lost everything. Don't be so daft. What's happened to my strong, determined sister? The Marnie I know doesn't give up when things get tricky."

"What do you mean?"

"Instead of worrying about what you've lost, start thinking about how to get those things back. You need to explain yourself properly to Sally, without Kitty there. And in time, you can mend things with Kitty. Will she help Sally and Roy in your absence? They need you. Sally will struggle without you, won't she?"

"Who knows? I've lost Kitty's friendship, but I'm not sure I actually want it back after what she's done."

"Don't be so hasty. How many years have you two been friends for?"

"Too many to remember."

"Exactly, and she was friends with Clara before that. I'm sure she doesn't approve of all Clara's life choices, but that doesn't stop them being friends. Give each other some time, let things settle down."

"Perhaps. In the meantime, is it alright if I stay here?"

"Of course it is. Will Sally manage caring for Roy by herself?"

"I suppose Kitty will have to help if she can't."

"Alright, I'll make you up a bed."

Chapter 56

November, 1944

Kitty trudged her way home feeling more despondent than she should for someone who had just done the right thing. It wasn't her who had given away a child as if it was worth no more than an old dress. An easterly wind howled around her, tearing her hair in all directions and refusing to give her the peace she craved. Damn Marnie for messing everything up.

As Kitty walked up to her cottage, she noticed a faint halo of light creeping around the edges of the blackout curtain. Was Stevie home already? He'd said he was working until seven, and usually squeezed in a pint or two on his way home. It had only been just after six when she left Sally's and Kitty had expected to have longer alone to collect her thoughts.

Kitty turned her key in the lock and pushed open the door. The house smelled different. What was it? She sniffed the air, something like a combination of diesel and seaweed reaching her.

"Hello?"

After closing the door behind her, Kitty hung her coat on the end of the bannister and kicked off her shoes. Her skin tingled, a sure sign something wasn't right. Was there an intruder in her home? But why would anyone break in when she had nothing of value to steal?

"Hello," she called again, frustrated by the shake in her voice. She was braver than this. With a deep breath and shaking hands, Kitty pushed open the sitting-room door. "Oh, my word." She let out a squeal that woke the sleeping figure in front of the fire. Kitty crossed the room in two strides, allowing just enough time for Bobby to climb out of his chair. "You're back. You're really back."

"I am, and I've got plenty of leave due to me."

"Why didn't you write?"

"From the middle of the English Channel?" asked Bobby with a laugh.

"They have WRENs to collect the mail. I saw it on a film when I went to the cinema."

"Not when you're as far out as we were," said Bobby, stroking Kitty's hair as she burrowed her head into his shoulder. "By the time we were closer to shore, I fancied the idea of surprising you, only when I got home you were out, and as soon as I sat in front of a warm fire, the months at sea caught up with me."

"So you're not back for good?"

"No, but I'm back for a good while."

"Do you want a cup of tea?"

"Tea can wait. I want to hear all your news, everything I've missed these past months."

When Kitty began sobbing, Bobby pulled a handkerchief out of his pocket.

"Whatever's happened while I've been away? Is it Stevie? Has there been more news of Simon?"

"No, it's nothing like that. I've had a falling out with Marnie," said Kitty with a sniff.

"Is that all? I'm sure whatever it is can be straightened out easily enough."

"I'm not sure it can. The thing is, I was so angry with her, I went and did something I fear may be unforgivable."

"It sounds like you're the one who needs tea," said Bobby. "Sit here, calm yourself down and I'll make a pot. Then you can explain to me exactly what's been happening in my absence."

Half an hour later, the mug cupped between her hands was empty and Kitty had spilled out the whole sorry saga with barely a pause for breath.

"I can't believe that of Marnie, I really can't. To give up a child like that?"

"I know, that's just what I thought. How could she do such a thing?"

"Then again," said Bobby. "I know something of the grief she must have felt losing Tom. You remember what I was like after his death?"

"Aye, of course, but surely that's even more reason not to go fooling around with some other chap."

"Perhaps, but grief can be awful lonely. It sounds like this chap Jack understood something of what she was feeling. Isn't it possible they were both looking for a little comfort?"

"Comfort or not, they did something foolish and should've faced up to the consequences."

"But didn't she do just that? It might not have been in the way you or I would have done, but she hardly chose an easy path, did she?"

"I'd say abandoning a child is far easier than having to raise one."

"Really? And how have you found these past years being separated from our bairns? Would you have picked that over having them under your feet?"

"You know I wouldn't. But it's not the same."

"Maybe not. I don't want us to fall out too, my love. I'm just trying to see things from Marnie's point of view. It strikes me none of the options available to her were pleasant ones."

"How can you say that after losing Al like we did?"

"I suppose there's a lot of time to think when you're away at sea as long as I've been. Anyway, sleep on it. Things might feel very different come the morning."

"I won't go running to Marnie with an apology."

"I'm not asking you to. But a friendship as long as yours is a big thing to give up on so easily. Hey," said Bobby, when Kitty went to argue, "Enough talk of Marnie for one night. I want to hear how our absent kiddies have been getting on, I want to know all about how Stevie's managing with his pirate leg, and I'd also like to know why you went and put yourself in harm's way by volunteering with the Red Cross."

Kitty worried he'd scold her for her volunteering, but Bobby's face spread into a grin and he pulled her closer to him. "I love you, Bobby Thorne."

"And I love you too, Kitty Thorne. How long do we have until Stevie gets home?"

"About an hour."

"Right, well, push all thoughts of Marnie and our children aside. We've got some proper catching up to do."

Kitty giggled as Bobby scooped her up into his arms, kissed her deeply, and carried her up the stairs to their bedroom.

Chapter 57

November, 1944

D espite her best attempts to pull herself together, there was no hiding the fact she'd been crying and Marnie had attracted sympathetic looks from fellow passengers as the train rumbled towards Somerleyton. There was no way of continuing her work on the nets while staying with Jimmy, but no reason she couldn't still work in the shop. It had been four days since she'd left Sally's, and Marnie still didn't feel any better about the situation. This bout of tears had been brought on by bumping into Kitty on her way to the railway station and being completely ignored. Marnie felt like a scarlet woman, an outcast, dirty.

The train pulled into the station and Marnie buttoned up her coat. It felt safer travelling these days, bombs few and far between, with not a single life lost so far that year. There was a feeling the world was turning a corner, even if her personal life was falling apart.

"That's us," said an elderly woman, pointing to the carriage door.

"Oh, sorry," said Marnie. "I was miles away." She opened the door and stepped down onto the platform.

"Marnie."

Marnie jumped and spun around. "Frank, what are you doing here? Why have you come all this way?"

"All this way? Marnie, it's not exactly far. I've been given a few days' leave. I was hoping to talk to you, but I can see this might not be the best time."

"What do you mean?"

Frank took a step closer to Marnie. He reached out a hand and stroked a finger down her cheek. "You've been crying."

Marnie shook her head and took a step back. "It must have been the soot from the train getting in my eyes."

Frank took Marnie's hand and pulled her closer to him. "Can we walk?"

"You can walk me back to the schoolhouse if you like? Though I'm still not sure why you've come all this way out here."

"I'm using my leave to visit my mother, but there's something I need to talk to you about and given you've not been at Sally's for a few days, I thought I'd best come to you."

"Has Sally told you what happened?"

"No, only that there's been some sort of falling out. I'll leave it up to you whether you want to tell me what it's about."

Flustered and confused, Marnie followed Frank down from the station and towards the lane that led to the village. Marnie had to run to keep up with his long strides.

"Can you slow down a bit?" she called. "My legs are half the length of yours."

"Sorry," said Frank. "I suppose I'm a little nervous and all that nervous energy is propelling me on."

"Nervous about what, Frank?"

"We need to talk about things. Personal things, between us."

Marnie groaned inwardly. After the past few days, tackling things with Frank felt like a bridge too far. "Do we? I think things are fine as they are."

"Really? You're happy with this... this... whatever this is going on between us?"

"I enjoy our friendship, aye."

"Marnie." Frank stepped into Marnie's path, forcing her to stop. She turned to face him and wrapped her arms around herself. "Please, Marnie, we're not children. Heck, we're not even young! Shouldn't we be able to admit to romantic feelings at our age?"

"It's not as simple as all that."

"Why not?"

"I have a child."

"I know, and I can't wait to meet her."

"I don't think you understand. It will be a big enough adjustment getting used to living with me, let alone bringing Annie home and introducing her to a strange man who's courting her mother."

"I'm not asking you to rush into anything. Haven't I proved my patience already? Do you have any idea how difficult it is living in the same house as you, sleeping just the other side of the wall, knowing I can't touch you, can't kiss you?"

"As you said, we're not children. Our lives are complicated. There are things I've done in my past that if you knew..."

"What? Nothing you say could change how I feel about you. Look, Marnie, I wouldn't expect to still be living with you if we were courting, it wouldn't be appropriate. But once the war ends, I could stay on in the town and get to know your daughter gradually."

"Please, Frank. Please don't do this." Marnie pushed past Frank, striding off along the lane. He jogged to catch up with her and this time took hold of her arm.

"Marnie Hearn, I love you and I'm not ashamed to admit it. I know you've suffered a great loss in your life and I may never measure up to Tom. But you can't deny you feel something for me, even if it isn't the deep love I feel for you."

Marnie forced back threatening tears. Over the past year, Frank had proved to be a kind, generous-hearted man who, under different circumstances, she would have been delighted to have by her side. But how could she admit her true feelings without being honest about past mistakes? And as Kitty had proved, it was all very well someone promising to think no worse of you, and quite another when it came to it.

"We can't be together, not that like."

Frank scrubbed his hands through his hair. "For goodness' sake, Marnie. If you don't have feelings for me, I would have hoped you'd have had the courage to tell me outright."

Marnie studied Frank, the salt and pepper hair, the crow's feet around his eyes. She pictured herself through his eyes, her blonde curls turning white, lines appearing on her skin. What were they doing, fooling around like youngsters? They were middle-aged and getting no younger. There was only one thing for it. Marnie squared up to Frank, a new steeliness in her eyes.

"I'm very sorry, Frank. I've not wanted to hurt your feelings, but the truth is I think nothing more of you than a friend. You're perfectly pleasant, and good company, but I see nothing more in our future."

"Perfectly pleasant?" Frank's eyes had widened, his hands brought to his hips. "Perfectly pleasant?"

"Aye, that's right." Marnie strained to maintain her composure. She wanted to jump into this lovely man's arms and tell him all the things she loved about him, but it would only lead to more hurt. It was better this way. "Perhaps we should spend less time together if you're not satisfied with a simple friendship."

"Yes, perhaps we should. In fact, do you know what? I'm going to go up to base this evening and ask to be returned to barracks. That should make things easier for you."

"What? You don't have to move out. I mean…"

"I think I do, and by the sounds of it, it will make your life far simpler."

"But, Frank…"

"What, Marnie? What more is there to say?" Frank spun around and marched back toward the railway station.

Marnie sank down on a grass verge, pulling her knees up and hugging her arms around them. Had she just made a huge mistake? Or had she saved them both a lot of heartache in the long run?

Chapter 58

November, 1944

"Today's the day," said Jimmy, laying a plate of toast and fried eggs in front of Marnie.

"Where did you get the eggs?"

"Don't change the subject."

"I'm not."

"You are. You need to go back today and sort things out."

"Had enough of me, have you?"

"You know I'd never get sick of you, but this has gone on long enough. Even if you end up coming back here tonight, you need to talk to Sally. She's got enough on her plate worrying about Roy without this falling out with you."

"She doesn't want to see me."

"How do you know?"

Marnie shrugged.

"And what about Frank? I know there's more to your feelings than you were letting on. You don't get as upset as you were the other evening if there's nothing beyond friendship."

"I can't bear to see the disappointment in Frank's eyes when he finds out the truth. No doubt Sally will have told him by now and he'll consider he's had a lucky escape."

Jimmy sighed and scrubbed his hands through his cropped curls. "You've got a day off from Chadds today, so use it wisely. Even if you don't speak to Frank, it's important you reconcile with Sally. Eat up, you're going to need your strength."

"Thanks for the vote of confidence."

"You're welcome," said Jimmy, popping a slice of toast between his teeth. "Off to work."

"I'll be here tonight, whatever happens. I'm not turning up at Sally's with my bags, even if she wants me to go back."

Jimmy waved a hand to show he was agreeable to the arrangement and left for the school. The thought of confronting Sally was enough to steal Marnie's appetite, but given the trouble Jimmy had gone to, she forced down the toast and eggs.

By the time Marnie found herself outside her in-laws' house, the sun was high in the sky and breakfast felt like a very long time ago. Marnie knocked on Sally's door and waited.

"Hello? Anyone home?"

Marnie put her ear to the door and listened. She heard the creaking of a floorboard and footsteps on the stairs.

"Marnie?" Sally opened the door, her hair dishevelled, her clothes giving off a musty smell.

"Hello, Sally. I thought it was about time we sat down and had a talk."

"I thought you'd be back sooner. It's been almost a week."

"I didn't think I'd be welcome."

"Yes, well, come inside."

Sally walked into the sitting room and waited for Marnie to join her. Only once Marnie was through the door did Sally sit down, her hands clasped in her lap.

"Sally, I'm so sorry. You must be so disappointed in me."

Sally held up a hand. "Before you start, I'd like to fetch Roy down. He needs to hear about this, too."

"Roy knows?"

"Of course he does. You don't think I'd keep something like this from him, do you?"

"I thought you might for the sake of his health."

"His health? What was I supposed to say? First Kitty turns up here harping on and getting in a lather, then you leave, and then Frank. Roy's body might be weakening, but he's not stupid."

"Frank's gone?"

"Yes. He told me you knew."

"He said something, but I didn't think he'd actually leave."

Sally sighed. "It strikes me you've got yourself into a right old muddle, Marnie."

"Aye, and I'm so sorry to have dragged you into the middle of it."

"It seems a bit late to be worrying about that. Come on, it will be easier if we help Roy downstairs together."

Helping Roy downstairs was no mean feat, but ten minutes later, Marnie faced Sally and Roy as they sat holding hands on the settee. She dropped her eyes to the ground, too ashamed to look at them.

"The first thing I need to say is how sorry I am. What happened in Padstow had nothing to do with Tom, at least, I mean, it had nothing to do with my feelings towards him. You know how much I loved him. I'll always love him. Nothing changes that."

"I think you'd better start from the beginning," said Roy. "From what Sal tells me there wasn't much sensible talking went on the night Kitty turned up here."

Marnie nodded and did her best to explain. "So you see," she said when she'd finished her sorry tale, "it wasn't about romance, it was about comfort, a very misguided sense of needing human comfort."

"Grief is a very lonely state of being," said Roy quietly. He reached across and took Sally's hand in his. "We know that better than most, but at least we've always had each other. Being all the way down there, you had to manage by yourself. We both know that can't have been easy."

"I wish I could blame this all on grief, but I fear it was more a lack of judgment."

"Whatever the cause," said Sally, "our issue isn't what happened between you and Jack. You know our history, you know we're in no position to judge. What we don't understand is why you didn't feel you could keep the child."

"I could never reconcile the idea of marrying Jack, nor him with me. Without a hasty marriage, the child, Grace, would have had to live a life shrouded in shame."

"Not if you'd brought her back here."

"People would still talk. They could do the sums and work out she wasn't Tom's child. And there was no way I could support two children by myself."

"You said part of the reason you abandoned her was because of us?"

"I thought you'd be horrified at what I'd done, and wouldn't feel comfortable having another man's child under your roof." Marnie's cheeks flushed as she realised how much she'd underestimated the kindness of her in-laws. "I can see now that was a wrong assumption," she said. "But I take issue with one thing you said. I didn't abandon Grace."

"She's being raised by Richard and Helen?"

"Aye. They've never been able to have children of their own. You've met them, you know what a wonderful couple they are, what wonderful parents they'd be."

"I must admit I don't remember much from our trip to Padstow," said Sally. "I was a bit of a mess, but the one thing I remember is Helen's kindness."

"I truly believe I did the best thing for Grace," said Marnie. "Even after all this distance and the passage of time, I stand by my decision."

"What about Annie?" asked Roy. "What does she make of all this?"

"As far as she knows, Grace is a refugee taken in by Helen and Richard. For all concerned, it's important it stays that way. Perhaps when she's older, I'll tell her the truth, but perhaps not."

"Thank you for coming here and explaining yourself to us," said Sally. "Whilst I can't condone your actions, I can understand them. You're our daughter in all but name, Marnie, and we'll always support you."

"That's more than I deserve," said Marnie, choking on tears.

"Don't be daft," said Roy. "After all you've done for us, there's none who could doubt our love for you is reciprocated."

"I have one more question," said Sally.

"Aye?" Marnie sat up straighter and squared her shoulders.

"When will you move back in?"

Marnie slumped back in her chair, laughing through her tears as relief flooded her. "Really?"

"Come here," said Sally, holding out her arms wide. Marnie crossed the room and kneeled in front of Sally, letting the older woman's arms wrap around her. "I still need to ask you about Frank," Sally whispered into Marnie's hair. "But those questions can wait for another day."

Chapter 59

December, 1944

Kitty stepped off the tiny platform and pulled her coat tighter around herself. All around her mountainous hills, barren and blackened in the winter light, enclosed her. She could see how beautiful such a place could be in fine weather, but at this time of year she found the view oppressive, having grown used to the wide East Anglian skies.

The only person to get off the train at this stop, Kitty stepped onto a narrow lane and looked around her. She pulled a small handwritten map from her pocket and studied it, turning left and beginning the long walk to the farmhouse.

When the latest letter arrived from Mrs Burrage, Kitty had hoped it might contain the offer of a lift, but to her disappointment no such kindness was offered. From the letter she received, she sensed Mrs Burrage disapproved of her desire to visit the farm. But Kitty had gone without her children long enough, and as a mother herself, she felt sure Mrs Burrage would accept the idea in time.

Kitty shifted her carpetbag to her other hand, grateful for all the layers she'd put on that morning. She thought Lowestoft was cold, but here a layer of frost clung to every surface, and the wind that whipped around her felt like icy fingers tugging at her coat to encroach on her warmth.

The four-mile walk gave Kitty plenty of time to think. It had been Stevie and Bobby who'd convinced her to come. Before Bobby was sent back to sea, he and Stevie had sat her down and told her things couldn't go on the way they were. Their words acted like a mirror, and Kitty had seen herself through their eyes, not just in the disintegration of her physical appearance, but in the hardness that had crept into her heart. Another advantage of having Bobby home was that for the first time in over a year, Kitty had managed a full night's sleep. With Bobby beside her, the nightmare left Kitty be, and despite Bobby heading back to sea a week ago, the nightmares were yet to return. The change a good night's rest brought had been remarkable, and her mind felt clear of the swirling darkness which had occupied it for so long.

A tractor trundled along the road, and Kitty pressed herself against a low stone wall. The driver doffed his cap as he passed, and Kitty gave him a small wave. A gust of wind caught her hat, and she grabbed it as it flew from her head, pulling it down tight once more. Kitty didn't want to turn up at Mrs Burrage's door looking as though she'd been dragged through a hedge backwards.

In the distance, Kitty spotted what looked like a low stone house, with several large outbuildings spread around a square-shaped court-yard. Certain this was the farm she was looking for, Kitty increased her pace, enjoying the warmth the exertion provided.

The thought of seeing her children spurred her on, a nervous excitement sending her stomach into somersaults. Would they be pleased to see her? Would they be happy to be coming home? Ever since the restrictions on entering coastal areas had been lifted, Kitty had longed for this moment.

But what if she'd forgotten how to be a good mother? What if the war had hardened her too much to compete with Mrs Burrage as a carer? Kitty's cheeks flushed as she thought of Marnie, and all the horrible things she'd said to her onetime best friend. She'd never understand Marnie's decision to give up a child, but that didn't mean she needed to judge her for it. Bobby and Stevie had helped her see how unkind her reaction to Marnie's confession had been, and yet Kitty hadn't yet been able to bring herself to say sorry.

All thoughts of home were banished as Kitty turned a corner and was welcomed to the farm by two lively sheepdogs, who ran up to her barking before jumping up and trying to lick her face. Taken by surprise, Kitty dropped her carpetbag to the ground and began stroking the dogs, laughing as they refused to leave her be.

A whistle pierced through the noise of the wind. The dogs' ears pricked up. A second whistle sounded, and the dogs sprinted towards the yard, where a young man stood, his fingers in his mouth.

Kitty tried to speak, but no sound came out. She cleared her throat and tried again. "Chrissy, is that really you?"

"Mum?" The young man strode towards Kitty, the two dogs docile at his heels. He stopped a few feet away from her. "Mrs Burrage told us you'd be coming, but we weren't sure what time you'd arrive."

Kitty stepped forward and stared at Chrissy. "Look at you." She took hold of his arms, needing to tilt back her head to meet his eye. "You've outgrown me and most likely your father, too. I sent away a young boy and have come back to collect a young man."

Chrissy laughed and took Kitty's hands. "It's good to see you, Mum. You must be freezing out here. Let me show you inside and you can say hello to the others. Mrs Burrage is keen to meet you, and she says she's bound to like you given you've raised such fine young men."

"Fine young men?" said Kitty, as much to herself as to Chrissy. So much had changed in the past few years, and yet as she followed him towards the farmhouse, Kitty felt the stirrings of optimism. She was at the start of a new chapter, one that promised to be far better than the last.

PART THREE

1945-1946

Chapter 60

January, 1945

"This is a bit different from the last time I made the journey."

"It seemed silly to travel such a long way and not do it in comfort," said Jimmy as he stored their luggage in the rack of their first-class cabin.

"Well, thank you, not just for the ticket, but for coming with me. I'm not sure I could've done this alone. In fact, I tried suggesting Annie make the journey by herself so I wouldn't have to travel west, but Helen wouldn't hear of it."

"Quite right too. Annie may be older and wiser than when you arrived down there, but I wouldn't fancy the thought of her travelling alone with all these soldiers about."

"I know. It was my cowardice that led me to suggest it. The thought of seeing Grace…"

Jimmy reached across and squeezed Marnie's hand. "Don't build the situation up in your mind. You don't know how you'll react to seeing Grace, but we'll deal with it together. You're looking forward to seeing Helen and Richard?"

Marnie smiled. "More than you can imagine. I've missed them so much these past few years, almost as much as I've missed Annie." Marnie's face clouded over again. "Do you think she'll remember me?"

"Annie?" Jimmy laughed. "Of course she'll remember you!"

"Alright, perhaps I don't mean that. I think what I'm trying to say is, what if she doesn't like me? Or what if she doesn't want to come home with me?"

"Of course she'll like you, and of course she'll want to come home. But that doesn't mean it will be easy for her. Think how hard you found it when you came home. Lowestoft has changed so much. You'll have to give Annie time to get used to how things have changed."

"I don't know what I'd do without my wise big brother," said Marnie with a smile.

"I've spent the last however many years trying to repay the kindness you showed me after my accident, so if I've gone some way to do that, I'm a very happy big brother."

"You daft old thing. You've repaid that debt ten times over, heck, more like a hundred times."

Jimmy laughed. "I'm pleased to hear it. Now, how about a game of cards? We've got a long journey ahead of us."

*

The passage of time had dulled Marnie's memories of just how tedious the journey from east to west could be. The train felt lazy, ambling through the British countryside like an elderly gentleman on a Sunday afternoon stroll. Despite Jimmy's best efforts to keep her entertained, Marnie's fingers tapped against the window, her legs jiggling with impatience.

In contrast to the lethargy of the train, crossing London was noisy and frenetic, and Marnie gripped Jimmy's arm tightly until they had safely boarded their connecting train.

By the time their third and final train pulled into Padstow station, Marnie was a bag of nerves.

"It will be alright," said Jimmy. "You know and love these people."

Marnie gave Jimmy a weak smile and waited for him to collect their luggage. There wasn't a lot to carry, as unlike the last time she arrived in Padstow, this trip would only last a few days.

"I hope Helen isn't upset that we're not staying with her."

"I'm sure she'll understand. She might be relieved. You're worried about seeing Grace, but she'll be worrying about that too."

"She has nothing to worry about where Grace is concerned."

"You know that, but she doesn't. For all she knows, you may reconsider and want to take Grace back to Lowestoft."

"Goodness knows leaving her was hard, but it was the right decision. I thought so at the time, and I think so now."

"Right, well, come on, let's get out of here. They'll be waiting for us, I'm sure."

As Jimmy opened the door onto the platform, Marnie's heart hammered in her chest. Bile rose in her throat and she worried she might throw up. She tried to smooth down her curls, which bounced straight back, then turned her attention to her dress, tugging on the hem before buttoning up her coat.

Jimmy stepped down onto the platform, then held a hand out for Marnie. "Here," he said.

Marnie took his hand and stepped down. She almost didn't dare look up, but when she heard a shout of "Mum!" Marnie lifted her eyes to see a beautiful young lady running towards her.

Marnie opened her arms as Annie flung herself into them, sobbing noisy, messy tears and clinging on to Marnie's coat for dear life. Marnie stroked the curls which were almost indistinguishable from her own were it not for the white which had overtaken the blonde in the past few years.

As Annie's tears subsided, she took a step back, suddenly unsure and awkward.

"Hello, my darling girl," said Marnie, reaching up and brushing a tear from Annie's cheek with her thumb. "My goodness, look at you! You're more like a woman than a girl."

"Hardly," said Annie, blushing and looking at the ground. "I'm only ten."

"Ten going on twenty," said Marnie with a smile. "You're almost as tall as me."

"She'll have outgrown you within a year," said Jimmy.

Marnie and Annie turned, as if only just registering Jimmy's presence.

"Uncle Jimmy," Annie whispered, her tears forgotten as in their place her face spread into a wide smile.

"You've not forgotten me then," said Jimmy.

Annie laughed. "It's not been that long." Awkwardness forgotten, it was Jimmy's turn for a bear hug which he eventually extricated himself from, laughing.

"It's very good to see my favourite niece."

"Only niece," laughed Annie.

Jimmy and Marnie exchanged a glance, which thankfully Annie didn't notice.

"Is Helen here?" asked Marnie, scanning the platform.

"Yes, she's just outside. She thought I should meet you alone, but she's been as excited as I am to see you."

"Then we'd best find her, hadn't we?" said Marnie, taking Annie's hand and kissing it.

"Helen made scones and even managed to get hold of some cream."

"Goodness me, we'll feel like visiting royalty," said Marnie, grateful that Annie seemed to have relaxed somewhat.

"And just wait till you see Grace. She's like a proper little girl now, and a lot more fun than when she was a baby."

Marnie squared her shoulders, took a deep breath, and let Annie lead the way out of the station.

Chapter 61

January, 1945

"Hello, Helen."

Helen, who had been staring out toward the harbour, spun around, her face spreading into a smile. "You're here."

"In the flesh." Marnie walked over and gave Helen a tight hug. "You remember my brother Jimmy?"

"Of course I do." Helen let go of Marnie and held out a hand to Jimmy. When he not only took her hand to shake but also kissed her cheek, Helen blushed and giggled. "Goodness me, what will the locals say?" she said, fanning her rosy cheeks.

"Let's go and see Richard and Grace," said Annie, tugging on Marnie's sleeve.

"Perhaps your mum would like to settle into her hotel first?" asked Helen, displaying the first signs of unease as her hands wrung together.

"There'll be plenty of time for that," said Marnie. "Besides, Annie said you've baked some scones and I remember how tasty they were."

"If you're sure?" Helen held Marnie's gaze.

Marnie nodded and reached across to squeeze Helen's hand. "Yes, I'm sure. I'd love to see how little Grace has grown." Marnie hoped her words sounded convincing. In truth, she had no idea how she'd respond to seeing her younger daughter, but now she was here, she'd rather get it over with.

Annie chatted all the way to the cottage, oblivious to the fierce breeze that tugged the water and nipped at their skin. She demanded to know all about Jimmy's time in Derbyshire and what evacuation was like for the children in his care. When he answered, "better for some than others," Annie frowned, considering his answer.

"I suppose I was lucky to have been evacuated without even realising it. It made it easier in the long run, I think."

Helen and Marnie shared a look. Annie seemed to have forgotten how difficult the initial separation had been, and Marnie was glad.

"Here we are," said Annie, as if Marnie was arriving for the first time.

Helen hung back, giving Marnie's sleeve a gentle tug as Annie dragged Jimmy inside. "Are you sure this is alright? I mean, I know this isn't easy, seeing Grace..."

"Honestly, Helen, I've made my peace where Grace is concerned. And if you've done half as good a job with her as with Annie, I've nothing but admiration for your parenting skills. There's just one thing, though. Is Jack here?"

"No, we thought that might be a step too far when you've just arrived. He asked me to let you know he'll be making repairs to his boat in the harbour all afternoon and evening if you want to see him, but to feel no obligation."

"Thank you."

Helen reached forward, gave Marnie a quick hug, then opened the back door. "We're home."

"Up here," came a voice Marnie immediately recognised as Richard's.

"You go on up," said Helen. "I'll put the kettle on and join you in a moment. It looks like Annie's already taken Jimmy upstairs."

With a smile, Marnie removed her shoes and climbed the stairs, each step bringing with it a greater feeling of trepidation. On the landing, she took a deep breath. From beyond the sitting-room door came the sound of chatter and the occasional burst of laughter. Marnie pushed open the door.

"There you are, Mum. Me and Uncle Jimmy thought you'd got lost."

Annie was curled up on the settee beside Jimmy, a sketchbook full of drawings open on her lap. Richard sat in an armchair, and at his feet a pretty little girl with a mass of bright red curls sat dressing a doll. She looked up, her green eyes meeting Marnie's blue. The little girl stared, then her face broke into a smile.

"Are you Annie's mummy?" she asked.

"Aye, I am. You must be Grace." Marnie took a step further into the room, knowing she should greet Richard, but unable to take her eyes off Grace.

"How do you know my name?"

"Your Aunt Helen has told me all about you in her letters."

Grace giggled. "Silly billy Helen. You know she won't let me call her mum, or mummy, or mother? But she is my mummy. Even if I didn't come out of her tummy. Everyone knows it."

"Do they?" Marnie walked towards Grace and sat down on the floor beside her. "Hello, Richard," she said, looking up.

Richard reached down and took Marnie's hand. "Hello, Marnie. It's good to see you after so long."

"And you. It's lovely to be back in your happy household." Marnie smiled a smile of genuine warmth. She'd yet to unpick the swirling mass of feelings that seeing both of her daughters had conjured up, but the overriding emotion was one of happiness, and a feeling of home.

"Marnie, would you like to see my bedroom?" Grace stood up, her hands on her hips.

Both Marnie and Richard laughed.

"As you can see, our Grace isn't backward in coming forward," said Richard.

"Just what I like to see. I'd love to see your bedroom if that's alright with your... uncle?"

"Yes," said Grace, her voice taking on a bored tone. "He's uncle, Helen's aunt, you'll get used to them soon enough."

"I see," said Marnie, trying not to laugh at the precociousness of the girl in front of her. No wonder she and Annie got on so well.

"That's fine by me," said Richard, "but don't be up there long, as the scones will be ready soon."

Grace's eyes lit up at the mention of scones. "Come on," she said, taking Marnie's hand, "we'd best be quick."

Marnie swallowed the lump in her throat at the feeling of Grace's hand in hers. From what she'd seen so far, Grace took most of her looks from her father, and Marnie wondered whether that had caused any speculation amongst the villagers.

"*Ta da*," said Grace, pushing open the door to the room Marnie once shared with Annie. "This room used to have a big bed in it, but my aunt and uncle swapped it for two little beds so me and Annie can share. They said Annie is going away soon. Is that true?"

"Yes, I'm afraid it is," said Marnie.

"But I don't want her to go. I don't want you to take her away." Grace folded her arms across her chest, her bottom lip sticking out.

"You'll be able to use the second bed for all your dollies once Annie's gone," said Marnie. "And I'm sure she'd like to come back and visit you in the holidays. Would you like that?"

Grace nodded. "And I'll get more helpings of scones once Annie goes away."

"Very true," said Marnie, her voice serious. "And I've tasted Helen's scones before, so I know how good they are. Shall we go down to the kitchen and see if they're ready?"

Grace smiled, grabbed Marnie's hand and dragged her away from her memories and in search of food.

Chapter 62

January, 1945

"Helen said you were coming for Annie."

"Hello to you, too, Jack."

Jack straightened up, rubbing his oil-covered hands on his overalls. "I'd shake your hand, only…"

"That's alright, I think we're past the stage of formalities, don't you?"

"If you say so."

"Problems with the boat?" asked Marnie, trying to steer Jack onto more comfortable ground.

"Nah, she just needs a bit of spit and polish, then she'll be right."

"That's good. I hear things have been fairly calm here lately."

"You heard right. Seems everything's on the up now we're winning. It said in the paper they've liberated that hellhole they call Auschwitz. The evil that went on in that place, it's hard to imagine. We're well away from it here, of course."

"And how are things with you?"

"Fine, same as ever."

"Helen tells me you spend a lot of time with Grace."

"If you've come to take her away with you…"

Marnie reached out and placed a hand on Jack's arm. "I'm not taking her away, Jack. I miss her and the thought of not being with her breaks my heart, but I made my decision a long time ago and I'm not about to go back on it now. I can see how happy Grace is, and what a wonderful job you're all doing to raise her."

"She seems happy enough," said Jack, looking at the ground.

"I'd say it's more than that."

Jack looked up at Marnie, meeting her gaze. "Do you fancy a walk?"

"Aye, why not?"

Jack jumped from his boat onto the quayside and gave Marnie a quick smile before striding off around the harbour.

"Slow down a bit, will you?" asked Marnie, panting as she struggled to keep up. "I'm not so used to hills as I once was."

"Sorry," said Jack, slowing his pace. "Is that better?"

"Aye, ta."

"You warm enough?"

"Thanks to this hill, more than enough," said Marnie.

At the top of the hill, Jack stopped walking and turned back the way they had come. "I bet you've missed this view."

"I have," said Marnie, shielding her eyes from the low winter sun. Pools of orange light butted up against the hulls of boats, disturbing the water and turning it back to blue. With boats moored up and the harbourside quiet, it was hard to believe there was a war on. "There's a lot about this place I've missed."

"You regret going back?"

"No, it was the right decision and Lowestoft is home, but Padstow will always hold a special place in my heart. How about you? Do you regret what happened between us?"

Jack kept his face turned towards the sea. "No," he whispered. "No, I don't." He turned to face Marnie, who was surprised to see his eyes glinting with tears. "Helen told me the name Grace means favour or blessing."

"Aye, that's right."

"Well, that's what Grace is, a blessing."

Marnie sat down on a patch of grass and Jack lowered himself down beside her.

"It must be hard for you, though."

"Aye, it is."

"Do you wish we'd done different? Married, perhaps?"

Marnie shook her head. "No, I don't. You?"

"No. I love Grace more than I thought it possible to love, but I've seen how Helen and Richard are as parents. I could never match that. I could never give her what they can. That's not to say I won't try. She'll always be my daughter, whether or not she knows it. I'll do my best for her, even if it's from the sidelines."

"I was worried about coming back. I couldn't imagine seeing Grace and not wanting to run off with her back to Lowestoft."

"And now?"

"When I walked into that cottage, I walked into a family home filled with love and happiness. I met a little girl who adores her parents as much as they adore her. She may call them aunt and uncle, but they're parents in the true sense of the word. It's right that I should find it hard, but I know in my heart I've given Grace the best life I could. If I feel pain because of it, so be it. Motherhood is all about sacrifice."

"She really is a wonderful little girl."

Marnie smiled at Jack. "She is that. I couldn't believe how grown up she sounds. She certainly knows her own mind."

"Another gift you've left her with."

"I'm not sure it's much of a gift," said Marnie with a laugh.

"And how is everything else with you?"

Marnie paused. She could talk about work, or war, or Roy and Sally, but there was something more pressing she wanted to tell Jack. "I'm not sure how to say this. I mean... I know we were never... but... given what happened..."

"You've met a chap?"

Marnie nodded, picking at a spear of grass. She jumped as Jack wrapped his arm around her shoulder and pulled her towards him. He kissed the top of her head, then released her. "I'm happy for you."

"Really?"

"Of course. It's about time you found a little happiness."

"That's very gracious of you."

Jack let out a bark of a laugh. "It wasn't like I tried very hard to woo you myself. I think I said I didn't want to marry you, but we should for the sake of the child. Or something to that effect."

"Aye, I wouldn't describe you as a romantic."

"No, I'm not and have never been one of those."

"You shouldn't close your heart to love either, though."

"Oh," said Jack, batting away the suggestion with a flap of his hand. "I have all the love a fellow could want, believe me. Now, I don't know about you, but I'm getting damn chilly sitting here in the cold. How about we head back to Helen's? I'd like to spend a bit of time with Annie before she leaves."

"I'm sure the feeling's mutual," said Marnie.

They stood, brushed themselves off, and headed back down the hill.

Chapter 63

January, 1945

The days went too fast for them all. Despite the weather taking a turn for the worse and Padstow not looking its best in the howling winds and torrential rains, it didn't matter a jot to those inside Helen's cottage. The days passed with games, shared meals, and long conversations that explored the heart of what would forever join them as family.

It was their final evening, and Grace was long in bed. Annie had followed shortly after, the warmth of the fire soothing any nerves about leaving and luring her to sleep.

"You'll be welcome back here any time," said Helen, topping up Marnie's glass with whisky.

"That's very kind of you, but I need to give you a chance to get on with your lives without me lurking around every corner."

"It would never be like that."

"You know, when I left here after having Grace, I was certain I'd never set eyes on any of you again, except Annie, of course. I thought it would be too painful for all of us."

"And now?"

"I won't lie and pretend to see Grace has been easy. On the one hand, she's a stranger, a fun, feisty little girl I'm only beginning to know, but then I catch myself, and remember she came from me."

"You know, legally, we have no right to keep Grace here. If you ever decide to take her..."

Marnie looked at Richard in horror. "You really think I'd do that?"

"No, of course not." Richard reached across and patted Marnie's hand. "I'm just wondering if we shouldn't put this arrangement on firmer ground."

"A legal adoption, you mean?" asked Jimmy.

"Yes, precisely."

"And it would bring you peace of mind?" asked Marnie, this time directing her question towards Helen.

"It would, but more than that, I think it would help Grace in the future, to know we went through a formal process to have her."

"She told me she didn't come from your tummy. It sounds like you've been quite open with her."

"As open as you can be with a three- going on four-year-old. She knows she came to us because the war meant she couldn't be with her birth mother. She seems satisfied with that knowledge for now."

"And if she wants to know more in the future? I've told you I don't want her knowing about me."

"Fair enough."

"But I'd be happy to go ahead with the formal adoption."

Both Helen and Richard let out a long breath. "Are you sure?" asked Richard. "It's a big decision."

"Aye, but one I'm happy to make."

"Thank you," said Helen. "You don't know how much this means to us."

Marnie crossed the room and embraced Helen. "I've seen what a wonderful mother you are, and how happy Grace is. That's all I need to know. This is the right decision. But I think we should make sure Jack is happy with the idea."

"I've already spoken to him," said Helen. "He said it was alright with him but that you should make the final decision."

"Then it's settled," said Marnie. "Now, I'd best make sure we have all Annie's belongings ready for tomorrow."

"I've gathered everything up in here," said Helen, passing a basket to Marnie. "I packed her clothes in a suitcase, so in the morning it should just be a case of popping her pyjamas in and you'll be ready to go."

"It's going to be hard for her to say goodbye," said Marnie.

"Hard for us too," said Richard, his voice gruff.

"Once the war ends, there's no reason you can't visit each other," said Jimmy. "I for one would like to bring Clara down for a holiday."

"Oh you must," said Helen.

"I think we should head back to the hotel now, Jimmy. We've got a long journey tomorrow, after all."

"Yes, you're right. Thank you for a lovely evening."

"You're welcome. We'll see you in the morning." Richard stood up and shook Jimmy's hand and hugged Marnie.

After saying their goodbyes, Jimmy and Marnie walked beside the harbour before heading back to the hotel. Jimmy linked arms with Marnie and she leaned into him.

"Are you sure about the adoption?" he asked.

"Aye, I am. It's the right thing for Helen and Richard, and more importantly, it's the right thing for Grace. You've seen with your own eyes how happy she is."

"But is it the right thing for you?"

Marnie smiled. "You know me too well, Jimmy Watson. Of course it's hard, it will always be hard, but it's what's best for Grace that matters in this situation."

"Very true. How do you think Annie will find leaving tomorrow?"

"Difficult. I'm worried being back with me won't live up to her expectations. And Lowestoft isn't the same place she left."

"You'll need to be patient," said Jimmy, "and allow her the time and space she needs to get used to being back at home. There'll be bumps in the road, but she'll get settled soon enough."

"I hope you're right. But I suppose time will tell."

Chapter 64

January, 1945

"Good morning, Jimmy." Richard greeted Jimmy with a robust handshake before offering a cup of tea.

"I don't think we've time for tea," said Marnie. "Is Annie ready?"

"Yes, she's up in her bedroom, but I should warn you she's been rather tearful this morning."

"I'd best go and see her," said Marnie, rushing to the stairs and taking them two at a time. She found Annie face down on her bed, crying into a pillow. Grace was sitting on the bed beside Annie, stroking her hair.

"Annie's crying 'cause she doesn't want to go," said Grace. "I don't think she should go." She stuck her bottom lip out in a pout and folded her arms.

"I'm afraid she has to," said Marnie. "Her ticket is booked and her grandparents can't wait to see her. Isn't that right, Annie?" Marnie sat down on the bed and brushed Annie's hair away from her face.

"I don't want to go," said Annie, sniffing and burying her head in the pillow once more.

"I know this is hard," said Marnie, "but you can come back for visits. Do you remember how upset you were at leaving Lowestoft in the first place?"

Annie shook her head.

"Well, from what I remember, you were pretty angry at the thought of leaving. The amount of tantrums I had to calm before I got you on the train, and look at you now. Going home is scary, I understand that, but you'll get used to it in no time. Nanny and Granddad are so looking forward to seeing you. They've missed you so much these past few years."

"I've missed them too."

"There, see, you've something to look forward to. Now, I don't like to rush you, but we don't have long before our train arrives, so had best be getting a move on."

"Can Grace come with us?" Annie pulled herself up and tucked her curls behind her ears. She reached across to Grace, pulled her onto her lap, and squeezed her tight.

"I'm sorry, but Grace needs to stay here."

Grace turned her head into Annie's chest and wrapped her arms around her neck. "I won't let you take my Annie."

Marnie sighed. What kind of mother broke such a strong bond between sisters?

"What's going on in here?" asked Helen, bustling into the room.

Marnie threw her hands into the air. "Annie doesn't want to go and Grace says she won't let her leave."

"Stop this foolishness now, girls," said Helen, pulling Grace off Annie. "You're behaving as though you'll never see each other again, which is nonsense. Annie, maid, you know you can visit us any time and once Grace is a little older, we'll make a trip to Lowestoft."

"Do you promise?" asked Annie.

"Of course," said Helen, trying to calm a wriggling Grace. "Grace, you won't be able to come and wave Annie off unless you have your shoes on. You've got one minute to run downstairs and find them or we'll have to go without you."

Grace dropped from Helen's arms and sprinted out of the room.

"You're so good with them," said Marnie.

"I've had plenty of practice these past few years, that's all. Now, Annie, give your face a wash and dry your eyes. You're off on a wonderful adventure so you can stop carrying on like you're being sent to jail. Go on, get on with you."

Annie climbed off the bed and slunk out of the room, her shoulders sagging.

"She's been so excited to see you," said Helen. "Don't take this reaction to heart."

"I always knew it would be hard for her to leave when the time came."

"No harder than for children up and down the country. You're doing the right thing, taking her back. As much as I love Annie, she needs her mum. She's missed you so much, Marnie. However difficult this next stage is, you'll do well to remember that."

"I'll try."

"We need to get a move on," came Richard's voice from downstairs.

"Coming," Helen called back.

After much fussing with coats, hats and gloves, all adults and children were out of the cottage, and Richard had locked the door behind them.

"I'm getting a terrible sense of déjà vu," said Marnie. "It only feels like yesterday we were heading to the station for you to wave me off. Now it's both me and Annie saying goodbye."

"But not forever," said Helen. "You know you'll always be welcome here, and can visit Grace whenever you like."

"I'll sign and send the papers as soon as they arrive," said Marnie under her breath. "That will put us on a clearer footing should we fancy a visit."

"Alright," said Helen. "If you're sure."

They reached the station and found the train already there, the driver moving the engine to the opposite end before setting off again. Grace looked on, mesmerised, as steam spilled from the chimney, pouring out across the station.

"Pooey, that's smelly," said Grace, holding her nose.

Annie laughed and picked Grace up, hugging her tightly and kissing her head. "You be a good girl for Aunt Helen while I'm away," she said. "I'll send you some drawings from Lowestoft, and me and Mum will come back to visit as soon as we can."

"I'll be a good girl, promise," said Grace, leaning forward and kissing Annie on the nose before giggling.

"Come here, you little pest," said Richard, scooping Grace into his arms and tickling her.

Marnie smiled at the sight of them. Grace looked so at home in Richard's arms, she couldn't imagine things turning out any other way. "Time to get on the train," she said. "Thank you both so much for everything you've done. Say your goodbyes, Annie."

Annie gave both Helen and Richard a tearful embrace before allowing Jimmy to take her hand and help her up onto the train. Just as Marnie was about to join her daughter and brother, Helen stepped forward and pressed a cloth bag into her hands. "Some food for the journey," she said.

"Thank you," said Marnie, kissing Helen's cheek. "For everything. I'll be in touch soon about you-know-what."

A whistle blew, and Marnie jumped up onto the train. She joined Jimmy and Annie, who were stowing their bags in their compartment. With a squeal and a spurt of steam, the train juddered forward. Marnie, Jimmy, and Annie pressed their faces to the glass, waving frantically to their friends on the platform. The train picked up speed, Padstow station slipped out of sight, and they were on their way home.

Chapter 65

January, 1945

They stood in their thick winter coats, waiting for the train to still. Marnie looked across at Annie, so ladylike in the fitted woollen coat Helen had treated her to that winter. Annie held her hands clasped in front of her, staring out of the train window, her brow creased.

"It will be alright," said Marnie, placing a hand on Annie's shoulder.

Annie nodded, a ragged breath shaking her. "You know you said the town's different?"

"Aye."

"Will I recognise anything?"

"Oh aye," said Marnie. "You'll recognise plenty. It's just some shops gone here and there, and a few houses too. I hope I haven't made it sound too bad, I just didn't want you having a nasty shock when we got back."

"Will Nanny and Granddad be meeting us at the station?"

"No, I'm afraid they're not too good at walking these days. They know roughly what time we're arriving and I'm sure Nanny will have laid on a special tea for you."

"Are you coming to Nanny and Granddad's?" Annie asked Jimmy.

"I was planning to, if that's alright with you?"

"Yes, I'd like you to," said Annie. She took hold of Jimmy's hands, squeezing hard. "Will Kitty be there too?"

Marnie glanced at Jimmy. "Um, no, I don't think so."

"Has she brought Sam and the others home yet?"

"I'm not sure."

Annie shook her head. "I suppose I'll just have to call round there myself and find out."

"What? On your own? I don't think so."

"Why not? Aunt Helen lets me go into the village by myself all the time."

"Things are very different here."

"You're telling me," grumbled Annie, kicking the carriage door with the toe of her boot.

Marnie pursed her lips together, trying hard not to let out the criticism on the tip of her tongue. It wouldn't do to reach Sally and Roy's under a black cloud. "Here we are," said Marnie as the train juddered to a stop.

Jimmy climbed onto the platform first, offering a hand to help Annie and Marnie off the train before retrieving their luggage. Annie looked around as though in a daze.

"Are you alright, Annie?" asked Jimmy.

"Yes, it's just different from how I remember. I suppose it's all the soldiers."

"Wait till you see the harbour," said Jimmy. "If you think there are plenty of soldiers around, just wait until you see how many sailors are in town."

As they walked out of the station and towards the town, Marnie remembered how shocked she had been all those years earlier and stole a look at Annie. Her daughter had her eyes fixed on the horizon, as though by focusing on the sky she could ignore the wreckage caused by the enemy's onslaught.

Annie's face was unnaturally still, as though by freezing her features, no emotion could leak out. Marnie reached over and squeezed Annie's shoulder. "I know it's sad seeing bombed-out buildings, but I promise you your nanny and granddad's place is the same as ever."

Annie nodded and followed Jimmy, who had gone a few paces ahead of them.

By the time they arrived at Roy and Sally's, Annie was visibly shaking. Marnie wrapped her arms around her daughter and squeezed her tight. "It's alright," she said. "You're home now." Marnie opened the front door, welcoming the wall of warmth that hit her. "Sally?"

"In here," came Sally's voice from the sitting room.

Marnie took Annie's hand and pushed open the sitting-room door. Both Sally and Roy were standing, their faces flickering between delight and uncertainty about how to greet their granddaughter. Sally took a step forward, then back, her hands wringing in front of her.

"It's very wonderful to have you home," said Roy, his voice thick with emotion.

If Annie was shocked by the physical change in her grandfather, she didn't show it. She stepped into the room, her face spreading into a smile. Roy was taken by surprise and almost knocked off his feet as Annie threw herself into his arms. She held out her right arm and Sally stepped into the embrace, the three of them swaying as tears mingled with smiles and gasps of 'how tall you've grown' and 'what have they been feeding you in Padstow?'

Jimmy stood at Marnie's side, brushing away a tear, the charged emotion of the gathering impossible to ignore. Marnie reached across and squeezed his hand, hoping that Annie's homecoming would continue in this positive vein.

"Goodness me," said Roy, stepping back and holding Annie at arm's length. "I can't believe you're actually here."

Annie laughed. "You are silly, Granddad."

"That I am. I think I need a sit down after all this excitement."

Jimmy stepped forward and helped Roy down into a chair.

Sally winked at Annie. "Wait here, love, I've got something to welcome you home. Marnie, I might need a bit of help."

Marnie followed Sally through to the kitchen. "Is that what I think it is?"

"Don't ask me how I got hold of the ingredients," said Sally, tapping the side of her nose. "Can you carry it through for me? I'll bring the plates."

Marnie picked up the cut-glass plate, a large fruitcake sitting on a doily at its centre. "Blimey, this is heavy." She carried it through to the sitting room, where Annie was now sitting on the floor beside Roy's chair, answering his many questions about her journey.

"Give the child a moment to take a breath," said Sally, placing plates down on a dresser. "Now, who's for a slice of cake?"

Annie's eyes lit up. "Yes please, Nanny."

"I'm glad to see they've taught you some manners down in Padstow," said Sally with a smile. She cut a slice of cake and handed it to her granddaughter. "I know I've already said it, but I really can't believe how much you've grown. You're like a proper little lady."

Annie grinned. "Uncle Richard says I'm like a beanstalk."

"Your Uncle Richard's right."

Marnie noticed a flicker of emotion pass across Annie's face. They were off to a good start, but Marnie knew they were in for a period of readjustment and that it wouldn't always be easy.

Chapter 66

February, 1945

"You off out, love?"

"Oh, hello, Roy. I didn't hear you get up. Yes, I'm off to get some bread and milk, and whatever else my ration book will allow."

"Mind if I come with you?"

Marnie paused. Heading to the shops with Roy in tow would be much more challenging than going on her own, but she didn't want to offend him. "Of course not. Is there anything in particular you're after? I could pick something up for you if you like? The weather looks frightful out there."

"No, there's nothing in particular I'm after, other than the chance to bend your ear."

"Oh, right, well, let's head off then."

"I'll just grab my stick."

Marnie helped Roy over the front step and closed the door behind her. The day was bitter, but with no hint of snow. Instead, it was one of those days when everything is grey; sky, sea, buildings. Marnie squinted and the world around her became one grey splodge. "There's not much to commend the weather today."

"No, even so, it's good to get some fresh air in my lungs."

Marnie smiled at Roy as he hobbled along the pavement. Annie's arrival had perked him up just as Marnie hoped it would. He was still frail, but a sparkle had returned to his eye.

"You know, I can see so much more of Tom in Annie's features now she's getting older."

"I thought the same when she arrived back," said Roy. "When she was young she was the spit of you, and she's still got your hair, but her face, now that's where we find our Tom. I wouldn't say anything to her. She might not want to be compared to a chap, but goodness me, Marnie, it feels like I've got part of Tom back."

"Aye, he certainly lives on through his daughter," said Marnie, linking arms with Roy. "Shall we head to the bakery, then pop over to the Corner Café for a cuppa? Then we can talk about whatever it is you need to get off your chest."

Roy tapped a hand against Marnie's arm in agreement and they made their way slowly along the street. Walking through the streets of The Grit no longer felt like stepping onto a battlefield. The soldiers training for invasion had long since put down their arms and houses now stood empty, bullet holes and shattered glass the only sign of their role in soldiers' training.

"There's a different feel to the place these days, don't you think?"

Marnie smiled and nodded to a neighbour and Roy doffed his cap as she stepped off the pavement to let them pass. "Aye, folk are that much more relaxed. And to have the sound of kiddies playing filling the air once more is quite something. We must be through the worst by now."

"All signs seem hopeful," said Roy.

They popped into Gray's bakery, and Marnie added a loaf of bread to her basket. Mr Gray had his wireless running all day, tuned to the latest news from the front. He kept Marnie and Ray talking for quite some time, keen to discuss the latest goings-on across the Channel.

Once they'd extricated themselves from the conversation, Marnie helped Roy navigate the pavement's curb and held his arm as they ambled the short distance to the Corner Café. Only once they were sitting at a table by the window with a pot of tea between them did Roy reveal what was on his mind.

"Frank came in to see me at the Seamen's Mission."

"Right, I see." Marnie looked into her cup, swilling the tea around inside. "And how was he?"

"He's looked better. You know he's living back at base?"

"Aye, he said that's what he intended."

"It isn't right for a chap of his age to be bunking in with all those youngsters."

"Perhaps he'll be housed with another family?"

"Unlikely with so many kiddies returning to the town. There aren't the spare bedrooms there once were."

"I'm sure he'll manage. If the war ends as soon as we all hope it will, he'll be able to return to his family up north and won't need to worry about where he stays down here."

"And that's what you want, is it? For Frank to head back up north and be rid of the problem?"

"I never said Frank's a problem."

"That's not how he sees things. Besides, even if the fighting on the Continent ends, there'll be plenty to keep our navy lads busy long after each side's downed their weapons. All those mines out to sea will need clearing for starters. No, Frank will be stuck in Lowestoft for quite some time yet, you mark my words."

"Drink up, Roy, your tea's getting cold."

Roy lifted the cup to his lips but kept his eyes fixed on Marnie's. "The poor chap had such a hangdog expression. I was minded to put him straight about why you turned him down."

"What do you mean, turned him down?"

"Oh, don't be so coy, Marnie. The poor chap asked my advice before telling you how he felt. Took a lot of courage, did that, coming to the father of your dead husband to ask for permission to court you. Of course, I told him he wasn't to worry about me and Sal, and that he should talk to you. I told him you'd have to be a fool to turn him down."

The implication Roy was now calling Marnie a fool hung in the air between them. Marnie topped up her cup from the pot.

"You know why I had to turn him down."

"Do I?"

"Yes. Because of what happened in Padstow." Marnie whispered the sentence, looking around her to check no one was eavesdropping.

"What's that got to do with anything?"

"Roy," hissed Marnie, "how could Frank still want anything to do with me after the way I behaved?"

"Goodness me, love, you're your own worst enemy. Give the poor bloke a chance to show what he's made of. If he's the fine fellow I think he is, he won't care a fig what did or didn't happen in Padstow, but whichever way it goes, you need to put him out of his misery."

"All right. I'll think about it."

"You do that, because having him moping around the Seamen's Mission is doing nothing for anyone's morale. Oh, and patch things up with Kitty while you're at it."

"Anything else?"

"No," said Roy, "I think that's enough to be getting on with."

Chapter 67

February, 1945

Marnie paused outside the door and closed her eyes. It was like going back in time, listening to the sounds of chaotic family life filtering through the door. The voices had deepened, their laughs turning gruff, but the sentiment was the same; a happy family lived between the house's walls.

With a crack of knuckles and a deep breath, Marnie knocked on the door. A young lad of Marnie's height opened it, his flame-red hair slicked down with a bucketful of Brylcreem.

"Sam? Is that really you?"

Kitty's youngest son frowned in confusion, then his lips spread into a smile as recognition dawned. "Marnie, good to see you."

"It's been a while," said Marnie, trying not to laugh as Sam held out a hand for her to shake. "Is your mam home?"

"Yes, come on in."

"I'll wait out here, if that's alright? Could you just let her know I'm here?"

"Of course. Back in a mo."

The door remained open a crack, and Marnie heard the thunder of footsteps on the stairs, the good-natured ribbing of one brother to another, and the cry of a father trying to regain control of his brood.

When Kitty came to the door, she looked a happy mess. Her hair stuck up in all directions, she wore a flour-covered apron, and her cheeks were flushed. She looked just how Marnie had pictured her while in Padstow missing her friend. She was back to the old Kitty, before war broke out and stole away her children and with them her joy.

"Marnie."

"Kitty."

"Would you like to come in?"

"Um…"

Kitty looked behind her and smiled. "No, you're right, it's chaos in there. Let's take a walk. Give me a moment to find my coat."

Marnie stamped her feet against the frozen ground and blew warm air into her hands while she waited. When Kitty appeared, Marnie gave her a small, shy smile. "You've got the boys back," she said as they began walking toward the harbour.

"Aye. They've been back a month or so. I couldn't bear the thought of another Christmas without them."

"And they've settled well?"

Kitty bit her bottom lip and frowned. "Some are better than others. Sam and Peter are happy to be home. Mark is worried he'll not find a cricket team to join down here, and Chrissy, well, I wouldn't be surprised if he's not living back in Derbyshire by springtime."

"Oh no, really?"

"Aye, he's got himself a lassie up there and by the sound of things, it's serious."

"What a shame, after just getting him back."

Kitty shrugged. "If the war's taught me anything, it's that you don't own your children. You can try your hardest to keep them close, but they've their own free will and will go where the wind blows them."

Marnie kept her eyes on the ground. Talking about children felt dangerous, like they were straying too close to the topic which had ripped apart their friendship. Marnie still had no idea if the wound inflicted by her actions would ever heal.

"How about Annie? Do you have plans to bring her home?"

"Oh," said Marnie, looking at Kitty in surprise. "I thought you'd have heard. She is home."

"I had no idea," said Kitty. "How long has she been back for?"

"Only a couple of weeks."

"Right. How's it going?"

Marnie shrugged and kept walking. She wanted to tell Kitty about the tears she heard Annie crying each night, about how despite her putting on a good show, she'd noticed her daughter growing thinner, restless, as though she couldn't settle into this new, old life.

"It's hard for them," said Kitty, interpreting Marnie's hesitation correctly as only a best friend could. "It's been hard for all my boys, but they've got a month's head start on Annie. She'll settle soon."

"I hope so," said Marnie, her voice quiet, her eyes filling with tears.

"Listen, Marnie." Kitty stopped walking and placed a hand on Marnie's arm. "I owe you an apology."

"You don't need to..."

"I do. First, for the way I spoke to you, and second, for what I did, going behind your back and telling Sally. I'm surprised you've come to me. I thought I'd damaged our friendship for good, but then again, you were always braver than me. Unless you've come to argue again rather than make up?"

Marnie managed a quiet chuckle. "I think there's been enough fighting in the world these past few years without us joining in. And you don't need to say sorry. You were right to hate me and to tell Sally. The last thing I am is brave. I should have told Sally and Roy what happened the second I got back to Lowestoft."

"I can see why you didn't. How are things between you and them?"

"Better, even more so since I brought Annie home. It's made the world of difference to Roy. He's really rallied these past couple of weeks."

"Did Annie get the train by herself?"

"No, me and Jimmy went to fetch her."

"So you saw your baby?"

Marnie laughed. "She's not much of a baby these days. I met a confident, talkative little girl. You might even describe her as bossy."

"Bossy? Surely not. Does she look like you?"

"No, she's the spit of Jack."

"And did you see him, too?"

Marnie nodded. "Aye, I did."

"And how was that? Any regrets where he's concerned?"

"No, it was good to see him, but only inasmuch as it's nice to bump into any onetime friend. He's a big part of Grace's life. That was good to see."

"And Helen and Richard? How were they?"

"Very well, better than I'd even imagined. Parenthood seems to have been the making of them."

Kitty sniffed, and when Marnie turned to look at her, she saw Kitty had tears streaming down her cheeks.

"Whatever's the matter?"

"I got things all wrong," said Kitty, pulling out a handkerchief. "It must have been so hard for you, leaving your daughter behind. All the while I thought you were the baddie in the situation, but Bobby helped me see you were the victim. It's you who's lost out. I should have recognised that and been there to support you, not hurling insults at you in the street like some barmy fishwife."

"But you are a fishwife," laughed Marnie, brushing away one of Kitty's tears from her cheek.

"I'm a fisherman's wife, not a fishwife," said Kitty, pouting.

"What a fine pair we are," said Marnie. "But seriously, Kitty. Are you alright now? I've been worried about you for quite some time."

Kitty sniffed, then smiled. "I still have my bad days, but on the whole I'm much better, thank you. I think I lost my way for a while back there. What with Al, the worry over Simon, Stevie's injury and all the others away, it was like I'd forgotten who I was. Add to that the things I've seen on the ambulance and it was like I spent a long time walking around in the middle of a black cloud. Not that it's any excuse for the way I treated you."

"I think we've both done enough apologising for one day. But I'd like to explain what happened in Padstow."

"There's no need."

"There's every need. It's important to me you understand. I've missed you so much these past few months."

"Alright," said Kitty, "but I fear I'm getting frostbite in my extremities. Can you tell me your story somewhere warm?"

"Pub?"

"I knew there was a reason we were friends," said Kitty, linking arms with Marnie and heading to the nearest drinking establishment.

Chapter 68

February, 1945

Marnie peered around the curtain. Had he received the message? Would he come? She flopped into an armchair, head in hands, praying she hadn't left it too late. She was in the same position when a knock came on the door. Marnie jumped out of her chair and ran to open the front door.

"Oh, I assumed you'd be at work." Frank picked at some peeling paint on the doorframe, refusing to look Marnie in the eye.

"I took the day off so I could speak to you."

"I thought you'd said everything there was to say?"

"No, I didn't say half of what I should. Are you going to come in? I know you don't owe me anything, but I really would like to explain."

Frank sighed and looked up. "I'm not sure what talking will achieve?"

"Please, just five minutes."

"Alright." Frank followed Marnie into the sitting room.

"I'm pleased you got my message, I was worried they'd forget to pass it on."

"The message said you had important post waiting for me."

"That was a lie, I'm afraid. Can I get you a cup of tea?"

"No, thank you. If it's alright, I'll listen to what you have to say, then be on my way."

Marnie waited for Frank to sit down, but he continued to stand in the middle of the sitting room.

"Alright. Well, first off, I need to apologise for lying."

"About the post?"

"No, not about the post. When I said I didn't love you, that was a lie."

"What?"

"Oh, for goodness' sake, Frank, please sit down. This is hard enough without thinking you're about to make your escape any minute."

After a moment of hesitation, Frank sat himself down in a chair, but perched on the edge, his hands on his jiggling knees like a coiled spring.

"You'll be wondering why I lied about loving you?"

Frank nodded and waited for Marnie to continue.

"When you asked me to marry you, I felt I didn't deserve it. I didn't deserve you. There are things in my past that I'm not proud of."

"We've all done things we're not proud of."

"I very much doubt you could compete with me on the shame front."

"Why don't you let me be the judge of that?"

"I'm going to start at the beginning, so you can perhaps understand how I was thinking at the time."

"Alright."

Marnie began her sorry tale, stealing glances at Frank to see how he was taking the news.

"Marnie, if this is too difficult, you don't have to explain."

"No, I do, I really do. So, after Tom's death, I muddled through. I'd intended to return to Lowestoft after six months, but then war was declared and that threw a right spanner in the works."

"I bet."

"Aye, everyone up here was so frightened and it seemed sensible to sit things out in Padstow for as long as we could…" As she introduced Frank to the idea of Jack, Marnie felt her cheeks growing hotter. She looked up at Frank, her eyes wide. "We're getting to the worst part," she said, her voice quiet.

Frank moved to sit beside Marnie on the settee. He picked up her hand and held it in his. "Marnie, nothing you say will make me love you any less."

Marnie pulled her hand away and twisted her fingers together in her lap. "… then one evening not long after the bombing, Jack was in a right old state. I went to comfort him and… and…" Marnie took a deep breath. "One thing led to another, and we made a terrible mistake."

"You mean…"

"Aye, *that* kind of mistake."

"So you were in love with this Jack?"

"No," said Marnie, shaking her head. "That makes it even worse. We were friendly, but not *that* friendly. Neither of us were looking for love. We just needed comfort and went about it in the most foolish of ways."

"You won't be the first or last person to make a mistake like that. I'd rather not go into my romantic history right now, but if it helps, I can assure you my wife was not the only romantic partner I've had in life."

Marnie sighed. "If only that were all that happened."

"You and Jack continued your relationship?"

"No, but I was left with the consequences of our liaison. Frank, I fell pregnant."

"Oh."

"Yes, oh. When Jack found out, he thought we should get married, but neither of us truly wanted that, so I made the hardest decision of my life to give up my baby."

"Your baby was adopted?"

Marnie nodded. "Aye, my baby, Grace, was adopted by Helen and Richard. Annie stayed with them too while I came back here, but now she's back home with me."

"Here? You went to fetch her?"

"Aye, she's out at school, but yes, she's living back here."

"Roy didn't mention it when I bumped into him the other week."

"It was him who persuaded me I needed to tell you the truth. I suppose Annie being back is part of that story."

"You saw Grace when you were down there?"

"Aye."

"How was that? Did it cause you to change your mind about Grace once you'd seen her? Were you tempted to bring her home?"

"No. I promised Helen that I wouldn't change my mind, and I didn't. Of course, it hurt to see the daughter I've lost, but it also confirmed I'd done the right thing. So there you have it, my sorry tale."

Frank took hold of Marnie's hands and twisted her around until she faced him. "Thank you for being honest. I just wish you'd told me the truth sooner. As if I'd love you less because you had a child outside of wedlock. What sort of man do you think I am?"

"A man with strong morals."

"Not that strong, good Lord, Marnie. I thought you were going to tell me you'd murdered someone. I understand why giving up a child must have been awful, but it really changes nothing where I'm concerned. You've been worrying over nothing."

"You don't think less of me?"

"Only for not telling me sooner, not for what happened in Padstow, no."

"What does this mean for us?"

Frank lifted Marnie's hands to his lips and kissed her fingers. "It means that I love you, and now I know you love me. But, I don't want things to become too serious between us just yet."

"I see."

"I'm not sure you do. The fact you couldn't trust me with the truth sooner suggests you don't know me as well as you might think. I'd like us to take longer to get to know each other before committing to a future together."

"So we carry on as before?"

"Not quite as before. I'd like us to put honesty first, and that includes being out in the open that we're courting. Oh, and, Marnie?"

Before Marnie could respond, Frank's lips met hers. As she sank into his embrace, a wave of happiness and relief consumed her. She was in the arms of the man she loved. For now, that was all that mattered.

Chapter 69

March, 1945

Annie burst through the door, her cheeks flushed from the cold, a smile on her face. "Good day at school?" asked Marnie.

"Yes, it was, although Sam Thorne is being as annoying as ever."

"That's only because he's sweet on you."

Annie screwed up her face and made a motion to suggest she felt sick.

"You could do far worse than Sam Thorne. I think it's sweet that he's held a torch for you all these years."

"Huh, I think it's disgusting. Where are Nanny and Granddad?"

"Down at the Seamen's Mission. They're having a bake sale, so Nanny helped Granddad down there and is manning the cake stall."

"Can we go there?"

"Yes, but there's something I need to talk to you about first."

"Alright." Annie pulled out a kitchen chair and sat herself down, elbows on the table, resting her head on a hand.

"I will take you to the bake sale, but I need to warn you that my friend will be there."

"Warn me? Doesn't sound like a very nice friend."

"No, I don't mean that." Marnie sighed and sat opposite her daughter. "Have Nanny and Granddad told you much about the sailor we had staying here while you were away?"

"In my room? Yes, they said he was called Frank and was very pleasant. Did he get sent overseas? Is that why he left?"

"No, he's still in Lowestoft. He left because we had a bit of a falling out, a misunderstanding of sorts."

"Oh."

Marnie took a deep breath. "You see, Annie, me and Frank, well, we're quite keen on one another. We'd like to start courting, but I don't want to do anything that would upset you."

"What about Dad?" Annie's voice was flat and she wouldn't catch Marnie's eye.

"My feelings for Frank change nothing about my feelings for your father. I loved Tom so much. Our marriage wasn't always easy, but he was my first love, and no one will ever take that away. Frank will never replace your dad, I promise you that."

"So I won't have to call him Dad?"

"No, of course not."

"Hmm." Annie fiddled with the salt cellar on the table, twisting it around in her fingers. Marnie let the silence between them stretch out, understanding her daughter's need to think through the revelation. "I don't like the thought of you being alone. Nanny and Granddad won't be around forever, and before long I'll be leaving too."

"Leaving? You're only ten years old!"

Annie giggled, reminding them both that although she'd grown taller, the little girl was still there. "You know what I mean."

"So, you don't mind?"

"I don't mind the idea of you courting, but whether I like you courting this Frank chap, well, I'll have to meet him to decide that, won't I?"

"You've got a wise old head on those shoulders, my girl."

Annie smiled. "Come on then, what are you waiting for?" She pulled on her coat, which had been slung across the back of the chair.

During the walk to the Seamen's Mission, Marnie's heart hammered in her chest. So much depended on this meeting going well, and she wished it wasn't going to happen in such a public environment. It had been Frank's suggestion for them to meet him at the fundraiser. He said it would take away some of the pressure, make the meeting more informal. As the Seamen's Mission came into view, Marnie hoped he was right.

"Welcome to our fundraiser," said an old fisherman manning the door. "Everything's happening in the main hall. That's where you'll find the cakes." He winked at Annie and rubbed his stomach. "I've sampled a few and they're very good."

Annie smiled, thanked the man, and popped a coin in his collecting jar. Marnie opened the doors to the hall, and they were met with a wall of warmth and cheerful chatter. Sally waved from behind her cake stall and Annie ran over to her, leaving Marnie to scan the hall for any sign of Frank.

A tap on the shoulder made Marnie jump. "Hello, Marnie."

"Hello, Frank." Marnie smiled, wanting to reach out and take his hand for reassurance.

"Is she here?"

"Aye, that's her over with Sally."

Frank looked over at Sally's stall. "Shall we?"

"I suppose so." Marnie took a deep breath, squared her shoulders and followed Frank across the hall.

"Ah, Frank, how wonderful to see you," said Sally as she noticed him approach. Annie kept her eyes lowered, stealing occasional glances at him from beneath her lashes. Sally looked from Annie to Frank and then to Marnie. "You know what, I'm parched. Would the three of you mind manning my stall while I fetch myself a cuppa?"

Marnie threw Sally a grateful smile, then waited for her to leave before making her introductions. "Annie, this is Frank. Frank, this is Annie."

"A pleasure to meet you, Annie." Frank offered his hand, and Annie looked up. After a moment's hesitation, she took it. Frank smiled, and Annie smiled back.

"You're older than I was expecting."

Frank let out a guffaw. "You're as plain speaking as your mother, I see. Yes, I'm afraid I'm no spring chicken."

"But neither am I," said Marnie.

"How are you finding being back in Lowestoft?" Frank asked.

Annie chewed on her bottom lip as she thought about his question. "It was hard at first. I miss Padstow, my friends and the family I was staying with. Has Mum told you about them?"

"Your Uncle Richard and Aunt Helen? Yes, she's told me lots about them. They sound like wonderful people."

"They are," said Annie. "And my friend Grace. She came to live with us when she was a baby, but she's three now and I worry she'll be missing me."

"I'm sure she will be," said Frank. "Have you written to her?"

"Yes, and sent her some of my drawings. I'd like to visit her, but Mum says we have to wait for the war to be over."

"Very sensible. I understand what it's like to miss a place. My family is up in Lincolnshire and I miss my mother and sisters a lot. Not to mention my nieces and nephews. Perhaps we could find a gift for you to send down to Padstow? There are a few craft stalls around by the looks of things."

"What a lovely idea," said Marnie. "I saw some knitted dolls on the table over there."

Annie shuffled her feet. "I don't have any money."

"My treat," said Frank. "Shall we?" He pointed toward the toy stall.

Annie smiled at Frank. "Thank you."

"I'd best stay here and watch the stall. You'll be alright with Frank?"

"Of course," said Annie.

Marnie watched the two of them walk off together across the hall. As first meetings went, Marnie thought it could've gone a lot worse.

Chapter 70

May, 1945

Roy lowered himself down into the wheelchair, scowling and muttering under his breath.

"Oh, for goodness' sake, Roy. It's not the end of the world."

"I still don't see why I couldn't have walked."

"You know why. Besides, the crowds will be quite something, I suspect, and it will be much easier if you're in this thing."

Roy humphed and squirmed into position. Marnie squeezed Frank's hand, and he planted a quick kiss on her neck before she took hold of the wheelchair handles.

"We're here!"

"Ah, Kitty, come on in."

"No, it's alright, Sally, there's that many of us we'll take over the whole house. Besides, it's too fine a day to be indoors. Perfect for the service at the Oval."

"Quite. Fine weather for a fine day. I always knew this day would come."

"Huh," laughed Roy, "you've been saying there'll be victory in Europe any day now since 1939."

"There's no harm in being an optimist," said Jimmy, earning himself a grateful smile from Sally. "Are you alright with the chair, Frank?"

"Yes, no problem."

"You look so smart in your uniform," said Sally, and Frank puffed out his chest.

"Come on, or we'll never get there," said Annie, dragging Marnie out the door and greeting Kitty and her brood.

"You look lovely," said Marnie, pointing to Kitty's dress.

"Thank you, Bobby bought it for me to celebrate VE day. I told him it's premature, as I won't feel like celebrating until war is over in the Far East and we get Simon home, but he insisted."

"It won't be long till they free Simon," said Bobby, "and he wouldn't want us missing out on the celebrations."

"Quite right too," said Roy as Frank wheeled him out of the house. "*HMS Europa*, here we come!"

Frank and Roy led the procession to the end of the street, where they joined crowds of locals heading in the same direction. The sun blazed down on them, joining with the surge of relief and optimism and turning the usually grey sea a delicate blue.

"Even the sea's joining in the fun," said Annie, pointing out the jewel-like reflections on the mill-pond-still water.

The crowds grew more dense the closer they drew to the military base. "Do you need to stand with the other lads from *HMS Minos*?" Marnie asked Frank.

"No, I reckon today anything goes. I'd like to celebrate with the folk I love, and I can't see anyone wanting to get in the way of that today."

All the churches had gathered for one joint service of celebration, thanks and remembrance. As locals and servicemen packed into the Oval, the mood was jubilant, but none had forgotten the battering the town had taken and the lives lost, and people carried loved ones in their hearts as they joined their voices in hymns and prayers of thanksgiving.

All throughout the service, Frank held tight to Marnie's hand. The small gesture filled her not just with comfort, but a hope for the future. Beside her, Annie stood on tiptoes, aware even at her tender age that she was experiencing a moment of history.

After the service, no one felt like going home. The day was warm and bright, but with the nearby beaches still a no-go area folk milled about the Oval, enjoying the weight that had lifted from their shoulders. Several spontaneous street parties had broken out nearby, and Marnie couldn't remember ever having experienced such a moment of unity in the town. It no longer mattered if folk were from The Grit, from up in the town, from elsewhere in England, or the other side of the world. What mattered was that it was over, or at least the immediate threat was. Hope had prevailed, and finally the future looked bright.

The bright blue sky faded, and the atmosphere turned to frenzied joy, fuelled by the many toasts shared with friends and strangers.

"They're lighting bonfires," said Frank. "I've just heard the Royal Hotel has torn down all their blackout curtains."

"In that case, let's head over there," said Kitty. "You're not getting too tired, boys?"

Kitty's sons laughed off their mother's suggestion they should head home, and ran off ahead.

"I'll catch them up," said Bobby.

The group walked through town, and as they reached the esplanade, the sun was sinking. It scattered pastel shades across the water and looked as though it were slipping into the sea.

By the time the sky turned navy, dancing patches of orange could be seen right along the curve of the coastline. Marnie held Annie's hand as they stood a safe distance from the enormous fire burning in front of them. Men hurled meters of black fabric onto the fire with whoops of delight. A group of women staggered beneath the weight of a large table, laughing as men joined their effort to hurl it on the fire.

"Why are they burning tables and chairs?" asked Annie.

"Goodness knows," said Marnie. "I think folk are mad with relief."

Frank joined Marnie and Annie and took her free hand. As she stood between her two loves, tears of happiness blurred the flames in front of Marnie's eyes. A single droplet warmed her skin as it slid down her cheek. After such a tumultuous few years, she couldn't wait for dawn to break on a new day, a new world.

Chapter 71

September, 1945

Kitty lay beside Bobby, an arm slung across his chest. "I can't believe it," she whispered, a tear leaking from the corner of her eye. "Read it to me again, please."

Once more, Bobby read the news that had been delivered first thing that morning; Simon had been freed from the camp where he was being held and was alive, if not well. The letter informed them he was in hospital receiving medical attention for malnutrition, but would begin the long journey home as soon as he was medically fit.

"But the fact that he's still in hospital, well, that's a worry, isn't it?"

Bobby laughed and brushed a curl from Kitty's eyes. "Can't we look on the bright side for once? A hospital is better than whatever sort of prison camp he's been held in up till now. And you heard what the letter said, as soon as he's able, he'll be on his way home."

Kitty brushed away another tear. "Happy tears," she promised Bobby, laying her head on his chest.

When VJ Day came and went without a word of Simon, Kitty had given up hope. They'd joined in the celebrations along with other locals, planting false smiles on their faces while others talked of the future and moving on. For Kitty, there would be no moving on until Simon had returned. Losing one son was bad enough. Then this morning, out of the blue, the news had arrived and she could barely take it in.

"Mum, can you have a word with those bloody boys?" Stevie burst into the room, not bothering to knock. "I've had enough. I'm a working man now, I need a decent night's rest, instead I've got those lunatics peeing about until God knows what time. It's not fair."

Kitty pulled herself up against the bedframe and patted an empty space by her feet. "Sit, I've got news."

In an instant, Stevie forgot all complaints about his younger brothers and sat on the bed. "Simon?"

Kitty nodded, then her face spread into a wide smile. She grabbed Stevie's hands. "He's in hospital, but as soon as he's well enough, he's coming home."

"Really? He's really coming back?"

Kitty handed Stevie the letter to read.

"Thank goodness for that. I'm sick of being the eldest. Perhaps my big brother can knock some sense into the little ones."

"You know your brother will have been through an awful lot and, just like when you came home, it will take him time to adjust. When he returns, me and Dad will sleep downstairs for a while and the pair of you can have our room. That way, you'll get some peace from the younger ones, but you'll be able to keep an eye on Simon."

Stevie left the room far happier than when he'd arrived. "What a long way that boy's come," said Bobby. "You know he's courting a young lady from Oulton Broad?"

"He's what? Why didn't he tell me?"

Bobby laughed. "Because he knows you'll be forcing him to bring her round to meet you. Let the boy have a bit of privacy, it's early days. It wouldn't surprise me if he's setting up a home of his own before long."

"And Chrissy's still insisting he wants to go back to Derbyshire. We'll have an empty nest before we know it."

The sound of boys fighting reached them and Bobby laughed. "What were you saying about empty nests? I don't think there's much chance of that for a while."

"I need to remember how much I hated living in a quiet house," said Kitty, "and feel free to remind me of it when I moan about my naughty boys."

"Will do," said Bobby. He gave Kitty a kiss, pulled on his slippers and went to act as referee.

No sooner had Bobby left than Missy appeared, sniffing the air to check Bobby was nowhere to be found. Satisfied she wouldn't get thrown off again, Missy jumped up onto the bed and nestled herself against Kitty's legs.

"You better not be letting that bloody dog into the bed," called Bobby.

"Of course not," said Kitty. She leaned back against her pillows with a smile. Bobby was home, her boys were home, Simon was alive, and although not gone for good, the nightmares were few and far between. When Bobby appeared with a cup of tea for her, Kitty wondered if life could get much better. She closed her eyes and listened to the sound of ordinary family life, the squabbles, the stresses, the mundane conversations that she'd missed so much. She picked up her tea.

"Mum, I need you!"

Kitty sighed and put the cup back down. She pulled on her dressing gown, tapped her leg for Missy to follow her and went to attend to her family.

Chapter 72

June, 1946

"I s this it?" Annie had her face pressed up to the window, her eyes wide as the island came into view.

"It certainly is," said Marnie, swallowing down her emotion at seeing it again.

"I can't believe you and Uncle Jimmy grew up on an island. It's so much more exciting than Lowestoft."

"I don't know about that," said Marnie. "It's much the same in many ways. You'll see when we get into the village how much fishing dominates island life, not unlike The Grit."

"Hmm, well, I think it's a very romantic place to grow up," said Annie, unable to tear herself away from the view.

Marnie laughed. "Romantic? Maye it was for Jimmy and Clara but never for me. I was too young to be thinking about romance when I was living there."

"I don't mean romantic in that sense," said Annie, tutting. "I mean a romantic setting, like from a novel."

"Right, I see," said Marnie, worrying that Annie would be terribly disappointed when they arrived and saw the village was much like any other.

"Is Aunt Clara going to be wearing a white dress?"

"I don't know, perhaps."

"Isn't she a bit old? I'd think a two-piece would be more appropriate for someone that ancient."

"Ancient? Crikey, Annie, Clara's not that much older than me."

Annie smirked.

"I can see you laughing by your reflection in the glass," said Marnie.

"Will I be able to see where you grew up?"

"The cottage? I'm not sure. My sister Sally moved in with her husband and children. From what I've heard, they're not the happiest of families, so I'm not sure how welcoming they'll be. You'll get to meet your Granny Rose, though. She lives with Clara at the hotel." Marnie shook her head and laughed. "There was a time I wondered if Mam and Clara would ever be friends, never mind living together. It's very generous of Clara, my mam is old and frail these days so needs someone keeping an eye on her."

"I wish I could have met my grandpa."

Marnie tried to imagine introducing her precious daughter to Alex Watson. She couldn't picture a scenario where that ever would have happened. At least he was long dead and didn't need to be factored into their plans.

"Granny Rose is very excited to meet you," said Marnie. "I think you'll like her. She got on well with your dad, and has mellowed in her old age."

"Everyone got on well with Dad," said Annie with a sad smile. "How much longer until we're there?"

"Only a few minutes. We'd best gather up our bags, as we'll need to get off at Beal. Uncle Jimmy will meet us there. It's a shame Kitty and Bobby couldn't travel with us, but there'll be up tomorrow."

"And Frank."

"Aye, and Frank."

"Why is he coming up a day later? And don't try telling me it's work. Have you two had a row?"

"No, of course not. It's just that I've a lot of ghosts to lay to rest on the island. And the last time I was there was with your dad. We both thought it best I have a bit of time by myself to say my goodbyes before Frank joins me."

"Will you take me to all the places you took Dad?"

"Of course I will."

"Sometimes, I can't remember what he was like. Is that awful?" Annie shuffled closer to Marnie on the seat. She held her hands in her lap and kept her eyes on the ground.

"Come here," said Marnie, pulling Annie close. "You were so young when you lost your dad, the memories you have of him are bound to fade. Added to which, a blooming great war has happened since then, turning your world topsy-turvy. Just because your memories grow weak doesn't mean you love your dad any less. And I can tell you for certain he wouldn't want either of us sitting at home pining for him."

The screech of a whistle broke into their conversation, and Marnie and Annie gathered up their bags. Jimmy was waiting to greet them, just as he'd promised.

"Whoa," he said, as both Marnie and Annie rushed into his arms. "You'll knock me over and I can't be injured before my wedding."

"We've missed you," said Marnie.

"And I've missed you too. Clara can't wait to see you, and Mam's dying to meet her granddaughter. Come on, the car's just out front."

Annie ran towards the motor car, determined to nab the front seat.

"Go on," said Marnie, when Annie climbed into the passenger seat. "I've seen it all before. You'll get a better view from there."

"Thanks, Mum."

Jimmy climbed behind the wheel, and the engine started with a roar.

"Is your leg alright for driving?"

"Yes, it is. I don't think I could get very far, but on short journeys like this, I'm fine. Here we go."

The car turned a corner, swooping down an incline, the tyres meeting with sand at the bottom. Annie gripped the door handle, her knuckles white. Jimmy pressed hard on the brakes and the car skidded to a stop.

"What are you doing, Uncle Jimmy? You almost drove us into the middle of the sea."

Jimmy laughed. "Don't worry. The tide's on its way out now. I came across to the mainland at the last low tide as I wanted to be there when your train pulled in. There's probably half an hour before the tide's low enough for us to drive across. You can get out, if you like?"

Annie climbed out of the car and walked towards the water's edge.

"Are you alright?" asked Marnie, coming to stand beside her daughter and wrapping an arm across her shoulder.

"I thought I'd be used to the seaside," said Annie, "having lived in Padstow and Lowestoft, but this is something else altogether. I've seen nothing like it."

Marnie tried to see the view through her daughter's eyes. Pink, orange and purple streaks of light played on a tide that raced itself, like separate ribbons of water being pulled at different speeds. Gulls swooped low, their stomachs almost skimming the water line. And all the while the island squatted on the horizon, cut off, but waiting to open its arms to them.

"It's like a magical kingdom," whispered Annie, as the water parted, exposing streaks of sand that would lead them home.

Chapter 73

June, 1946

"I'm glad to see you've got a good appetite," said Clara, clearing away Annie's breakfast dishes.

Annie grinned at her aunt, who she'd taken a shine to from the moment they arrived at Clara's hotel. Although they'd met once before in Padstow, Annie's memories of Clara were hazy, but that hadn't stopped an instantaneous bond developing between them.

"Do you know you're named after my mother?" Clara had asked Annie the night before when they'd sat in the garden watching the moon rise over the harbour. "Well, she was actually called Anna, but Annie is a tribute to her memory."

"What was she like?"

Clara smiled, a far-off look in her eye. "She wasn't born on the island, so there was always something a little exotic about her to my mind. And my, was she beautiful, and kind, so very, very kind. Losing her so young was one of the hardest things that has ever happened to me."

"I know how that feels," said Annie.

"Of course you do," Clara had said, taking Annie's hand.

That conversation had cemented their bond, and now, two days into their stay, Annie had taken to following Clara around the hotel like a shadow.

"Morning," said Marnie, walking into the dining room with Rose holding her arm for support. The physical change in her mam had shocked Marnie at first. The once sturdy Rose had shrunk, her back hunched and neck stooped. But her eyes lit up in the presence of Annie, and she seemed to relish the excitement of the upcoming nuptials. It warmed Marnie's heart to see the bond between Rose and Jimmy, and she was grateful her mam had lived long enough to see her only son wed.

"Good morning," said Clara. "I was just admiring your granddaughter's appetite, Rose."

"It must be all the fresh air," said Rose, smiling at Annie. "The island suits you, lass."

"Are there any last-minute wedding preparations you need my help with?" asked Marnie.

"No, I think everything is in hand. The weather is set to be fine tomorrow, which is a blessing. I told Annie I'd take her for a walk to see the north shore this morning, if that's alright with you?"

"Aye, of course. Why don't I come too?"

"Ah, I think Frank has other plans this morning that involve you."

"Oh, right, I see."

When Frank came down to breakfast, Marnie asked what his plans were, but he just tapped the side of his nose in a move which infuriated Marnie. All Frank would say, was that Marnie was to meet him outside the hotel at eleven a.m. When she asked what he'd be doing until then, he just grinned, wolfed down a slice of toast, and left before Marnie could interrogate him any further.

"Frank looked like he was in a hurry," said Jimmy, walking into the room and kissing Rose's cheek before sitting down.

Marnie tore her eyes from the view she'd been staring at and shook her head. "I don't know what's going on with that man, but he's up to something. He wants to meet me here at eleven and Clara's taking Annie off to the north shore, so I have a couple of hours free. Do you fancy a stroll with your little sister?"

"Nothing would please me more," said Jimmy.

"We should probably see if Kitty and Bobby fancy it, too."

"I've not seen them yet this morning, and to be honest, it would be nice to have a bit of time, just the two of us. There are plenty of shared memories to unpick. Do you mind, Mam?"

"Of course not," said Rose with a chuckle. "I struggle to get out of a chair these days, never mind out for a walk. Besides, I've promised Clara I'll make the bouquets this morning. Set me up at a table with all I need, and I shall be fine on my own until lunchtime."

"It's just you and me then," Jimmy told Marnie.

"I'll get my coat."

Ten minutes later, Jimmy and Marnie were walking through Market Square, stopping frequently so Jimmy could greet locals and discuss wedding plans. Most looked at Marnie with curiosity, then finally recognition and delight.

"Folk are pleased to see you back," said Jimmy, as they followed the road past the Presbyterian church.

"I'm surprised they remember me at all. I was so young when I left, and I was only back for a few days when I came here with Tom. How are you finding being part of a village community again?"

Jimmy took a moment to answer. "Hmm, well, it's very different from Somerleyton. There, no one knew about my history. They knew me as a well-spoken headmaster and nothing more. Here, everyone knows everything about my past, and it's as though that gives them the right to know everything about my present. Does that make sense?"

"Aye," said Marnie. "It does. Some days it will be a blessing to be living in such a small community, other days it will be a curse. You don't regret coming back here?"

"No, not for a second. Part of me regrets not coming back sooner, but there's no point thinking like that. It's wonderful to have repaired my relationship with Mam. And being with Clara every day, waking up beside her, well, it was worth waiting a lifetime for."

"I'm so happy for the pair of you."

"Shall we head down here?" Jimmy pointed to a narrow path that snaked its way beside the school and into fields beyond. Marnie followed Jimmy as he began walking, pushing aside brambles and nettles as he went. In front of them the sky stretched out as though on a canvas, meeting a line of silvery sea below. "Do you remember coming down here to look for Cuthie beads when we were bairns?"

"Aye," said Marnie. "I think so. Didn't we come with Clara sometimes?"

"Yes, that's right. There was that one time she fell back into the water and got a soaking. Goodness me, I felt terrible about that."

"I remember," said Marnie, "although I must have been so young."

The path banked steeply down onto a shingle beach. Jimmy and Marnie walked towards the water's edge, their feet sinking into the sand.

"Blimey, that smell takes me back," said Marnie, sniffing the air.

"Aye, there's something unique about island seaweed," said Jimmy. "I've never quite found a match for it anywhere else."

Marnie laughed and linked arms with Jimmy as they stared out towards the mainland. The tide was in, sunlight bouncing off water that swirled around the island, separating them from life beyond. A small boat bobbed along the channel, barely enough wind to fill its sails. Gulls perched on top of poles sticking out of the water, ready to guide pilgrims who would cross the sands once the tide made a retreat.

"It's good to be back here with you," said Marnie. "It feels right, like we've come full circle."

"That makes this sound like an ending," said Jimmy, "but there's plenty of life yet to come for us all. Speaking of which, while I could stand here staring at this view with you forever, you have a young man waiting for you with big plans for today."

"Young? Are we thinking of the same man?"

"Younger than me," laughed Jimmy.

"Actually, I think you and Frank are the same age."

Jimmy sighed. "Away with you, go on, go to Frank. He'll be itching to reveal his surprise."

Chapter 74

June, 1946

On the way back to Clara's hotel, Marnie passed Kitty and her brood.

"I said we were going to buy a postcard, but we seem to have gained several bags of sweets," said Kitty, standing outside the post office and trying to share out the sweets in a way that would make everyone happy.

Marnie laughed. "I'm told I'm needed by Frank, but would you like to go for a stroll together later?"

"That sounds lovely, but you get on. When we left the hotel, Frank was pacing up and down outside, waiting for you."

"All right, I'll see you later."

Marnie walked on through the village. She passed the cottage where she'd spent the first part of her life, but didn't knock on the door. She would see her sister and brother-in-law tomorrow at the wedding, but had no desire to spend more time with them than was necessary. Instead, Marnie rushed past, finding herself out of breath by the time she reached the hotel.

"Oh good, you're here," said Frank.

"With five minutes to spare," said Marnie, grinning. "Come on, Frank, what's all this about?"

"Follow me."

Frank took Marnie's hand and together they walked across a field which led to the harbour. The tide was on the turn, but boats still bobbed gently on the calm waters, a few fishermen on the shore, doors to their sheds flung open as they readied their equipment for upcoming voyages.

"Let's go this way."

"You've been getting your bearings," said Marnie, impressed, as she followed Frank up onto the Heugh. "Wait a moment," she said, turning to view the island in all its fullness. "I'd forgotten how beautiful it is here and how much the castle looms over the harbour."

"I love the ruined priory," said Frank. "There's such a sense of history when you walk among the ruins."

"Is that where we're heading?"

"No," said Frank, taking Marnie's hand once more.

They walked on in silence. Below them, seabirds swooped down across the water before finding themselves a perch on the cliff. The sound of waves on stone and sand reached them through the still air.

They began climbing down a path that would lead to the priory. "This way," said Frank, turning sharply to the left and following a tiny path that ran along the cliff, halfway between the beach below and the cliff top above.

"You know about the caves?" asked Marnie, her mouth falling open as Frank edged his way along the secret path cut into the rock face. "But how?"

"Jimmy," Frank called over his shoulder.

"Of course."

Marnie giggled as she followed Frank along the perilous path. She felt young again, and in the middle of an adventure. When she reached the caves cut into the rock face, Marnie's hands flew to her mouth. Frank reached out a hand, and she stepped towards him.

"You've done all this?"

Frank nodded, pulling Marnie down onto a picnic blanket he'd laid out. Around them were bunches of spring flowers, tied with ribbon and filling the air with their sweet scent. Frank leaned back into the farthest recess of the cave and pulled out a basket.

"What have you got in there?"

"Aha," said Frank, pulling out a selection of food and laying it on the blanket. "I'm afraid I can't take credit for this. Clara's chef rustled up the picnic for us."

"This is so thoughtful, thank you," said Marnie. She leaned across and kissed Frank.

"There's one last surprise," he said, reaching into his pocket and pulling out a small velvet box. He opened it slowly, the ring inside catching the sunlight and throwing silver shapes across the roof of the cave. "I'm afraid I'm a bit too old to be getting down on one knee, but I'd like to ask you something, Marnie. Will you make me the happiest man alive by agreeing to be my wife?"

Marnie threw herself at Frank, knocking him onto his back. She smothered his face in kisses, laughing as he fought against her.

"Watch out," he said. "I don't want the ring falling over the edge of the cliff."

Marnie sat up and laughed. "You are a dark horse, Frank Merton. I'd given up hope of you ever asking me to marry you."

Frank smiled. "I wanted Annie to get used to the idea. It took her such a long time to settle back into being home, springing a wedding and step-father on her too soon seemed cruel."

"That's one thing I love most about you, you know."

"What?"

"Your kindness. And what's more..." Marnie looked down at the ground, took a deep breath and raised her eyes to Frank's. "What's more... I think Tom would have very much approved of you. He would have wanted me to be happy, but the concern you've shown for Annie's happiness, well, that confirms it for me."

"Is that a very long way of saying yes?"

"Wasn't the kiss enough of a yes?"

Frank shook his head. "No, I'd like to hear you say it."

"Frank Merton, the answer is yes. Nothing would make me happier than to be your wife."

"Thank goodness for that," said Frank, slipping the ring onto Marnie's finger.

"Surely you weren't worried I'd say no?"

"Well, there was a lot riding on getting a yes from you."

"Such as?"

"Our wedding being tomorrow, for starters."

"What? But that's not right. It's Jimmy and Clara getting married tomorrow."

"And so are we. If you're worried about stealing their thunder, don't be. It was their idea."

"They knew you were going to propose?"

"In the absence of a father to ask permission for your hand, I went to Jimmy and Roy. Thankfully, both gave their blessing. I also asked Jimmy if he could suggest any romantic spots for a proposal and he suggested here."

"You really are such a dark horse, Frank."

"Not just me. Annie's in on it too. She picked out a dress for you, and a bridesmaid's dress for herself. You don't mind, do you?"

"Why on earth would I mind?" asked Marnie, her eyes wide as she tried to take in what Frank was telling her.

"I thought you might be cross that we've planned it all without you. I know the day can never match up to your first wedding to Tom, so I thought this would be a way of making it completely different."

"I'm beyond touched that you and everyone else have planned all this."

"Good," said Frank, leaning over to kiss Marnie. "Now, we'd better get on with lunch, as several people are waiting anxiously to know the outcome of our picnic."

Chapter 75

June, 1946

Kitty poked her head around the door and smiled. The church was full. Jimmy's father Alex had tainted the Watson family name, but there was plenty of goodwill towards Jimmy and Marnie, and the entire island had turned out to share in their celebration. She spotted Jimmy and Frank waiting at the front of the church. They both looked handsome in their smart suits, but judging by the way they wrung their hands, they were both rather nervous. Kitty gave Bobby a little wave, then crept back outside.

In the churchyard, Kitty made her way over to the bridal party, who were sharing a joke with two late arrivals.

"Oh, there you are," said Kitty. "I was just looking in the church for you. Did Ben find you all right?"

"Yes, and what a kind chap he is. You must be so proud of your brother," Sally told Clara. "He couldn't have done more for us these past couple of days. We've been made so welcome in his home."

Marnie was brushing away tears with a borrowed handkerchief. "I just can't believe you came all this way. You have no idea how much it means to me. It's the best surprise I could've hoped for."

"And I'm so pleased you were both able to come today," said Clara. "Jimmy will be delighted to have you here."

"We wouldn't have missed this for the world," said Sally. "Both Jimmy and Frank have become surrogate sons to us. Not that they've replaced our precious boys, but they've brought happiness to our lives we didn't think we'd feel again. And, Marnie, you know we see you as our daughter. Of course, we wouldn't have missed your wedding."

"Kitty's idea of spreading the journey over several days was a good one," said Roy. "I'm not sure we could have done it otherwise."

"Enough chatter," said Sally. "We'd better get in the church, Roy, or we'll be behind the brides!"

"We can't be having that," said Roy, waving to the assembled women as Sally pushed the wheelchair towards the door.

*

Frank took a deep breath, straightening his jacket and cracking his knuckles. "It's jolly good of you to let us join you today," he told Jimmy, twirling his cufflink as he stared out into the congregation.

"It's a pleasure," said Jimmy. "I'm delighted you're marrying Marnie. How are you feeling?"

"Nervous as anything," said Frank. "I know both Marnie and I have done this before, but my first wedding was rather low-key."

Jimmy laughed. "You can't get away with low-key for an island wedding. You know about the traditions?"

"I've been given fair warning."

Both men looked up as the heavy church doors creaked open. "False alarm," said Bobby from the front row.

"Hold on a minute," said Frank. He grabbed hold of Jimmy's arm. "Isn't that..."

Both grooms set off down the aisle of the church to the confusion of the gathered congregation. Heads turned to watch as Jimmy and Frank ran to greet the small elderly lady trying to heave a clunky wheelchair through the door.

"But how?" asked Jimmy, staring open-mouthed at the sight of Sally and Roy.

"You didn't think we'd miss this, did you?" asked Roy, his face spreading into a lopsided grin.

Frank stepped forward and hugged Sally, while Jimmy shook Roy's hand.

"Let me help you with the chair," said Frank, taking the wheelchair handles from Sally.

"Just put us somewhere in the back," said Roy.

"Not a chance," said Frank. "Unless... unless... if you'd rather not have a good view, I mean, I know this must be a difficult occasion given... well... Tom..."

Roy grabbed hold of Frank's sleeve and pulled him down. "Frank, you listen to me, lad. There is no one we'd rather see our Marnie marrying than you. She's like a daughter to us. Do you think I'd have given my blessing if I weren't happy about it? Not a day goes by that we don't miss our Tom, but we've taken on his job of caring for Marnie and Annie, and we couldn't be happier with this match."

"And besides," said Sally, "do you think we would have travelled all this way if we didn't want to see you wed?" She laughed and shook her head. "Now get on with you, Frank. Don't you have a girl to marry?"

Frank smiled, took hold of the wheelchair once more, and pushed Roy to the front of the church. Islanders craned their necks, wondering who these guests of honour were and how they fitted into either family.

*

Kitty stepped forward and clicked open the heavy wooden doors. "Are you ready?" she asked Clara and Marnie.

Marnie and Clara nodded to each other. "As we'll ever be."

"And what about you, Annie?" Annie grinned and gave Kitty a thumbs up. "Right, then I think we're all set. Lead the way, Bill."

Clara's father, Bill, held out his bent elbows and Marnie and Clara each linked arms with him, one on either side. The organ struck up the wedding march, and the congregation stood. With slow, careful steps, the bridal party moved forward. Jimmy and Frank stood at the front craning their necks and were rewarded by the sight of Marnie and Clara, resplendent in their happiness. As he walked between them, Bill's back was hunched with age and the many years he'd spent at sea, but his face was filled with pride, his eyes shining.

Kitty walked behind Clara, careful not to tread on the full-length green silk gown that set off her auburn hair. In contrast to Clara, Marnie's dress was pale pink, its hem skimming her ankles. Kitty considered them a fine pair of brides and felt a wash of pride that she was a maid of honour to both.

Kitty turned her head to Annie. "You all right?" she mouthed. Annie nodded and smiled.

Both Kitty and Annie wore dresses covered in roses, not only matching the colour of both bridal gowns, but in acknowledgment of Rose, who, when she saw the dresses, had burst into uncharacteristic tears. In the same vein, both brides' bouquets were filled with pink and white roses.

It was a detail Jimmy had insisted on, and Kitty noticed his eyes filling with tears as he took in the full effect. She saw his hand delve into his pocket and knew his fingers would wrap around the shilling he'd put in there as a reminder of the healing that had happened since his return to the island.

Over several whiskies the night before, Jimmy had told the story of his island life, his escape, and subsequent return. From what he'd said, the Watson family still had its dark corners, but the hold Alex had once had over them all was well and truly broken. They were ready to embrace a new future, and Kitty felt honoured to be playing a small part in it.

The tiled floor in front of her blurred as Kitty fought the tears that threatened. Never had she been present at such a poignant occasion, where loss combined with happiness, memories of the past colliding with the present.

Marnie and Clara reached the front of the church, and a hush descended. The vicar stepped forward and Kitty signalled to Annie that this was their cue to take the bride's bouquets from them.

With Marnie's bouquet of roses in her hands, Kitty moved to stand beside Bobby, who gave an appreciative smile at the sight of his wife all dolled up.

"Dearly beloved, we are gathered here today..."

By the time the ceremony was drawing to a close, Kitty had soaked not only her own hanky but also Bobby's. Stevie grinned at her, shaking his head at the emotion painted across her face. Beside him, Simon did his best to stay upright, still weak after his return home at the beginning of the month. The younger boys filled the rest of the pew, all smart in the new suits Jimmy had insisted on buying for them.

The organ struck up, and Kitty handed her handkerchief to Bobby. "See you outside," she whispered. "According to Clara, there's to be a bit of gunfire. Perhaps best wait with Simon in the church and bring him out when it's over." Bobby nodded his agreement as Kitty stepped into her position next to Annie.

The happy couples walked back down the aisle to cheers from the congregation. Kitty's younger boys slipped down the side of the church and were ready and waiting to pelt the wedding party with confetti the second they stepped through the doors.

"What happens now?" asked Annie, brushing confetti from her face and hair.

"Well, if what Clara told me is true, there are some interesting traditions to get through before we get our hands on any cake."

"Like what?"

"The fishermen will make an archway with their guns for the happy couples to run through. The brides have to jump the petting stone, there's some sort of toll and something to do with smashing the cake plate."

Annie shook her head. "I love this place, but it can be mighty strange."

"I couldn't have put it better myself," said Kitty with a giggle. "Come on, we don't want to miss the spectacle."

Chapter 76

June, 1946

Marnie looked out onto the lawn where Simon sat gazing out towards the harbour. Kitty came over and stood beside her.

"How's he getting on?" Marnie asked. "I'm sorry. I've not caught up with you properly since we arrived."

"You've had plenty else on your mind," said Kitty. "He's alright, on the whole. Very thin, as you can see. There's a lot going on in his head and plenty of nightmares. Can you believe he and some of the other lads were told not to tell anyone about what happened to them?"

"Why ever not?"

"Apparently, the country wants to move on and people don't need to be reminded of the dark days of war."

"As if that's going to help those poor boys."

"Just what I thought. I've told Simon that what he was told is a load of old rot. It was talking to Joe that helped Stevie all those years ago, and Stevie made sure Simon knows there's always a listening ear should he need one."

"Is this a private conversation, or is it alright to come in?"

Marnie turned to see Clara standing in the doorway. "As this is your own hotel, and your own wedding day, I'd say you've a right to go wherever you want." Marnie held out a hand and Clara walked over and took it.

"What are you two doing up here hiding away?"

"Just taking it all in," said Marnie. "It's hard to catch your breath down there among all the action."

Clara laughed. "My thoughts exactly. That's why I came up here, too."

"Are you sure you don't mind me and Frank crashing in on your wedding day?"

"Of course not! I never would have met Jimmy again if it weren't for you. It's an honour to share the day with you."

The three friends stood side by side, watching as the next generation came spilling out onto the lawn.

"You know Annie says she wants to live here?" said Marnie, turning her head to Clara.

"That'll be the islander in her. She may have Hearn as her last name, but she's a Watson, too. The island always eventually calls them back." Clara held a hand to the window. At that moment, Jimmy looked up, smiled, and blew her a kiss. "You know Annie is always welcome here with us, whether for a holiday or something longer."

"That's very kind, but I may not tell her that just yet. I'd like to keep her in Lowestoft for a few years. When she reaches sixteen, she can do as she wishes."

"Look at them all," said Kitty. "They're the future, aren't they?"

"Then I'd say we're in safe hands," said Marnie, smiling as Kitty's boys dragged Jimmy, Frank and Annie into a cricket match they were setting up on the lawn. Rose, Bill, Sally and Roy watched on from chairs set up around the lawn.

"I know we're all hurtling towards old age, but today I felt like a youngster myself," said Clara.

"Less of that old-age talk, please," said Kitty with a frown. "We're women in our prime and I'll have none say otherwise. We've lived through two world wars and held everything together. I'd say it's our turn to have a little fun."

"In that vein, how about we go down and join the cricket?"

"Race you there."

Marnie hung back as Kitty and Clara ran giggling from the room. She turned back for one last glance beyond the window. All her favourite people together in one of her favourite places. The island would never be a home for her again, but if Annie still felt its pull in a few years' time, Marnie wouldn't stand in her way. If she'd learned anything over the past few years, it was to look forward, not back.

Marnie felt for the locket around her neck. Helen and Richard had declined her invitation to the wedding but invited Marnie, Frank, and Annie to visit in the summer. Their wedding gift was something Marnie would always treasure. She flicked open the clasp and stroked the lock of red hair hidden inside. Grace was thriving down in Cornwall, Annie was excited about the future, and she had just married the man she loved.

"Hey, you there."

Marnie laughed as Frank cupped his hands around his mouth, calling to her. He beckoned her to come outside. With a smile, Marnie closed the locket, placed it against her heart, and went to join her family and friends.

* * *

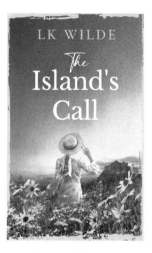

Lowestoft, 1953

Annie's return to Lowestoft after the war should have felt like coming home. Instead, a sense of restlessness lingers, only deepened when she stumbles upon a mysterious letter hinting at a long-buried family secret. While family members expect her to settle down with her childhood sweetheart, Sam, Annie's heart pulls her in another direction.

When a catastrophic flood upends her life, Annie takes it as a sign to embark on a journey of self-discovery. With Sam's blessing, she sets off for Padstow, where her suspicions about her family's past grow stronger. Determined to uncover the truth, she travels to Holy Island, where she finds solace at her aunt and uncle's hotel and forms a deep bond with her grandmother Rose.

For the first time, Annie feels like she belongs. But just as she starts to feel grounded, she befriends someone who isn't what they seem. By trusting the wrong person, Annie risks shattering her newfound happiness—and losing Sam forever.

As family secrets come to light, Annie must confront the past and learn to forgive. Only then can she truly discover where her heart belongs.

Acknowledgements

Until I began researching this book, I had no idea just how vulnerable Lowestoft was during World War Two, or the important role it played in the war effort. Figures suggest almost three hundred people were killed across eighty-three separate air raids, and I can only begin to imagine the level of strain Lowestoft residents were under during these war years. To detail all the devastation wreaked on the town would have required more than one book, but I hope by highlighting some events, in a small way I've drawn attention to the town's history, and the remarkable resilience of its residents.

With so much history to unpack, visits to the various museums at *Sparrow's Nest* (*HMS Europa*) proved very useful. If you ever get the chance to visit the town, The Lowestoft Maritime Museum and the RNPS museum are great to explore among others.

I spent a lot of time poring over history books during my research, and my particular favourites were; *Port War,* by Ford Jenkins, *When Will I See You Again?* by Christopher J Brooks, and *The Grit* by Dean Parkin and Jack Rose. Thank you to Ian Fosten and Sally Middleton for providing me with so much reading material. I came home from one trip to Suffolk armed with about thirty research books!

Thank you to Jo for your wise editing advice, Julia Gibbs for your expert proofreading, and Jarmilla Takac for putting together such a lovely series of covers.

Thanks to my family near and far for their continued support, and finally, thank you, reader, for taking the time to explore Marnie's story.

Also by LK Wilde

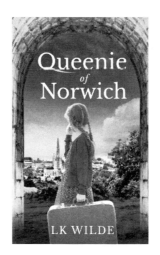

People say you get one life, but I've lived three.

I was born Ellen Hardy in 1900, dragged up in Queen Caroline's Yard, Norwich. There was nothing royal about our yard, and Mum was no queen.

At six years old Mum sold me. I became Nellie Westrop, roaming the country in a showman's wagon, learning the art of the fair.

And I've been the infamous Queenie of Norwich, moving up in the world by any means, legal or not.

I've been heart broken, abandoned, bought and sold, but I've never, ever given up. After all, it's not where you start that's important, but where you end up.

Based on a true story, *Queenie of Norwich* is the compelling tale of one remarkable girl's journey to womanhood. Spanning the first half of the 20th century, Queenie's story is one of heartbreak and triumph, love and loss and the power of family. It is a story of redemption, and how, with grit and determination, anything is possible.

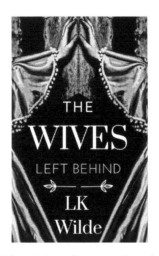

1840, Cornwall. The victim, the accused, and the wives left behind. Welcome to the trial of the century...
Based on a true story.

When merchant Nevell Norway is murdered, suspicion soon falls on the Lightfoot brothers. The trial of the century begins, and two women's lives change forever.

Sarah Norway must fight for the future of her children. Battling against her inner demons, can Sarah unlock the strength she needs to move on without Nevell?

Maria Lightfoot's future looks bleak, but she's a fighter. Determined to rebuild her life, an unexpected friendship offers a glimmer of hope...

With their lives in turmoil, can Maria and Sarah overcome the fate of their husbands? Or will they forever remain the wives left behind?

Book 1 in the Cornish feel-good *The House of Many Lives* series

Kate is stuck in a rut, She works a dead end job, lives in a grotty bedsit and still pines for the man who broke her heart.

When Kate inherits a house in a small Cornish town, she jumps at the chance of a fresh start. A surprise letter from her grandmother persuades Kate to open her home and her heart to strangers.

But with friends harbouring secrets, demanding house guests, and her past catching up with her- can Kate really move on? And will her broken heart finally find a home?

About the author

Author and musician LK (Laura) Wilde was born in Norwich, but spent her teenage years living on a Northumbrian island. She left the island to study Music, and after a few years of wandering settled in Cornwall, where she raises her two crazy, delightful boys.

To keep in touch with Laura and receive a 'bonus bundle' of material, join her monthly Readers' Club newsletter at-

www.lkwilde.com

Or find her on social media- @lkwildeauthor

Finally, if you enjoyed *The Hope She Found*, please consider leaving a review or rating on Amazon. Reviews are so important to indie authors as they're the best way to help more people discover the book!

Printed in Great Britain
by Amazon

48049280R00200